ALSO BY CHRISTINA KOVAC

The Cutaway

WATCH
US FALL

A Novel

CHRISTINA KOVAC

SIMON & SCHUSTER

New York   Amsterdam/Antwerp   London
Toronto   Sydney/Melbourne   New Delhi

Simon & Schuster
1230 Avenue of the Americas
New York, NY 10020

For more than 100 years, Simon & Schuster has championed authors and the stories they create. By respecting the copyright of an author's intellectual property, you enable Simon & Schuster and the author to continue publishing exceptional books for years to come. We thank you for supporting the author's copyright by purchasing an authorized edition of this book.

Copyright © 2025 by Christina Kovac

All rights reserved, including the right to reproduce this book or portions thereof in any form whatsoever. For information, address Simon & Schuster Subsidiary Rights Department, 1230 Avenue of the Americas, New York, NY 10020.

First Simon & Schuster hardcover edition December 2025

SIMON & SCHUSTER and colophon are registered trademarks of Simon & Schuster, LLC

Simon & Schuster strongly believes in freedom of expression and stands against censorship in all its forms. For more information, visit BooksBelong.com.

For information about special discounts for bulk purchases, please contact Simon & Schuster Special Sales at 1-866-506-1949 or business@simonandschuster.com.

The Simon & Schuster Speakers Bureau can bring authors to your live event. For more information or to book an event, contact the Simon & Schuster Speakers Bureau at 1-866-248-3049 or visit our website at www.simonspeakers.com.

Interior design by Wendy Blum

Manufactured in the United States of America

10 9 8 7 6 5 4 3 2 1

Library of Congress Cataloging-in-Publication Data:
Names: Kovac, Christina, author.
Title: Watch us fall : a novel / Christina Kovac.
Description: New York : Simon & Schuster, 2025. | Summary: "By the author of The Cutaway, a work of psychological suspense set in the days leading up to and following the mysterious death of one of Washington, DC's hottest investigative reporters"-- Provided by publisher.
Identifiers: LCCN 2025005768 (print) | LCCN 2025005769 (ebook) | ISBN 9781501141720 (hardcover) | ISBN 9781501141744 (paperback) | ISBN 9781501141751 (ebook)
Subjects: LCGFT: Psychological fiction. | Thrillers (Fiction). | Novels.
Classification: LCC PS3611.O74942 W38 2025 (print) | LCC PS3611.O74942 (ebook) |
DDC 813/.6--dc23/eng/20250210
LC record available at https://lccn.loc.gov/2025005768
LC ebook record available at https://lccn.loc.gov/2025005769

ISBN 978-1-5011-4172-0
ISBN 978-1-5011-4175-1 (ebook)

*FOR SHARON TAYLOR,
WHO GAVE ME A WINDOW FULL OF BLUE
WHEN I NEEDED IT MOST*

WATCH
US FALL

PROLOGUE

PEOPLE STILL TALK ABOUT WHAT HAPPENED TO ADDIE AND JOSH. Some of what they say is true, most of it is not; you know how people are. I figured the talk would drift away like fog across the Potomac, but there'd always been something intriguing about the two of them. Maybe it was their doomed romance, the fairy tale told with that final nasty twist. Or maybe it was Josh's celebrity. Everyone thought they knew him, thought they knew what happened, but they didn't. Who could? *We* didn't even know.

I had what my mother used to call the catbird seat. For a long time, Addie and I were best friends, and that was everything to me. She called me her sister. We watched each other's back. I nursed her through that heartbreak with Josh—or tried to anyway. I was in the middle of it all.

Even now I still see them, Addie with her strong cheeks and pixie-cut black hair, her warm, copper-brown skin like a penny in the sun. In my mind, she's always running. On a good day it's toward me. Sometimes I imagine Josh still there alongside her, as though he couldn't get close enough, the golden guy with his father's face and eyes like gas burners that made you feel seen.

He really should've known better. Not everyone wants to be seen.

PART ONE
THE SWEETIES

January

CHAPTER ONE

ON JANUARY 20, DURING THE BIGGEST SNOWFALL TO HIT DC IN A decade, Josh Egan disappeared. He was thirty-one years old, wealthy and handsome, a TV news star who zinged through the city on celebrity rocket fuel and left contrails in his wake. He was born of a famous political family. His father had run for president before tragedy struck. To this day, the Egan name is spoken in a kind of nostalgic hush.

And I know, *I know*, you've probably already heard all that from sources more reputable than me. From me, people want the straight dope, the insider's take, to be able to say, *Okay, well, the best friend, Lucy Ambrose, told me this . . .* but it's not so easy. Trying to figure out how all this happened is like being a kid again, back home on the dock, trying to cup truth like water in your hand, watching it pour out.

The thing to understand: We didn't know Josh, not really. Except for Addie, none of us were given privileged glimpses into the complications of Josh's big brain, and that's not for lack of trying.

In the beginning, Addie didn't even tell us they were dating. At the time, we were still living as postgrads in a Georgetown row house I'd wanted to live in more than anything. Offer me eternal life or a short time in that house with those girls, and I'd choose the row house every time.

It was a beautiful old Victorian corner unit on O Street, a stone's throw from our alma mater, where the four of us had been rooming together since fate (aka Georgetown University housing) did me a good turn and assigned me track phenom Addie James of Washington, DC, California party girl Estella Warbler, and premed mama hen Penelope Zamora of Potomac, Maryland, as roommates. We named our friend group after that first freshman-year dorm suite, calling ourselves the sweeties.

We were tighter than family. We'd lived like one for five years. We told one another everything—well, *almost*. Prior to Josh, our favorite topics had always been men and sex and sex with men, discussions that spun for hours, usually over huge vats of wine.

Then came last summer, when unbeknownst to us, Addie met Josh. She'd stay away for days on end with her phone location services turned off and Do Not Disturb turned on. We'd catch her sneaking home with the sunrise and ask where she'd been. She always said the same thing: "Out."

"Out" got to be the big joke around our house. We'd tell her to say hello to "Out" for us. "Out must be treating you pretty good," we'd say, "you're looking amazing for Out."

And it was true. That summer Addie was radiant.

But why all the secrecy? We started to worry she'd gotten involved with a married guy or a cult leader, or maybe her boss at her new job at the Smithsonian. Under the guise of bringing Addie lunch, we pulled recon missions at the history museum, cornered a docent by Dorothy's ruby slippers. A hot historian by Jefferson's lap desk denied knowing Addie James before asking us to please leave him alone. That's how young we were—a year out of college and acting like it.

Fast-forward to the end of last summer: at a Labor Day party, a friend told Estella she saw Addie enter a posh Foggy Bottom condo with *oh my God, Josh Egan*. We were floored. Next chance we got, we cornered Addie in the kitchen. Penelope cued up a video of Josh on the set of his network's *Morning Show* and shoved the iPad under Addie's nose. "Oh, look, here's Out, he's anchoring the news."

"His tie matches his dreamy eyes," Estella said. "You choose Out's tie for him, Ads?"

Addie was always too smart to let anybody ruffle her. She simply explained she was afraid to talk about dating a guy everybody thought was a big deal before she figured out whether he was a big deal for her. Plus, she didn't like the thought of people gossiping about her. She asked whether we thought they would.

"Probably not," I said, telling her what she wanted to hear.

"Maybe?" Penelope, the worrier, worried.

"Of course they will!" Estella was thrilled. "We'll be so famous!"

Addie dropped her head in her hands. "That would be a disaster."

But Estella was undeterred. "He's great in bed, isn't he? That's what's got your brain scrambled." She kicked out a kitchen chair and patted its seat, but we never got one sexy word out of Addie.

Four months later—a week before Josh disappeared into the snowstorm—he and Addie broke up as mysteriously as they'd gotten together. All Addie would say was that he'd scared her in a way she never wanted to be scared again. We asked questions, but she told us to drop it, which we did; Addie had always made the rules. For years they'd been very good rules and had served us well. Until everything fell apart.

THAT FATEFUL SATURDAY the forecasters were calling for a major snowstorm. I knew nothing of snow. I'm a Georgia girl from the low country, where we don't do winters, and DC itself is considered a snow hole. Blame it on the city's geography, its low elevation, two rivers to stabilize its temperatures. In my five years living in DC, I'd never seen more than a dusting.

I woke up that morning full of excitement. I raced to the window, but our cobblestone street was still dry, the old trolley rails glinting under a gray sky. I left my attic room and went downstairs with romantic thoughts of being snowed in with my friends, maybe roasting marshmallows in the fireplace.

At the turn in the stairs, on the landing between two floors, I stopped as always and pinched myself at the view of the foyer. I loved its high Victorian ceiling and wedding-cake cornices, the half-broken chandelier I hadn't yet figured out how to fix. I've heard it said people whose families are lost to them have a big appetite for home. All I know is, the first time Addie showed us this house, my hunger gutted me.

That morning, the front parlor was abandoned, its big hearth messy with ashes from the fire the night before. By the front door, the shoe tray was empty. Addie's favorite running shoes, her hot-pink Nike Vapors, were gone.

I thumbed open my phone's Find My Friends app: Estella was still out on a don't-ask overnight. Penelope was at the hospital, working intake at the Saturday psych clinic, her weekend gig. Addie's blue dot was moving homeward at a fast clip from the C&O Canal towpath. I went into the kitchen and made a pot of coffee. While it brewed, I scarfed down a day-old bagel before I headed back to my room.

I was halfway up the stairs, hot coffee mug in hand, when the front door slammed. My phone said 10:19. I remember this very specifically—10:19. In the foyer below, Addie was back from her run.

She was a stunner, tall but delicately made, athletic, with muscles that were lean and subtle. Her short hair, always perfect even after runs, was tousled—I assumed from the wind. She was dead-bolting the door. We never dead-bolted the door.

"What's going on?" I said from the staircase landing.

She swung around, startled, and looked up. "Nothing." She said this in a tone that suggested she meant the opposite. Her track jacket, the one with CAPTAIN stitched across its back, was wadded by her side. This was her lucky jacket. Addie had worn it to break the mid-Atlantic four-hundred-meter, a record she holds to this day.

She came bounding up the stairs. As she passed, I clocked the bruise on her cheek.

"*Did someone hit you?*" I said.

She rounded the corner to the next set of stairs, gone.

Wind shook the big French windows. I turned back to the front door, puzzled over the lock. What—or who—was she trying to keep out?

I followed her up the stairs.

WATER WAS RUNNING in the hallway bathroom. Through the open door, I could see Addie was sitting on the side of the claw-foot tub, still in her sweaty running clothes. Steam rose from the tap. I knocked on the doorframe and went in, saying, "Hey, are you okay?"

She glanced over her shoulder. "Can you help me get this out?"

I stood over the tub. Her track jacket was soaking in water that was pink with blood. The air sparked with electricity, or maybe that was my anxiety. "Where are you hurt?"

"The blood's not mine."

Then she put down her head and cried. I hugged her, feeling scared, looking down at that blood in the water. Whose blood? What happened? And I'd never seen Addie cry. Not when she busted her knee at a track meet and thought running was over for her. Not even when she and Josh had broken up—not that she'd let us see, anyway.

I asked her to make room for me on the tub. She slid to the side. Everything would be all right, I told her, despite having no idea what was going on.

"Want to tell me what happened?" I said. "Maybe I can help."

She sniffled. "The sleeve is a mess. There's blood all over it. Why isn't the blood coming out?"

Hot water sets stains, every woman knows that. Addie was just too freaked out to think straight. I turned off the tap and let the tub drain before starting again, this time with cold water.

"Hand me the soap?" I said, and when she did, I noticed a bruise forming on her wrist. I gritted my teeth but chatted as though we didn't have a care in the world. Dove soap was genius, I said. It was gentle, good at getting stains out. Look, the jacket was better already.

Then, as if we were gossiping about something that had happened to someone else, I said, as casually as possible, "So, this happened on your run, I'm guessing?"

IN ADDIE'S WORLD, unlike mine, there was no room for rehashing or revisiting or obsessing. She never tossed in bed at night cringing over stuff she'd done. *That race has been run*, was Addie's saying, and sometimes she was talking about people. When she was done with someone, she'd cut them from her life. I'd seen it happen. It was a trait I found to be simultaneously exasperating and terrifying.

So when she started telling me what happened, I knew to pay attention. She wouldn't repeat herself.

Around half past nine that morning, January 20, Addie left our Georgetown row house for her typical Saturday long run. These were generally ten-milers, sometimes longer. She'd always take the towpath, which starts in Georgetown and winds westward into the C&O Canal National Historical Park. Addie picked up the path five blocks directly south of our house and headed into the woods.

Those woods were perfect for running, the path flat and smooth and sheltered by tree canopy, the woods thicker and city streets seemingly farther the more miles west you ran. On the towpath, you didn't worry about bus exhaust or stop signs at every corner or cars that creamed DC pedestrians at grisly rates. You could run all the way into Maryland if you chose, and Addie often did. On a day with better weather, you'd be surrounded by other runners and hikers, cyclists and dog walkers. People said hello. That park was known to be a friendly, safe place to run.

On this particular morning, Addie kept a fast pace, trying to get her run in before the snow started. At her one-mile mark, coming up on the boathouse, she noticed a man sitting on the hill leading to the boathouse parking lot. There was something familiar in the set of the man's shoulders, though he was too far from the path for her to be certain. So she kept running a mile or so farther before she noticed the clouds darkening and looped back for home.

"I did everything the way I was supposed to," she said.

"I know." Though I didn't, not yet.

"I wore my open-ear headphones. I had my phone and my watch." Her watch had an SOS button. When she came up on the boathouse again, the man from the hill was gone. "You know our cut-through?"

She was talking about the secret passage through the brush to our hideaway, our hangout since freshman year, the one I'd followed her through countless times. "That's where it happened," she said. "He was in the brush, waiting for me."

"Who?"

"The guy from the hill. The one who jumped out at me."

My blood ran cold. "What was he trying to do?"

"I don't know." She lifted her hands. The bruise on her wrist was swelling. "I came around the bend, and he was just there, waiting, and I tried to get around but he grabbed my wrist and wouldn't let go." She struggled for a moment, blinking back tears. "I thought he was trying to drag me off. I swung on him. I had no idea a nose would bleed that much."

"You broke his nose?"

She nodded slowly. "Think so."

"Good," I said. I was wringing water from her warm-up jacket like it was that asshole's neck. I hadn't been this hot since I'd seen my father deck my mother. I waited until the heat left my face. "Want to report it to the police?"

"I'd rather forget it happened."

"Okay," I said. "I get that." Forgetting was pretty much my modus operandi, too.

So no cops.

Maybe I should've handed her a stiff drink and gotten out of her way. But our row house was on a busy street, a major cut-through between the university and the bars and shops of Wisconsin Avenue. Addie had become, if not a celebrity, at least recognizable for dating Josh these past six months. I didn't know whether her attacker knew who she was, or followed her on social media, but if he did, he'd have seen her posted run routes, which always started here at this house—which meant he knew where we lived.

Penelope and Estella and I could watch her back. I felt uniquely capable of this, as if my entire life before now had been one big warm-up exercise for this task of keeping my best friend safe.

"What do we look out for?" Now that I had this job I wanted to get started this minute. "What does he look like?"

Addie got up from the tub. She brushed the fog from the mirror above the sink and gazed at her reflection. Her eyes were too large. I wondered whether she was in shock.

The radiator hissed. Naked tree limbs clattered against the bathroom window. Below, the sidewalk was clear—for now. "You said he reminded you of someone?"

"I'm only bruised," she said. "Bruises heal."

And blood tells. My mother's warning to my father. Meaning dad's lineage was trash but also, keep it up, jackass, blood is evidence. Stupid me, I washed all that evidence down the tub.

"I'll drop it"—I knew I wouldn't— "if you just tell me who to look out for."

"Promise not to tell anyone?"

I crossed my heart and hoped to die. "I'll take it to the grave."

"You won't believe it," she said.

"I always believe you."

Her eyes met mine in the mirror. "He looked like Josh," she whispered, scared. "We collided on the towpath, and I thought, oh my God, it's Josh."

CHAPTER TWO

I COULDN'T STOP THINKING ABOUT WHAT ADDIE HAD SAID. HER attacker looked so much like Josh she mistook him for Josh? I wondered whether she was talking in code. I'd grown up listening to code and was attuned to its nuances. When my mother said my father was "in a mood," what she was really saying was "run" or "hide." When she'd been "clumsy," she was saying don't hug her too tight, he had hurt her again.

So when Addie said "oh my God, it's Josh," she was saying Josh had attacked her outside the entrance to our hideaway, where she'd once taken Josh.

How Addie had ever found that hideaway to begin with, I had no idea. The first time I saw it was Parents' Weekend, freshman year, during a particularly difficult bout of homesickness. For reasons that aren't remotely clear to me now, I'd been so sure my mother would visit that weekend. When she didn't, I went to bed, told everybody I was sick.

Sunday afternoon, after the parents all left, Addie barged into our room. "I understand you're hurt," she said, "but Estella and Pen and I are going on an adventure, and we don't want to leave you behind. Will you come?"

Soon the four of us were racing past athletic fields and dining halls. We crossed over M Street to the towpath and followed it into the park. Deeper in the woods, the air was cooler, rich with the brackish smells of the Potomac River.

For a mile or so more, Addie guided us through brush that opened into a clearing with a white tree at its center, the most beautiful I'd ever seen. Long, witchy branches and a trunk knot like an eye. Roots knuckled under the black rocks that jutted up dangerously. Addie stood by the tree and threw her arms wide. "Anybody up for a swim?"

All along the path had been warning signs. DO NOT SWIM. DANGEROUS RIVER CURRENTS. STAY OFF ROCKS. ROCKS ARE SLIPPERY.

Addie toed off her shoes. Estella and Penelope wiggled out of their cutoffs. I moved carefully across the rocks and at the edge looked down. The cove below was dark. I knew I couldn't jump—and couldn't explain why. At that point, we'd only lived together a month, and I was still afraid of saying the wrong thing. "It looks cold."

"Cold's the point, dum-dum," Estella told me.

"No worries, I'll go first." Addie flashed her daredevil smile. With a wink, she sprinted across the rocks and in a great leap hurled herself off the ledge with an arm-winding, leg-kicking, joyous yawp.

We ran to the edge and looked down. Addie shot to the surface with her hair plastered to her skull, screaming with laughter. "It feels great! Come in!"

"You don't have to tell me twice," Estella said, and cannonballed in. Penelope held her nose and jumped.

I climbed the white tree and watched them swim as naturally as I used to, as if they were born for water. Penelope was the first to climb out. She slipped on her blouse, buttoning it with pruney fingers, and joined me on my tree branch. "You don't know how to swim?"

"My mom taught me to swim before I could walk." That's how we did it where I came from.

"I'm sorry your parents didn't show," Penelope said.

"We're estranged." Estranged—that was a good word for it.

"I don't talk to my father either." She told me about her dad abandoning her family to start another one in Florida, and how, psychologically, she got really screwed up. She began dating this old guy, Mr. Dennison, at her mother's tennis club. She was only sixteen when her mother caught her kissing him in a Safeway parking lot. "He kisses like a snake. Seriously, he dives in like this." She opened her mouth wide and came at me.

"Stop, gross," I said, laughing, my hand up.

"Mom made me see a therapist. The doc said I was re-creating the Dad dumping me scenario with Mr. Dennison. You know, hurt the guy this time, instead of me being hurt."

"Did you?"

She rested back against the trunk, finger combing her wet hair as she tried to remember. "Meh, who knows? But I was more interested in the science of being screwed up than in being screwed up, and I think that healed me." She looked up from her wet hair. "Something bad like that happened to you?"

"I'm good."

"Yeah?" she said, not buying it.

"Honestly. See?" Then I hopped out of the tree to prove it. My heart banged in my ears as I marched across the rocks. Before I could think about it, I stepped off the edge, shoes and all.

Splash.

Down I went, my body gone rigid. My lungs told my brain it needed oxygen. My brain told my arms and legs to get moving. But I was paralyzed with an old fear. The water grew colder the deeper I plunged.

Addie must've jumped in after me. I felt her shoulder under my armpit, and her arm locked around my rib cage, as she propelled me up toward the wavering sun. We broke the surface, coughing and spitting, and climbed out of the river using tree roots as handholds.

After that, Addie told us to hold hands as we warmed ourselves on the rocks. She promised everything that had happened to us before now was washed away. From here on out, there was only the four of us and this new life together.

A baptism of sorts.

———

BACK TO THE snow day: By late morning, the wind was ripping up O Street, but still no snow. I don't remember what time I left Addie, maybe eleven, maybe a little earlier. I hung out in Estella's suite of rooms on our second floor, waiting for her to come home. I loved her sitting room with the pillowy sofa under the big window and her art from the Cady's Alley gallery where she worked. On her bookshelves was a rainbow of her Birkin bags that could've paid off my student loans.

I nicked a sheet of monogrammed stationery from her desk, don't ask why. Estella was the most generous person I'd ever met. Once she even let me borrow her so-called Keira Knightley Green Dress Worn in the Movie *Atonement* that her mother bought at auction for a truckload of money and may have even been real. That was the kind of person she was—she'd lend you the Maybe Keira Knightley dress off her back.

At her desk, I wrote my weekly letter to my mother. For the life of me, I can't remember what I said, or why the police would later make such a big deal about it. You can imagine how boring and repetitive my weekly letters to my mother were. I'd talk about my mediocre starter job, my three best friends, and a great guy I'd been dating for years. I must've closed the letter its usual way: *I miss you, don't worry, I'm okay,* and addressed it to *Katherine Ambrose c/o Sheriff Ed Brown, Glynn County Sheriff's Department, Georgia.* When I heard Estella's footsteps on the stairs, I shoved it in my pocket.

Estella leaned against the doorjamb, looking like an all-nighter gone wrong—strapless black dress under a large men's leather jacket, blond hair tangled and nose pink. "What are you doing behind my desk?"

"Looking for a stamp."

"Don't think I have any." She sauntered past me and dropped onto the sofa with a groan. "Ugh, I'm so hungover. My kingdom for a Motrin."

In her bathroom, the cabinet was filled with a dozen different meds. Some to sleep, some to wake up. Painkillers in plastic containers rubbed shoulders with mini bottles of vodka we swiped from hotel parties. I scooped up a handful of medicine bottles and carried them back. "Let's see, I've got Tylenol five hundred and what's this . . . are these for your migraines?"

Her eyes were closed. She tapped her fingernails on the table. "Leave it all right there. I'll figure it out, thanks."

"Want something to wash it down?"

One eye opened. "You got vodka?"

I filled a dirty mug with tap water from her bathroom faucet and carried it to her. She told me I was a sweetie, thanks, then swallowed her pills. The effort brought some of her color back. She told me about a party I missed last night. "Jenna Taylor brought her cute little dog, a Yorkie," she said.

"A Yorkie's not a dog. It's a cat that barks."

"She carried it in a pink Coach satchel made especially for her dog. I wouldn't mind having a dog like that. What do you think?"

"I worry you'd forget the dog was in your satchel," I said. "You'd forget to come home and feed it. Penelope would end up taking care of the dog you shouldn't get."

She frowned. "Well, I need something, Lucy. The rest of you have your careers. What do I have? A job at a gallery cutting my hours. You might've noticed I'm floundering."

"Any day you're going to land something that'll wow even yourself," I said, trying not to think about my career she envied at the "fancy" political messaging firm. It wasn't much more than an entry-level job. "Speaking of which, I have to run into the office," I said. "Can you keep an eye on Addie for me?"

"You're not working today? It's the weekend."

"It's just a few hours," I said with a shrug. I had sky-high rent and student loans I could barely afford. If I had any hope for a raise, I needed to impress the boss.

Estella straightened, suddenly alert. "Can you stop by the store on your way home? I need Solo cups for the Danger Punch party tonight. We're making Danger Punch slushies with snow. A bulk pack should be fine."

Estella's parties were always fun. But I couldn't help feeling that a Danger Punch party tonight was a terrible idea. "During a snowstorm?"

"Only walking-distance friends are invited. Not more than thirty people or so."

"Maybe you should cancel? There's zero chance Addie wants a party."

"Last night she was thrilled about the party."

I thought about how Addie looked when I left her by the tub. How I promised not to tell anyone about her attack. "Check again," I said. "And were you listening? I have to go into the office for a few hours. Keep an eye on Addie, okay?"

Her eyes narrowed. "What's going on? You're acting cryptic."

"Just do it, okay?" I said. "Text if she needs anything."

IT WAS A short walk to work. The Andrew Lee Strategies building, where I'd worked since I graduated a year and a half ago, was seven stories of glass on the Potomac River. In its street-front window I watched myself approach, a woman in a dark parka and hat with red hair spilling out, storm clouds behind me.

I swiped my badge to get in. A football game blared from a TV inside the security office. Bruce, the head of security, came out wearing Dad Snow Day clothes. He tapped the sign-in tablet. "Put your John Hancock here so I can get back to the game."

"Who'd you piss off to get stuck working a Saturday?" I joked.

He shot me a *get serious* look. "Mr. Lee's here."

Mr. Lee founded the firm, considered one of the city's most prestigious marketing and political messaging firms. His clients were a who's who of businessmen and politicians in need of reputational makeovers. I signed my name with a flourish. "Anybody in the mail room?"

"Mail guy called in sick with the snow flu."

Damn it. "I have a letter to get out to my mother."

Bruce and I always chatted about our families. He had two grown kids who texted but sometimes Bruce wished for a letter or a card, something that lasted.

"Hang on." Bruce ducked into the security office and came back with a mail-room key. "Drop it back here before you go. Are you going to be long?"

"A few hours, thanks."

I was halfway across the lobby when he said, "That's really special, how you're always thinking about your mother."

I WORKED ON the third floor as a dirt digger, aka an opposition researcher. Addie thought it was a hatchet job, and it was, but it was also the best-paying job we could find. Addie had started right after graduation, the same day I did, hatcheting right alongside me until she landed her dream job at the Smithsonian.

The project I was woefully behind on was for a client you've probably heard of, though I can't say his name. I signed an NDA when I was hired. Anyway, this politician had what Andrew Lee called a "reputational" problem; he was a pig. He got "involved" with a pool boy when the pool boy was still technically a boy, and this election year, the boy was now a grown man and was threatening to talk to reporters.

My job was to do a background check on the pool guy and find dirt on him, which I wasn't exactly motivated to do. For one thing, our client deserved whatever he got. For another, my thoughts kept wandering to Addie, how eight days ago Josh had scared Addie in a way she'd never been before, and then this morning, she was attacked.

Had she really meant Josh? A lonely trail, bad weather, no one around to help her—

I could see it. My father only ever picked on my mother when we were alone. If it was Josh, would he come after her again?

I opened a separate browser window and started another background check. Josh Egan had no arrest record, no civil judgments, no police calls to his house or to any place he'd lived when he went to school in New York. No #MeToo stuff about him on social media. I dug a little deeper. In a private Facebook group for newscasters I infiltrated, one lousy photo of a fist-sized hole in a newsroom wall was captioned "Egan's Artwork."

I ran my fingers through a knot in my hair. Josh punched the walls of his workplace, and people thought it was funny?

My mother's letter crinkled in my pocket. I grabbed the key Bruce had given me from the side of my desk and carried the letter down to the mail room.

AFTER THE MAIL room run, I told myself to get serious. I settled back into work. My office didn't have a window, so I had to keep googling *is it snowing*. Sometime midafternoon, Google told me *yes, it is*. Around six o'clock, Bruce knocked on my door. He told me Mr. Lee had gone home and ordered the office closed.

"How bad is it out there?" I said, handing Bruce the mail room key.

"Sidewalks are a mess," he said. "I'll give you a ride home."

Inside Bruce's Tahoe, I turned up the heat on the leather seat. Outside the window, fat snowflakes drifted through flickering gas lamps. Brick storefronts were dark with their awnings rolled in, with M Street abandoned to the snow. This was Georgetown as it must've appeared centuries ago.

At the top of the hill, our corner row house was all lit up. Someone climbed our stoop and opened the door, revealing our crowded foyer. I had forgotten about Estella's Danger Punch party! Estella's Solo cups! I thanked Bruce for the ride and hopped out of the Tahoe. The snow came up over the boots Addie had given me.

Inside our foyer, the sweeties were nowhere in sight. I hugged and air-kissed my way past our friends, saying, "How have you been? I haven't seen you in so long!" I darted up the stairs to find them pregaming in Addie's room.

Addie sat cross-legged on her bed, a mess of clothes around her. She wore a faint, tipsy smile. Estella sat across from Addie, applying makeup to Addie's eyes. "Ouch, you poked my eye," Addie complained.

Estella leaned back. "Stop moving."

"I didn't move."

"Something moved." Estella glanced around and spotted me in the doorway. "Hey, Luce, is the room moving?"

"Don't think so," I said.

Someone laughed and said, "Oh you're here, good!" and I came into the room to see Penelope on the love seat, curled up with a bottle of Fireball. She winked at me. "I didn't think we'd see you till spring. I thought you had plans to get snowed in with Connor tonight." I'd been dating Connor for four years, and Penelope liked to tease me about him, mostly because she liked him so much.

Penelope had streaks of purple in her dark hair and enough nervous energy to light up the waterfront. The purple streaks were to impress the kids who got therapy at the pediatric psych clinic where she worked in the hospital; she thought her hair made her relatable. She worked full-time at the clinic and often volunteered at an Anacostia health center, all while navigating the hellscape called the med school application process. Last year, while pulling an all-nighter studying for the MCATs, she got up from her desk and promptly fainted, slamming her head against a century-old iron radiator. She came to, bandaged her forehead, and knocked back four Advil so she could finish studying.

"Any word?" I said, meaning, had she heard back from any med schools yet?

Penelope lifted a bottle of Fireball. "Not yet," she said.

"They'll want you," Addie said. "Everyone will want you." Her voice wandered off. Suddenly the room felt too quiet. There was a big party downstairs, and we were up here. "Know what we need?" Addie said, perking up. "Music!"

Penelope clapped her hands. "Pull up our pregame playlist, will you, Stelly?"

"Stelly?" I laughed.

Penelope gave me a sly grin. "Pet name coined by the guy whose clothes Estella has been wearing home each morning."

"I wear my own clothes, thank you very much," Estella said with dignity. "I merely borrowed a jacket after forgetting mine. And anyway, it's not like you think. We just hang out."

Penelope winked at me. "He dropped her off several mornings this week. I saw it with my own eyes. He's downstairs, you know. What's his name? Muscles?"

"Henry," Estella said.

"Oh, I love that name," Addie said. "Such an old-fashioned name. Wait, I know! Let's dance on the roof."

"Dibs on Addie's boots," Estella said.

They crowded into Addie's closet, knocking into each other as they snatched up boots, running shoes, whatever was at hand. Estella put her hand on Penelope's shoulder and stepped into an old running shoe, and with the other foot a hiking boot. Penelope lost her balance, and I caught her bottle and took a long gulp that burned going down.

Addie put her shoulder against the window frame and forced it open. We climbed onto the flat, snowy rooftop. Everything was blue, our faces, the snow. Out on that roof, we had nothing to worry about anymore. Nothing bad could happen. Not in all our happiness.

"Crap, I'm cold," Penelope said.

"You'll numb in a minute." Estella took the bottle from me and poured Fireball into Dixie cups snatched from Addie's bathroom. She handed us each a drink. Then Addie hit play as we formed our circle, and the song started.

Everything was exactly as before. We screamed lyrics about London werewolves and Chinese menus into the winter sky over Washington, with Addie's voice—which was truly terrible—loudest of all. We danced with our drinks lifted like an offering. Then came the famous refrain, and we tilted our faces to the moon, and we howled.

The song ended, and I realized the moon was out. The snow had stopped. Behind us, someone banged on Addie's window.

"Stelly?" a man called through the gap between the window and its sash. "You out there?"

"Stelly," Penelope mouthed at us.

Estella rolled her eyes. "He can't even figure out how to open a window," she said, and shouted at him, "The window sticks, Henry. Put your shoulder into it. Use your big, strong muscles and . . . push!"

"I tried," he said. "It's possible I've had one too many Danger Punches. I feel quite drunk."

"Then a snowy roof isn't the place for you, don't you think?" Estella said.

He turned his face sideways in the gap. "It's dark out there. Is Addie with you? There's a detective downstairs asking for her."

"Asking what, Henry?" Estella said.

"If we've seen Josh Egan," Henry said. "The detective says nobody knows where he is."

CHAPTER THREE

THE DETECTIVE WAITED ON THE LANDING ABOVE THE FOYER. SHE had a rigid bearing. Ex-military, maybe. The shoulders of her wool coat glittered wet with snow. In the foyer below, the party raged on.

"Detective Rayne Kelley, Second District," she said, shoving her ID in Addie's face. She was laser-focused on Addie, who folded her hands in front of her.

"What's this about Josh?" Addie said.

The detective asked whether Josh was here. Addie said he wasn't. The detective said Josh never showed up at work this afternoon. His coworker's attempts to reach him by phone were unsuccessful. Josh's boss then called Detective Kelley's boss to ask what could be done. "So I'm out here doing what we call a welfare check for Mr. Egan." She said "welfare check" the way you say "no big deal" and then "Mr. Egan" with the same inflection you'd say "grown-ass man." "The boss doesn't like it when the VIPs go MIA," she said. "Mr. Egan's condo concierge thought he might be here. You're on my way back to the district station, so . . . ?" Her voice petered out.

"You won't find him here," Addie said. "Josh and I broke up last Friday."

Detective Kelley made a sympathetic noise. "I'm sorry to hear it."

"What about his car—maybe he drove somewhere? Does his car have one of those finder thingies?" Addie sounded rattled.

Kelley lifted her eyebrow, amused. "Thingies?"

"Maybe his car got stuck in the snow?" Addie said.

"She's saying maybe you can track him?" Penelope chimed in.

"Mr. Egan's personal vehicle is in his garage," Detective Kelley said, rocking back on her heels. "Okay, so none of you have seen or talked to him today?"

Addie shook her head, and then we were all shaking along with her. Downstairs, somebody flipped on more lights, and someone else turned down the music. People were eavesdropping.

"Probably he got confused," Addie said. "His work schedule is all over the place. Mornings, nights, I could never work like that. What time was he scheduled in?"

"Three this afternoon," the cop said. "To anchor the evening news."

Addie looked like she'd been lightning-struck. "*Anchor?*"

"His boss said Josh had agreed to fill in."

"That is a big, big deal," Addie said. "A show can't go on air without its anchor. You understand how big a deal that is?" She glanced around at us, and we were all like, not really. Kelley, too. "Detective, could we have a word privately?"

Kelley nodded. "Sure we can."

"We can use my sitting room," Estella told them.

"Thanks but I'll meet with Addie privately," Kelley said.

THE THREE OF us went downstairs to bust up the party—confiscating Danger Punch slushies and shoving coats at guests, pushing our friends into the storm. An argument broke out in the front room. Estella, our very own Captain Chaos, who was never so happy as when she had an antagonist, was fighting with Kevin Thompkins, an old track mate of Addie's. It was getting loud.

Best I could tell from the insults Estella hurled: Kevin had surreptitiously taken a picture of Addie talking to the detective on the staircase, then posted that picture to social media, tagging it *#DCPolice interviewing Addie about #JoshEganMissing.*

"You made it sound like Josh disappeared!" Estella seethed.

"She's exaggerating," Kevin told me. "I didn't say disappeared. I hashtagged 'missing.' And I was standing right there when the detective asked where he was. Meaning, he's missing."

Estella said, "You took a picture of my friend in my house at my party and posted it without permission! You make it sound like something bad has happened!"

"A police detective is questioning Addie," he said with an eye roll. "Does that sound like something good's happening?"

"Delete the post," Estella shouted.

"No way! You know how many new followers I've gotten?" Kevin said. "It's already my most popular post!"

Estella lunged for the phone. "Careful," I told her. "Don't break the phone."

"His phone, hell," she gritted out. "What I'm going to break is his neck!"

A crowd closed around us. Someone came in from the snow, shouting "Stelly!" and next I knew, Henry was pushing his way through, inexplicably wielding a shovel. He snatched Kevin's phone and threw it onto the marble floor, where he proceeded to beat it with the shovel. I begged him to stop. "How the hell does a smashed phone take down the post?" I said.

Henry looked up, confused.

Just then, Detective Kelley came down the stairs; seeing the fight, she shook her head in disgust and went out the door.

AFTER THE PARTYGOERS had cleared out, I went up to Addie's room. She was zipping up white ski bib pants over a dove-gray turtleneck, looking like a model for some ski resort advertisement. She was getting bundled up to leg it to Josh's condo. "Don't even try to stop me," she said. "I've got to talk to Josh."

"But Detective Kelley said Josh wasn't home."

"Maybe he is now."

Going to Josh's was not a good idea on so many levels. It was nearly midnight. We were still Fireball drunk—or at least I was. There was a foot of snow outside our door, and Josh lived more than a mile away. Even if she made it to Foggy Bottom in all that snow, what if Addie got snowed in with Josh? What would he do to her? What had he already done?

"Why not wait till morning?" I said.

"I can't! He's in trouble now."

Was I missing something? "Did that detective say he was in trouble?"

"She barely said anything!" Addie said, outraged. "Just that he's a grown healthy man, so he'll *probably* turn up soon! Ugh."

Okay, so Addie only *thought* he was in trouble. But still, once Addie got an idea in her head, you couldn't crowbar it out. "Okay, let's review the facts. Josh blew off work. Whoop-de-do."

Addie's eyebrows shot up. "Whoop-de-do?"

"Think about it, Ads. I've blown off work. You've blown off work." Not many times, but. "Everyone's blown off work. Who wants to work at the height of a snowstorm?"

"Josh doesn't blow off work. He's the most ambitious person I've ever met." Coming from Addie, whose parents were renowned physicians who worked insane hours, this was something. "Josh has a compulsion. It's called his job. He has to prove he made his own way all by himself, not on his family name. He's afraid he'll get lost in his father's shadow. His not showing up to anchor a show, the most important job in a career that's oxygen to him? That spells trouble, okay? Plus, he's not answering my calls!"

"Is it possible he's giving you the space you said you needed?" I asked carefully. "You had a bad morning on the towpath." An understatement. "The breakup was scary, too. You're upset with him. He's upset with you. Why not give him time to calm down?"

"But there's something wrong now!" Addie was pacing in front of her wall of Angela Bassett classic movie posters. Angela dancing on a white beach with a hot man. Angela walking away from her man's Mercedes that she torched. Angela with her coven of witches. She pressed a fist to her gut. "And I still love him, all right?"

I guess it made sense. Josh was her first love, and she'd been wild about him for months. Everything had turned bad so fast. Of course she wasn't over him. They'd only been broken up a week.

"Okay, Addie, you love him, you need to do something," I said, nodding. "If we could do one thing to make you feel better tonight, what would it be?"

"I'm going to Josh's," Addie said. "If he's still not back, I'm going to look around the condo for something to explain what's happening. Soon as I know he's okay, I can rest."

"Sounds like a plan," I said, starting for the door. "I'll borrow Henry's shovel and dig out Pen's Jeep. I'll let you know when we're ready to go."

"You'll help me?"

She'd pulled me out of the river. She'd taken me in and made me feel DC could be home. Aside from my mother, there was no one I loved more on this planet. How could I let her go to Josh's alone? What if she couldn't get away from him this time?

I said, "I'll do anything for you."

HENRY DID US one better than lending his shovel—he said we could use his car, which was garaged two blocks away. Soon enough, his brand-new, tricked-out Range Rover pulled up in front of our house.

He helped Estella into the driver's seat. "You'll take care of my baby, right?" he asked.

"You bet," she replied, and slammed the door in his face.

"Does Henry know you've never driven in snow?" I asked.

"He knows I'm from California," Estella said, and floored it.

Snow flew past our windows. Penelope white-knuckled the oh-shit handle. I assumed the crash position, praying to any god who'd listen to please take the wheel. Addie pressed her nose to the glass, telling Estella when to turn onto Josh's street.

Josh's condo was a massive white cutout against the darkness. It had long sweeps of toothy balconies. Estella skidded the Rover to a stop under the portico. We argued over what was happening next.

We decided that Addie and I would go up to the condo and Penelope and Estella would stay with the car. Addie and I passed through the most luxurious lobby I'd ever seen. Marble and gold and rich wood and artwork. I could almost hear my father sneer, *Here you go again, getting above your raising.* Addie stopped to chat with the concierge. I stood there, gawking.

We went up the mirrored elevator and got off at the penthouse floor. Addie banged on Josh's door—no answer. Addie slipped her key in the lock and opened the door slowly, leaning through the opening. "Josh?" she called into the dark apartment. "You here?"

Nothing.

She felt for the wall switch, and the overhead lights came on. According to Addie, this had been Josh's parents' home, and except for a short time away at school, Josh had lived here all his life. After his mother passed a few years back, Josh inherited the apartment but hadn't changed much. You could see that in what was left of the faded floral wallpaper and the scatter of fussy tables shoved between the more modern stuff, obviously Josh's—the leather sectional, the huge TV over a granite hearth. The wall of windows framed bright white monuments along the black river.

Nothing seemed to be out of sorts. My take on all of this was that Josh had screwed up badly with Addie at the park today and now was smartly giving her space, *as he should*. I figured he'd gone off with the sulks.

Addie tossed her coat on a settee by the door. "I'm going to do a quick check of the bedrooms. You stay here, okay?"

"Fine by me."

I stood by the coat closet. I've got a thing about closets, as in I don't like their doors closed. First thing I'd do whenever I came home was check the closet. Make sure there was nothing scary inside. That's what I did with Josh's closet.

The man was a serious coat hog. Behind all those coats, leaning against the wall, was the official portrait of Senator Elliott Egan. I pushed coats aside and studied the senator.

He was good-looking, for an old guy, though he looked mean, and I had no idea how anybody could vote for mean people. He had a long, stubborn jaw and cool blue eyes like Josh's.

Why would Josh stuff him in the closet? If I had an almost-president for a dad, I'd stick his portrait in the middle of our foyer. I might even haul it into work, so the bosses would give me every promotion, all on account of having this famous dad.

I made my way to the kitchen. I looked for notes or mail, any kind of correspondence, a calendar that might show what he was up to today, but there was nothing. I checked the trash can (emptied), the recycle bin (also dumped, damn it). The refrigerator, big as my closet, was full of perishables. Yogurt and cut berries, a takeout container of sushi rolls that warned any minute Josh could come back to finish that sushi.

"Hey, Ads? You almost done?" I shouted.

From somewhere in the back of the condo, her voice said, "Need a few more minutes."

I gave her those few minutes before I started down the long hallway. "The girlies are probably getting cold," I shouted toward the end of the hallway, where a door was open. "And you know, any minute Detective you-know-who might come back and catch us here."

Would Kelley arrest us? Probably not, since Addie had a key. "Let's go, Ads," I said. "You back here?"

At the end of the hall was a bedroom with a huge platform bed, dumbbells in the corner, an enormous TV over a bureau—bingo, Josh's lair. Glass sliding doors showed a snowy patio overlooking the Kennedy Center, a hell of a view. The man never met a curtain he liked to close. "Where are you anyway?"

"Don't come back here, seriously," Addie said from behind a partially closed door. A slant of light shot through. I crossed the bedroom and pushed the door open.

"Woah," I said.

CHAPTER FOUR

IT WAS A HUGE DRESSING ROOM WITH A THICK LAYER OF PAPER strewn across the floor. I'm talking about hundreds, maybe thousands of pieces of old, yellowed paper. Some balled-up, others ripped to shreds, and still more spilling out of storage boxes on their sides. Addie sat in the middle of the mess. Beside her, an EGAN 2004 bumper sticker had been ripped in half. An empty bottle of Jack Daniel's lay on its side.

I'd seen every episode of *Criminal Minds* twice. I knew exactly what was going on here. "What were they looking for?" I asked.

Addie smoothed out a document and took a picture with her phone's camera. "Who?"

"FBI search team. SWAT team. Whoever busted up the place."

"The police didn't search here," Addie said, not even glancing up from her picture-taking. "The concierge let Detective Kelley in, walked her around to make sure Josh wasn't having a medical emergency, and left." She gnawed at her lower lip. "The apartment wasn't broken into. Concierge also said Josh hasn't had visitors today. No, I think Josh did this."

"*Josh?*"

She looked up, annoyed. "Yes, Josh."

I turned slowly in a circle. On the far wall was Josh's wardrobe. Fancy suits. Crisp dress shirts, blinding white, hanging neatly. Silk ties in every color. In the middle of it all, the huge paperwork mess. The mess Josh had made.

I kicked aside the Jack Daniel's empty and picked up a ball of paper, unraveled it: *Des Moines Iowa Itinerary, July 2004, staff contact list.* "What is all this crap anyway?"

"It's not crap," Addie said primly. "This is his father's legacy. Campaign documents, speeches, I'm not sure what else. Everything that hadn't been sent to the National Archives after Josh's dad died. There are personal notes in here, too."

"So what? He's angry at his dad?"

Addie didn't say anything. Probably she couldn't conceive of anybody hating a parent. She and her father were tight.

"Unless Josh has got a Dr. Jekyll, Mr. Hyde situation going on?" I suggested. "One minute he's a nice guy, then night falls and he turns into a raging monster?"

She laughed shortly. "The things that get in your head. There's no evil side here." Then she let out a sigh and set the document beside her. "This room wasn't like this when I left Josh. I wonder what's been going on with him. Maybe I mishandled the breakup."

I sat on the floor across from her. "He scared you. You got away. That's the right way to handle being scared."

She told me how, after Detective Kelley left our house tonight, Addie had called Josh's closest friend at work, a producer named Marcus. The newsroom, Marcus said, had been buzzing about Josh all week. Word was, Josh had been getting threatening calls. Others noticed Josh had been coming in late, blowing off meetings, ducking out of the bureau at odd times. He'd even missed a news story—unheard-of for Josh. Marcus had reached out, but Josh ducked him, too.

"That was why, aside from the fact that Josh would never, ever, ever miss a chance to anchor, or put his show in jeopardy by skipping out, the bureau chief contacted the police right away. There'd been this ongoing level of worry for Josh around the newsroom this week. Now I'm looking at all his father's stuff and wondering, what if, the night we fought, I'd stayed and tried to understand whatever was really going on with him? What if instead of getting upset and scared and running away, I stuck around and tried to help him?"

My take? Marcus had primed Addie to see Josh as a person who needed help. You could also look at this room and see it as evidence of a spoiled TV star's tantrum.

When a person scares you the way Addie had been, you have three options: fight or run or play dead. That's it. If you ask me, running is always the best option.

"You never said what the breakup was about."

She looked up at me from under her eyelashes. "Maybe you don't want to get dragged into all this?" she said.

Was she kidding? Getting dragged into exactly this was what friends were for. I'd been waiting. "Drag me," I said.

Finally, she opened up. You could see what a relief it was for her to talk. It all started with Josh wanting her to move in with him. "He was like, *move here right now*," she said. "You know me, I need a minute. I just wanted time to think. All he would hear was that I was choosing my friends over him."

"So he wasn't listening."

"Right? And then he started saying obviously untrue things about my friends, and that if I loved him, I would believe him. Then it all escalated. His face got all contorted. He seemed like a stranger, and he wasn't making sense. He punched a wall, Lucy. It's right there, in the bedroom, if you don't believe me."

I believed her. I'd seen that private Facebook post. The fist-sized hole in the wall. *Josh's artwork*, they called it.

"So I grabbed my stuff and ran out," she continued. "He followed me to the elevator. He got on the elevator with me."

My hand flew to my mouth. Through my fingers I said, "Did he hit you in the elevator?"

"What? God, no. Why would you say that?"

"Okay, all right." I was still suspicious though. She was being so careful, like she was handling me. She had that tendency. And I knew she was still holding something back—I could *feel* it, and it was *big*. "You said he talked about your friends? You mean us?"

She chewed her lip.

"What did he say?"

Then she started this roundabout story about how Josh had a bee in his bonnet about lies, anything he called "fake." She suspected his work as an investigative reporter chasing down bad people had made him overly suspicious. "He's like that kid in *The Sixth Sense*," she told me. "The kid character who sees dead people everywhere? Josh sees liars everywhere."

"Wait a sec," I said, bristling. "He sees liars *in our house*?"

She gave me the sweetest look, full of love. She reached over and took my hand, gently. "I need you not to hate him, okay?"

"Okay, I don't hate him. Now tell me."

She was looking at me now intently. I tried to pull my hand away, but her hand slid to my wrist, and her grip tightened.

"It wasn't Pen and Estella he accused of lying," Addie said. "He was talking about you."

PART TWO

HE SAID, SHE SAID

CHAPTER FIVE

JOSH

Seven Months Earlier

THIS WAS HOW THE WHOLE MESS STARTED: JOSH EGAN GOT A message on his tip line from an anonymous caller. The caller described himself as a friend of Josh's dad. Josh, who prided himself on fairness, decided not to hold it against the guy (in retrospect, a big mistake).

The caller provided his bona fides, taking up half the recording (and most of Josh's patience) talking about the view from Josh's dad's old office in the Russell Senate Office Building—the West Front and its gardens, the Washington Monument in the distance, blah-blah-blah. The caller had been in Dad's inner sanctum, bragged about seeing Dad's gold desk clock that spun and the campaign map all marked up and color-coded as if Dad were General Eisenhower invading Normandy. Details Josh hadn't remembered until the caller brought it up.

The caller, Josh knew, was working hard to make Josh trust what he was about to say. Josh yawned. He circled his finger, like *get on with it already*. Finally, the caller did.

According to the tip: the honorable Congressman Whit Frank had a rap sheet as long as his femur, under a few different aliases. Not to mention an ex-wife shaking him down—saying he needed to pay up or she'd reveal his false identities. As he had so many times in his career, Josh thought, God love the ex-wives of the crooked and shameless. He couldn't do his job without them.

Josh was an investigative reporter specializing in crimes of all types. This was a very good thing since Josh worked in DC, and in DC the only other thing to report on was politics, and Josh would rather eat glass than cover politics. But this politician was a liar who'd broken the law, which was Josh's wheelhouse. Also his obsession.

It wasn't commonplace lies Josh was obsessed with. *No, you look great. Nothing's wrong. I only had one beer.* Josh himself lied, though he considered himself an honest person.

He was obsessed with a very specific kind of lie: those told to gain control over people. If Josh had taken a minute to reflect—he was allergic to reflection—or to tug at his terrible memory, he might've realized it wasn't Whit Frank who set him off. Who he really needed to have it out with was the old man. But he couldn't do that, could he? His sainted father was dead.

So instead Josh became a reporter who investigated jerks like Whit Frank. After that news tip, first thing Josh did was reach out to his pal at FBI's Public Integrity Section.

Turns out, Whit Frank's legal travails were not unknown to the FBI. The pal pointed Josh to the rap sheet—gun charges and domestic assault complaints, the declinations to prosecute, everything under former names. By that afternoon, Josh had talked to the ex-wife, who told Josh to get the little weasel before she did. He called the weasel's office and left messages.

That night, Josh flirted with a staffer at party committee headquarters who slipped him the congressman's burner phone number. Josh called the congressman's burner phone with his own burner phone, saying, "Hello, Congressman, this is Josh Egan—"

The congressman hung up.

Thus began the weeklong game of cat and mouse, which for a variety of complicated reasons—mostly to do with the congressman's errant belief he could duck Josh (he could not)—ended with Josh and his photographer driving two hundred miles north of DC into the hinterlands of the congressman's district in Pennsylvania.

Josh left the same message on every phone number he had for the congressman, explaining what he was reporting and the documentation he had to back it up, along with the ex-wife's interview on camera. Josh was offering Whit Frank the opportunity to defend himself on camera. He knew the congressman was back in his home district. Josh could be at his house in half an hour or less.

The congressman called back, saying "bring it, you prick," along with a variety of clever insults regarding where Josh could shove it, before hanging up again. Josh grinned at his photographer, Claude, who was driving, and said, "We got him. Let's go."

THEY PARKED ON a horseshoe driveway in front of the congressman's replica of an English castle. Josh knocked on the front door. He noticed a curtain moving just before the front door flung open. The congressman shouted for them to get off his property in this weirdly theatrical way that made Josh glance around for a camera rolling. Then the congressman pulled a pistol from the back of his waistband.

Josh thought, *Gun*, and his insides zinged as though he'd knifed a toaster and was riding the electric current, unable to let go. He shouldered Claude out of the way and slapped the gun from the congressman's hand. He kicked the gun and it went skidding across the football-field foyer. Then his hand curled into a fist.

From behind, his collar was being yanked. "Let's go, Rambo," Claude said, and, thank Jesus, dragged Josh back to the car.

Next Josh knew, he was blinking sweat from his eyes as the highway lines sped past. The car sweltered. Slowly Josh's thoughts came back to him. He'd almost punched a sitting US congressman.

Not a good congressman, no. Probably he wouldn't be a congressman for much longer, either. But still, if Claude hadn't grabbed hold of him, Josh's career would have been over.

"You think he would've killed us?" Claude was saying.

One half of Josh was still live-wire buzzing, the other sinking lower and lower in the passenger seat. He'd almost hit someone, Jesus. He'd never hit anyone in his life. He'd wanted to, sure, but grown-ups didn't actually punch people.

Claude laughed. "For a fancy dude, you do all right. I'd go into the foxhole with you any day."

He barely heard Claude over his mother's voice in his head: *Imagine how that looks, Joshua.* When he was a kid, he'd often disappointed her like this. *You have to behave as if everyone has a camera. Our enemies are all around us. Everything you do reflects on your father.*

In other words: do not show you're afraid. And when he was a boy, Josh was afraid a lot. So he'd push his feelings down, or he'd run off and hide where no one could see.

The truth was, Josh had been rattled before they arrived at the congressman's house. He'd been off his game since that caller, his dad's friend, had started talking about his father.

THEY WERE STILL north of the city when Claude agreed to drop Josh back at his place. Josh would write the script in the quiet of his home. He'd take a shower, have a drink, watch the sun set over the Key Bridge as he wrote. That would relax him.

Fifteen minutes outside the city, his work phone chimed the *Law and Order* ringtone he'd assigned to his boss's calls. Linda, the Washington bureau chief, was saying Congressman Whit Frank's chief of staff had called to allege Josh had assaulted the congressman after trespassing on his property.

Over speakerphone, Josh offered to Linda the contemporaneous electronic notes he'd already gathered like an exhibit to a legal brief. He'd recorded the congressman's "bring it" phone call, since he always recorded these kinds of calls. The Google Maps timeline, which he screenshotted, showed their drive to the house *after* the invitation. "The minute the congressman said we were trespassing, we prepared to leave," Josh said. "He pulled the gun anyway."

"No one was hurt, I hope," Linda said.

Claude said, "Thanks to Josh, I'm good, Linda, thanks."

"Excellent," Linda said. "Neither of you saw a 'No Trespassing' sign on the property?"

"No signs anywhere," Claude agreed.

Linda let out a long sigh. "Also very good. Without signs indicating otherwise, you have the right to knock on a door without having a gun stuck in your face. Congressman Frank had the right not to answer or interact. But your records help our cause, Josh. As always, you're the bright one. Just be sure to stress the phone call invitation when you talk to Legal."

"Tell me they're not killing the story? That's why the congressman pulled this stunt, you know. He doesn't want the story to air."

"The minute the folks with the law degrees give it the okay, it will air. And Josh? I'm glad you're okay." There was a smile in her voice. "You are dear to us."

THE NEXT DAY, in his office, the red light blinked on Josh's desk phone. This particular light indicated a message left on the anonymous tip line. It was that caller again, the friend of his father's.

"I didn't see the story last night," the caller said. "Everything okay? You need more info? Claire Ryan is handling the congressman's damage control.

Her Virginia firm is partnered up this month with Andrew Lee Strategies. You can catch her at their Georgetown building. You know Claire Ryan, right? Worked for your dad."

The message ended. He wished he could listen to the message again, but it automatically deleted after playing, a safety measure for his whistleblowers and anonymous sources. The government can't subpoena what doesn't exist. Plus, it was James Bond cool.

Josh jotted "Claire Ryan" on his notepad.

The name did feel familiar, though Josh remembered almost nothing of his childhood. His father had died the day Josh turned twelve, a day Josh remembered not at all. What few memories Josh had were little more than impressions from old news clips and documentaries about the senator who'd run for president.

Elliott Egan had been young—for a politician—and handsome, a rock-star candidate. Josh had seen video of his father working a rope line bulging with screaming crowds, mostly women wanting to touch him.

He was aware of his father's platform—end war and childhood hunger and poverty. Fix carbon pollution, as his father called it in 2004, a term Josh wished had caught on. Dad had been right. Carbon was polluting the planet to death. Josh probably would've voted for the guy.

Whenever he tried to see his father as, say, a father, a real person he loved, his memory crusted over like ice across a windshield. Whenever he pushed the memories hard, he got a headache. So he stopped trying.

But Claire Ryan . . . did he know her?

He searched her name, and Google spit out her bio. She'd been the former campaign manager for the Elliott Egan for Senate campaign in 2000 and the Elliott Egan for President campaign in 2004. Nothing between 2005 and 2014. After 2014, she hopped the fence, reinvented herself as a messaging consultant for the other team.

He clicked on her image: an attractive blond in her fifties maybe, a heart-shaped face, soft hazel eyes. He'd been doodling on a notepad as he read about her. He blinked down at the sketch. Without thought, he'd drawn elements of his recurring dream—a brown creek, a wooden bridge with a red house on it.

In the dream, Josh was running to this house, sometimes away from a hotel room. Inside was always the same woman, so pale she was nearly bloodless. A red sash, or was it a tie, was around her neck.

He looked up from the sketch and squinted at Claire Ryan's image on the computer screen until his head hurt. *Do I know you?*

No, he decided. He did not.

AT LUNCH, HE walked the five blocks to the M Street Bridge and crossed over into Georgetown. His favorite falafel place was on Potomac Avenue, and the Andrew Lee Strategies office building was around the corner. Two birds and all that.

He went into the office lobby and asked to speak to Claire Ryan. The security guy, who had clearly recognized Josh, said, "I don't know any Claire Ryan."

Josh was only good at what he did because he knew lies when he heard them. Lies had a sound—mellifluous, overly simple.

"I was told she worked here," Josh said.

The security guy laughed without humor. "I think I'd know who works here."

"How about Andrew Lee?"

"Him, we got."

"Ha ha," Josh said. "Can I talk to him?"

What was he even doing? So Andrew Lee says yeah, let me get Claire Ryan for you, then what? He didn't need a Claire Ryan response to a story already in the can and scheduled for air tonight. It's not like he could say, *Ever since someone mentioned your name this morning, I've been wondering whether I know you.* Or, *I have what I think is a recurring dream, and in the dream I'm a kid being chased in the woods by a creek, and when I saw your picture, it felt connected to that dream somehow. Do you know what I'm talking about?* At which point she would say, *No, you're mad as a bag of ferrets, and I'm sad to see Elliott's son turn out whack.*

The security guard was saying, "You can't just walk in without an appointment and expect to meet with someone like Andrew Lee," which was exactly what everyone always said to Josh the moment before they agreed to talk.

"Could you please put in the request, thanks," Josh said.

Across the lobby, an elevator dinged, and its door opened. A woman came out with a file box in her hands. She had big eyes and boyish hair, sharp cheeks and warm, brown skin. He liked the way she moved despite the awkwardness of the box. Like a dancer, or an athlete. Someone joyful in their body.

The woman carried the box into the atrium and chose a sofa in the sun. She wore the expression of a sun-warmed cat. He wondered what she was so content about. Nobody he knew was even remotely content.

"Tell Andrew Lee I'm waiting for him in the lobby," Josh said, and followed the woman into the atrium.

He sat in a chair diagonal from her. She didn't glance his way. He liked that. He wondered whether she knew who he was or had seen him on TV. Maybe she knew and didn't care. That was best of all.

Inside the box on her lap was a tablet in a brown leather case, a green gym bag, a handful of picture frames unfortunately turned the wrong way. Not that he was snooping. Given the box, he assumed she was a soon-to-be ex-employee. Leaving on good terms. Otherwise, the brawny dude behind the security counter would've walked her out. She stretched her very nice, very long legs, and the box rattled. He noticed the mason jar filled with Jelly Bellies. A purple ribbon with the words WE'LL MISS YOU tied around its neck. "Those are literally my childhood," he said.

She swiveled on the sofa and met his eyes. "I'm sorry . . . what?"

"The candy. My mom used to buy huge barrels of them for my father. They were his secret addiction." Funny he was remembering this now. "I've tried every combination. You ever put together two pale greens with a cinnamon red?"

She was smiling now. "I have not."

"Tastes like apple pie. I swear it," he said with his hand to his heart. "Runner-up combo? Two colas with one cherry."

"But surely more on the nose?"

"I don't like the recipes that try too hard. They're overly complicated."

She laughed. "Are we still talking about jelly beans here?"

"Jelly Bellies," he corrected. "The gold standard."

She leaned over the box, as if she was about to share a great secret. In a low voice she said, "These are a going-away gift from the guys in the mail room. It was very kind. I didn't have the heart to tell them I don't eat candy."

"Wait. Never?"

"No."

"Huh." He sat back. He thought about it. "So . . . a going-away gift? Going far?"

"Just across town. The Smithsonian." A slow smile crossed her face. He felt the punch of attraction all the way to his gut. "At the American History Museum. I've waited a year for this job. I'm so happy."

"Wow, huge congrats," he murmured. "I'm Josh by the way."

"I know. I've seen you on the backs of Metrobuses."

Ugh, those bus ads. How anyone thought his giant face on the back of a bus would help ratings was anyone's guess. He was about to ask her for her name when his phone sounded the *Law and Order* ringtone. She smiled when he said it was his boss. "Could you excuse me a second?" Josh said, then hit the accept button as he walked toward the window. "Linda, hello."

She wanted him to hop the next flight to New York. *The Morning Show* needed him to fill in on the anchor desk for Peter, who'd had a medical emergency.

"Anchor? *The Morning Show*?" Josh said, giddy.

"Yes, congratulations. Good things are happening for you. Do you want it?"

"That would be a huge yes. Thank you, Linda."

"Plan is for you to do your story from the evening news New York studio," she said. "Afterward you can meet with the *Morning Show* EP and he'll walk you through tomorrow. Your flight is booked, wheels up in two hours."

Josh slid his phone in his pocket. He'd need a change of shirt and jacket and tie and an Uber ride and a rundown of stories to read on the plane. All in that order, all of it ten minutes ago. He dug around in his wallet for a business card and held it out to the woman.

"Listen, I have to go," he said. "Could you call me on the cell phone number listed?"

She took the card. "You want me to call you?" she said, confused.

"So we can finish our discussion."

"About?"

"Anything you like, just call." He was walking backward to the door, still watching her. "You're going to call me, right?"

She laughed. "I don't know."

"How about this? When you call, what name's going to pop up on my screen?"

"Addie," she said.

He made an impatient circling motion with his finger, *give me the rest of it*. She gave him that smile again, the one that went straight to his gut.

"I'm Addie James."

CHAPTER SIX

THE NIGHT OF THE SNOWSTORM, WE GOT HOME LATE FROM JOSH'S. I went straight to my attic room and climbed into bed beneath the electric blanket and cranked it up high.

It had started snowing heavily again. The wind rattled the copper rooftop. Sometime around three, the snow changed over to sleet that tapped on the windows—*tap, tap, tap*, like somebody begging to be let in.

I kept going over what Addie told me in Josh's dressing room. How he'd claimed I was a liar. He warned her not to trust me. I was hiding something awful, he just knew it. He told her he worried about her *with me*.

This was laughable. She'd told him, "You do realize you're talking about my best friend in the world? Also what you're saying sounds a bit . . . well, unhinged."

She said she'd defended me, which I believed. She'd told him she knew me better than anyone did—also true. She would not tolerate people saying bad things about her friends. Above all, Addie was loyal. He asked whether she was calling him the liar. Then he lost his shit and punched the wall, and then he'd chased her into the elevator.

Horrible as all this was, I knew this to be the condensed version, the sanitized, more palatable one. She was still trying to manage my feelings about Josh.

I didn't want to be managed. I deserved to know what he'd accused me of. "What exactly were these supposed lies?"

She held me in her gaze. There was love in that look, but a question, too. "He told me your mother is dead."

MY MOTHER WAS not dead. It made me angry that I should have to say that. Addie had seen the letters I'd written home through the years.

Still, my anger was tempered by an inconvenient guilt. Josh was right that I had lied to the sweeties, though only once. It happened when I was seventeen and still back home in Georgia, before the four of us were even friends. One June day the summer before leaving for college, I got a group text initiated by an Addie James. It said: hello, i think we're all roommates? did everyone hear from housing?

One by one we all chimed in. We texted for weeks. They seemed so glamorous to me, these funny, witty girls with astonishing lives. They had beautiful clothes and big houses, the kind you saw in magazines. They told me their parents were doctors (Addie), inventors of energy bars (Estella), people with money from so far back she didn't want to know where it came from (Penelope). Then they asked about me.

My thumbs moved across the phone before I could think better of it. I told them I grew up along the Georgia coast among the barrier islands (true); my mother ran eco kayak tours (which also had been true); and my father owned beach resorts. This last was not even remotely true, although he had once been fired from a beach resort.

They texted pictures from their vacations—south of France, backpacking through Europe, a summer in Martha's Vineyard. Well, I had what I had. I texted golden-hour sunrises over the ocean, action shots of ospreys with fish in their talons and dolphins arcing over waves and pelicans swooping in great squadrons. Of bay grass and cattails so tall a child could hide in them.

One of the islands had wild horses, and Addie loved them best. I'd spend long afternoons in thigh-high marsh water, mosquitos buzzing around my head as I tried to get a decent shot of a pony. I'd tell Addie how the horses warmed their salt water–bloated bellies on blacktops and survived storms by herding their young to the island's highest land. How they were quick to kick and bite, elusive—like happiness, was how I put it—disappearing for weeks on end, and when you were at your lowest, a pair would appear ghostlike on the dune, fog-drenched, tails twitching.

I only lied so I could fit in. I was afraid the sweeties would pick another roommate. I was already a little in love with them. Once I got to college, I told myself every day I'd come clean but never found a good moment. Then the day would pass, and the next got harder. The lie had become too big, so much of how they saw me. I gave myself the deadline of Parents' Weekend, when my mother would visit campus. She'd help explain it all.

But she didn't show. Then Addie took us to her hideaway and rescued me from drowning. We dried on the rocks and promised each other the past was gone. Addie gave me this new life. Soon I forgot there was any other way to live.

As soon as Josh came home, I'd have to say the truth I'd never been able to tell. That I don't know where my mother is, and it kills me.

AT DAWN, I gave up on sleep and went out to shovel. The snow came to my knees and was heavy, but the work cleared my head a little. I dug Penelope's Jeep out of the alley first. Then I cleaned the sidewalk around our house to our stoop. Our neighbor's was a mess, so I shoveled that, too.

I was freeing her copy of yesterday's *Washington Post* from its icy sleeve when Mrs. Dalton opened her front door. She was old and frail enough to break if you looked at her sideways, and boy did she have a way with words. "If I wanted my stoop cleared," she said, "I'd have paid someone to do it."

I leaned on the shovel and smiled. "Want me to put the snow back?"

"I want you to make people pay you." She talked like this whenever I did stuff for her, carried in her deliveries, took out her recyclables, picked up her arthritis meds at Morgan's Pharmacy. "You're a woman. They'll make you work for nothing if you don't demand money."

"All right," I said sweetly. "Pay me."

She ignored that. "And why on God's green earth do you girls behave as stupidly as you do?"

"What'd we do now?"

"The way you treat Elliott's boy. It's a scandal."

Elliott Egan's son. Josh, she meant. Mrs. Dalton had known Josh's dad from back in the day, the same way she'd known all the important people. Mrs. Dalton was a name-dropper who'd go on forever about long-ago parties with Pam (I had to google Pamela Harriman, but okay, she was fly) and the Bradlees and Jackie, who, sixty years later, still needed no surname in the neighborhood.

"In my day, Elliott's boy would've been snatched right up," she said. "But there you idiots are, making that boy stand out in the cold."

"That boy? *Josh?* Where?"

"Last night. Right there." She flung her arm out, pointing to a spot on the sidewalk beneath our windows.

"Josh *Egan*?" I said. "You're sure? Last night?"

"Are you deaf? That's what I said."

I considered this. Last week I'd found her wandering Wisconsin Avenue, confused about how to get home, even though she'd lived only blocks away, same house for more than fifty years. When I asked whether I could help, she accused me of interrupting her window shopping.

"You think I wouldn't recognize that boy?" she said. "Built just like his father. Those shoulders, my goodness."

"What was Josh doing?"

"Staring up at your roommate's windows like he was Heathcliff on the moors."

Could Josh really have been here? The idea made me dizzy with relief. If he'd been here last night, when he was supposed to be at work, that meant he'd been fine!

"What time?" I asked. "It must've been dark, right? Are you sure? You got a good look?"

"You think I can't see in the dark?"

"Was he out here during the party?"

She got a confused look. "What party?"

I KICKED THE front door closed and dropped the shovel, which clattered by the boot tray. "Addie!" I shouted.

She came out of the front parlor with her finger over her lips and a phone to her ear.

"That Josh?" I mouthed.

She shook her head no.

"I have news." I couldn't wait another second to tell her. Addie put her phone on mute. I told her what Mrs. Dalton had just said.

"He was here? When he was supposed to be at work?" she said, shocked. "How did he look? Did he look okay?"

"Like Heathcliff on the moors."

"Huh?" she said, then waved me away. "I'll talk to her myself. Let me finish up this call."

OUR KITCHEN WAS old-world cool with black and white tiles I kept sparkling clean. True, the appliances were better suited for the Smithsonian, but they had charm, and they sometimes even worked.

Penelope and Estella were at the kitchen table, huddled over Penelope's phone, going through her Tinder account. Penelope was in search of a romantic life she could fit in during her work breaks. When I came in, Estella was saying, "Why not just hook up with one of your dorky doctor friends in a bunk room?"

"Only happens on TV," Penelope said.

"Well, this swipe right? He's too young for you."

"Sigh, I know," Penelope said. "Still at the university."

"University?" Estella said, laughing. "He's Georgetown *Prep*. But at least he's eighteen."

Penelope grabbed the phone in a panic. "How did this happen? But he was talking about school. *Our* school. Didn't it sound like that?"

I poured myself a huge mug of coffee, famished from the morning's shoveling. "Anybody got chocolate?"

Estella pointed to a corner cabinet. "Box of Snickers. Top shelf."

I scarfed down the candy bar in three bites. "Who's Addie talking to?"

"Detective Kelley, I think?" Estella said.

I told them about Mrs. Dalton's Josh sighting. I bet Addie was informing Detective Kelley right now. The mystery would be resolved.

Estella's eyes narrowed. "Why are you so wired?" she asked, and then Penelope was looking at me the same way. Estella said, "You've been shoveling forever. You should be exhausted. Have you hit my medicine cabinet?"

"Just happy Josh is fine," I said.

Penelope put her hand on Estella's forearm. That was the Penelope signal to be quiet. That whatever needed to be said next required Penelope's gentle touch.

"You were wired on the drive home last night, too," Penelope said. "Was it because of Josh's closet?"

"Josh's closet isn't a closet," I pointed out. "It's a room as big as this kitchen. Rooms don't scare me."

Closets though?

I can't sleep with a closet door closed. Years ago, Penelope had asked why

I always had to check the closets as soon as I came home. "I'm looking for monsters, naturally," I had joked. The four of us had had a good laugh.

They never pressed me on it. They were thoughtful, sensitive people. Penelope has a saying: "Everyone has their stuff." Addie, a fervent believer in the gospel of privacy, prided herself on being discreet. Even Estella, who was loud and wild and apt to say the wrong thing at the very worst time, would never intentionally make anyone uncomfortable.

Since last night, after Addie said Josh had called me a liar, I'd wondered whether my reluctance to talk about certain things gave him space to criticize me. Was not talking about a thing the same as lying about a thing? Of course not. But I could be more open.

Baby steps, I decided. "Want to know why I'm scared of closets?"

A surprised silence. Estella recovered first. "Only if you want to tell us," she said.

WHEN I WAS little, my father left us a lot. Usually to shack up with other women. He always came back though, until one day, when I was seven or eight or nine, I don't remember, my mother told him no, he had to stay away.

That made for a not-good day. Neighbors called the police. Our friend Sheriff Ed Brown talked my father into leaving the property peacefully. Then Ed stayed on to make sure my mother was okay—and me too, I guess, though Ed loved my mother more than he did anyone.

That night, Ed took us out for dinner at a pizza joint. He gave me quarters for an old arcade game, Ms. Pac-Man. I ate enough pizza to fall into a food coma. Later that night, I drifted off to sleep with the radio playing low in the kitchen downstairs and the sound of Sheriff Ed talking my mother into leaving Dad for good.

Then I heard the monster. Stealthy footsteps in the room across the hall, my mother's room. I called for my mother. A monster was in her room, I said.

We did our usual monster check. We turned on her bedroom light—nothing. We looked behind the curtains and under the bed—no monsters there either. My mother tried to turn the closet doorknob. The door was being held from inside.

She threw her body against the door and told me to get out. Halfway down the stairs, I heard her say, "Sam, you son of a bitch."

PENELOPE WAS BLINKING hard. "That was your dad?"

"What was he going to do?" Estella said.

"I don't know." Not for sure, anyway. Though I'd seen the knife that Sheriff Ed took off my dad. Its curved blade, the ripping edge.

I forced myself to shrug. It happened long ago, and my mother didn't press charges. Later she even let him come back, though I've never understood that either. "Anyway you can't be upset about something that didn't actually happen."

"Yes," Penelope said, "you can."

I WENT OUT to see Connor, who co-owned a coffee shop near the canal with two good friends. Connor and I had been seeing each other since sophomore year, when we'd met in Ancient Greek Warfare class, a mistake class for me since I was the only female student in the lecture and kept getting interrupted in every discussion. One day, when I'd decided enough was enough and was going to drop the class, Connor stood up and said, *Would you all please shut the fuck up and let Lucy finish her point? I for one would really like to hear it.* And I thought, *Oh but he's the one for me.*

It was a short but treacherous walk to his coffee shop. Most sidewalks were still covered in snow. The ones that weren't had a thin sheen of ice I stepped carefully over. A shopkeeper stopped shoveling and moved aside for me to pass.

On Potomac Street, sand was scattered across the café's sidewalk. Through the storefront window, I saw Connor coming out of the back room. He was lean-hipped and handsome, with a boy-band flop of brown hair. He had no customers. Usually by now, there was a line out the door.

The bell over the door clanged as I went in. Connor glanced up and said, "Hey, Red," same as always, and then he gave me his secret smile. "Missed you last night."

I went around the counter to greet him properly. "You smell like fresh baked bread."

This, he knew, was my favorite smell. He gave me a sexy look. "It's not like I'm fighting off customers here. I could close up shop, call it a snow day, and we go upstairs and binge a show or something."

Connor had a wonderful upstairs apartment with a window that overlooked the canal. In the warm weather, Connor and I liked to sit on the sill at night and drink wine, watching the city lights blink on one by one as Wisconsin Avenue became a carnival beneath us.

This was a tempting offer. But I didn't have time. "I'm only dropping by to make sure you got through the storm okay. I've got to get back soon. Addie's a wreck."

"Oh no. What now?"

"I don't even know where to start."

The door chimed behind us. Nikki Banks came in with her golden-doodle, Baxter. Nikki had once been Estella's friend. They were both blond Californians with communications degrees and similar ambitions. Nikki had landed a job as assistant to Lena Leamas, the famous columnist and self-proclaimed DC media maven. She sidled up next to me at the counter. "Cute boots, Lucy."

"Thanks." They were cute. Addie gave them to me.

Nikki thumped her satchel on the counter and ordered a flat white. Connor slid a smoked salmon and egg breakfast sandwich in front of me. I took a bite. "Wow, this is amazing."

He grinned. "Right?" He tossed the dog a hunk of bread.

"Baxter's on a low-carb diet, Connor," Nikki said, then turned her high-wattage smile on me. "Funny I should run into you. I've been worried about Addie. You know what everyone's saying, don't you? The police are looking for Josh."

Connor looked up from the counter, eyebrows up to his hairline.

"And his network bosses are acting so shady," Nikki went on. "All I've gotten so far is a no comment. Even though I heard he didn't show up for work either."

"Sounds like gossip."

"That's your comment?"

"I don't have a comment. I'm eating my breakfast." I slouched over the counter and took a huge bite of sandwich.

"Know what else I heard?" she said, leaning closer. "Kevin Thompkins posted a picture of Addie being interrogated by the police, but I can't find the picture anywhere. I reached out to Kevin but no luck. Word is Estella's latest boy toy threatened to kill Kevin if he talked. Is it true?"

"That Henry kills Kevin? One can only dream." I pushed my plate away with a sigh. "You're bothering me about a person who, best I can tell, is on a work assignment."

I explained Josh's job as basically the plot of *All the President's Men* minus a president. He was an investigative correspondent who hunted dark crimes and shadowy people, going under the radar for days, sometimes weeks. I almost sounded like I knew what I was talking about. I didn't even watch TV news.

"So it's not true about their breakup?" Nikki said. "No one's seen them together in ages, you know."

"More gossip. Consider sticking to facts."

Nikki laughed. "What a secretive little girl gang you four have always been. Practically cultlike." She grabbed her flat white from the counter and dragged her dog to the door. Over her shoulder she said, "Makes me think there is something to what people are saying."

The door closed behind her. Connor turned to me. "Why didn't you tell me Egan was missing?"

CHAPTER SEVEN

JOSH

Six Months Earlier

WHENEVER JOSH THOUGHT OF ADDIE JAMES, AND HE LET HIMSELF fantasize about her quite often, his heart quivered. *Chordae tendineae.* Heartstrings, according to WebMD. He'd had no idea heartstrings were real, or that he had any, or why, for the first time in his life, he actually felt them. Because of a woman he'd met exactly once.

It'd been a month, and she hadn't called—he'd been so sure she would. He'd looked her up and found her phone number in two seconds flat, but in the end decided not to chase her. If she had wanted to talk, she would've called him.

He had really thought that today might be the day she did, though. It was his thirty-first birthday, not that she knew that. He lazed around his apartment before powering up his work phone, making an exception to his hard-and-fast birthday rule.

Since his father died on Josh's birthday, he found it less stressful to spend the day alone, unplugged, doing a news fast, keeping the drapes closed to the outside world. It had always been like this, since he was a boy. Later, he had the clause written into his employment contract: on this one day of the year, he should not be called into work unless it was a national emergency, a nuclear war, or an act of God.

He went into the kitchen in boxers and a T-shirt, his hair a wreck. On the counter were party-sized bags of Doritos and a six-pack of IPAs he'd gorge on from his sectional while anesthetizing himself on Investigation Discovery shows—*Fatal Vows* and *Deadly Women* and the marathon starting at midnight, *Evil Lives Here*. Pizza was likely to be the main meal.

He felt good today—this surprised him. He picked up his phone and checked his messages at the office. Another exception to his hard-and-fast birthday rule. There was a message on his anonymous tip line.

"Happy Birthday, Josh."

It was that friend of his dad's who'd left the tips last month about the sleazy congressman. He'd stepped down from his position after the FBI charged him. Josh recognized the caller's deep voice, the rasp a vague reminder of someone—who? In the background was the rumble of a truck, a commercial jet roaring loud overhead; the guy was calling from outside the city. Near a highway, Josh was pretty sure.

"I was thinking about that last party with your dad," the tipster said. "What were you? Twelve?" He described his father's Senate office filled with balloons. A conference table piled high with presents. "Such a tough day, isn't it?"

Suddenly Josh could see himself with his mother on that long-ago Yellow Cab ride to Capitol Hill. His mother was in her signature black-and-white dress, and he wore squeaky shoes and a scratchy collared shirt. They rode the Senate subway, his favorite thing, to his father's office, coming out at the Russell Rotunda, where tourists took pictures of his mother. He remembered racing up the stone steps—don't run, his mother had said—to the second floor. Had he stopped to pet Senator Kennedy's water dogs out for their walk? Or was that another day?

Inside the office, silver HAPPY BIRTHDAY balloons bounced along the ceiling. He remembered that, and the Wiffle bat wrapped, one of the staffers holding it up, laughing and telling him to guess what it was. Phones ringing. Suitcases everywhere. The typical last-minute travel chaos for another long campaign swing, or so they thought. Later that evening, his father would be wheels up.

Sometimes he woke from dreams of that plane. The cabin lights dim, windows black with night. In those dreams he'd feel the sharp jolt his father must've felt, followed by the ear-shattering crack, the scream of shearing metal, as out of nowhere, a starlit sky appeared where the cabin used to be. In his dreams, the blue and white 737 carrying Elliott Egan would fall from the sky, his father gripping Josh's wrists, pulling him down with him.

THIS BIRTHDAY, THOUGH, he kept his personal phone on. It was a four-year-old iPhone that had been his mother's and was still registered under her name and felt like a "safe" device that wouldn't be hacked back to him.

On that phone, he treated himself to another read of the article about Addie James breaking the mid-Atlantic collegiate record. He went out onto the sunny balcony. Birds chattered on the cherry trees below. He clicked on another article, a more recent one, a short feature in the *City Paper*:

> Addison James, Georgetown University alum and record-holding track star, has started *Addie on the Run*, a smart blog that mixes sports advice and self-help, posts trail maps and snapshots of Washington's most well-loved paths. The aim of the blog, James says, is to get would-be and veteran runners back to the trail. She writes about setting routines and listening to your body, training past discomfort but short of pain, which James admits is the most difficult balance.
>
> "Running," James says, "is an act of will."

Josh clicked open her Instagram page, where she'd recently posted a video of her walking along the towpath, talking about getting out under the trees. Outside, where you felt freer, lighter, happier. He wanted to feel that.

Then he noticed the pattern to her posts. Every Tuesday and Sunday, she posted runs through Rock Creek Park for #hillruns. For #longruns, every Wednesday and Saturday, the C&O Canal towpath. Monday and Friday were #speedwork at the #GeorgetownTrack.

Lucky for him, today was Friday. #HappyBirthday to Josh, the day to treat himself.

HE CLIMBED INTO the cab, wearing his new running shoes. The driver saw his face in the rearview mirror and did a double take. Over the angry blare of talk radio, the cabbie asked whether he was that guy. "You investigate the truth?"

"Try to," Josh said.

The cabbie turned down the radio. "You look into what happened to your father?" He talked about the worldwide plot Josh's dad had allegedly uncovered (he hadn't) and how the CIA killed him (they didn't). Josh used to try to explain the NTSB report, the black box and voice recording that proved the crash was due to mechanical failure, but it never did any good. People only ever heard what they wanted to hear.

The cabbie turned in his seat to look at Josh as he explained his theories with more excitement than Josh thought healthy. "You're driving into oncoming traffic," Josh pointed out. The cabbie swerved but kept talking.

Josh texted Marcus: currently in cab with driver talking about aliens mating with government officials, satanic rituals may be involved

Marcus: get out of the cab, bro

Josh: dad allegedly uncovered plot so CIA blew up plane

Marcus: calling police, where are you

At the intersection of Wisconsin and Prospect, the light turned red. Josh handed the driver a twenty and got the hell out of the cab. The humidity pressed down on his shoulders. An old woman passed, walking a dog in a doggy raincoat. He hurried to the Georgetown track.

From the gate he saw her stretching by the bleachers. Willowy arms skyward, her long frame elegant even in running clothes. He knew the moment she spotted him. She held her stretch a beat too long. He crossed the track.

"I didn't know you worked out here," she said, grinning, and he felt it all again, the punch of attraction, that wild high.

"You posted your Friday run here. Was it weird of me to notice?"

She laughed. "You think I post on Instagram so people won't notice?"

"You didn't call. Maybe I'm being pushy by coming here. I don't want to make you uncomfortable."

"I thought about calling," she said, serious now. "It just wasn't clear to me how often you give out your card, or for what purpose."

He knew what she was asking. "I've asked women to call me before, but I've never been so disappointed when someone didn't. I woke up this morning wondering, why shouldn't I do the one thing I want more than anything?"

That got her laughing again. "Work out at the track?"

He shook his head slowly, smiling. "But I'm happy to run as many laps as it takes if you'll have a coffee with me afterward. Or a drink. Or dinner. Whatever you want."

She took pity on him and stayed on the outside lane at an easy pace. After the first lap he was winded. By the fifth, his lungs threatened to fly free of his ribs in search of a better body. She kept trying to get him to talk. "You should be able to hold a conversation," she said, so easily. "We should slow down if you can't talk."

"I'm good," he panted out.

She glanced over. "Does your face always get this red?"

"I'm fine." On his tombstone, that's what it'd say: *He was fine.*

Afterward, he collapsed on the bleachers. She went to the line for her speed work. He watched her crouch and shoot forward so fast and easily, he knew he was witnessing magic. A woman at the height of her athletic powers.

She sauntered back, her skin glowing as if a fire burned beneath. He felt himself grinning like an idiot. "Did I mention today was my birthday?"

"Happy birthday, Josh."

"It is," he said. "It really feels like it."

THAT SUMMER THE planets were aligned, Jupiter showed itself in the eastern sky, and Josh Egan was in love truly for the first time. The wonder was that Addie told him she felt the same way.

One night after Labor Day, when they were tangled in bed, and he was still a little sex-dazed, she lifted herself on her elbow and said, "What are we doing here, Josh?"

"What? You want to do it again?" He grinned. "I'm game."

"I'm serious."

He sat up with his back against the headboard and listened. She wanted to know why they never went out in public. Was she his secret? Even her friends had noticed this strange thing about them. He could see he'd hurt her feelings without meaning to. He'd been selfish, wanting to keep her to himself for as long as he could. He explained how it felt safer for them up here, in the privacy of his home.

"Sometimes people can be a bit intrusive," he said.

He was trying to think of examples she would understand, but the truth was, though he knew his life was strange, it was his. He was used to it. Take the strangers who came up to his box at ballgames without being invited. Others who sat at his restaurant table to debate the merits of a story he'd aired, as though they were old friends. He'd had people follow him home from bars. On a walk, a woman came out from behind a tree and flashed him, nearly giving him a heart attack. Strangers sent gifts to his news studios. The DMs were the weirdest.

He explained it the best way he could. He was thankful people watched him on TV, because this was how he kept his job. The medium itself was weird though. People started to think they knew him, that they were friends. "I'm not complaining. I chose TV, and any time I could walk away. It's you I'm worried about. I don't want you to be scared off."

"You think I'm afraid of the celebrity thing?"

"I wouldn't really say I'm a celebrity. I'm a journalist."

"Anyway," she said, drawing letters over his chest with her fingernail. The first letter was *A*, the second *J*. "I don't scare easily."

"You sure?"

"I'll tell you if anything gets too much for me."

"Deal," Josh said. "So what's our first date in public? Think of the most conspicuous place we can go. I want everyone green with envy when they see you with me."

"How about you meet my friends?" Addie said.

THAT FRIDAY NIGHT, they walked, holding hands, from his condo in Foggy Bottom to Georgetown. He could see heads turning. He figured everyone was looking at Addie, who was particularly beautiful in a white gauzy number that floated around her like a dream. While they waited for the light at Wisconsin Avenue, a group of women asked him to take a picture with them. He lifted his hand in Addie's and said, "Do you mind if I decline? I'm on a date." That got the ladies aflutter. They hit him with questions:

"Where are you going, someplace romantic?"

"What's your name, honey? Are you on TV, too?"

"Is she your girlfriend?"

Addie got adorably flustered. He laughed and said, "Girlfriend? Hmm," and pretended to consider this. He smiled down at Addie and said, "It's more accurate to say she's everything to me."

With that, they'd officially gone public.

———

ON THE FRONT stoop to Addie's house, she stopped and put her hand on his chest. "Tonight, let's skip the interrogations, okay?"

"Do I do that?"

"Charmingly," she said. "Estella would love it, and Penelope won't mind, but Lucy's shy. I think her life has been harder than she lets on."

"I'm sorry to hear that."

"And I want everyone to like each other."

"Then we will," he said, so sure of himself.

Inside, the Victorian was more run-down than he'd expected. She was showing him around the house with a pride of ownership that felt a little like magical thinking. Here, the walnut banister—gorgeous, she said—even though it wobbled. Original hardwood planks moved beneath his feet. She loved the century-old chandelier with exposed wiring they'd fix, but why? It wasn't theirs. They'd never own the house.

Penelope hurried out of the kitchen to greet them. She was a pretty girl with purple streaks in her hair and big black glasses she pushed up her nose. "Thank you for coming to dinner. I'm so thrilled to finally meet you. Addie has told us such wonderful things." She said this all in a long, nervous rush, then turned to Addie: "Everything's ready, but Lucy's running late. What do you want to do?"

Just then the front door opened. A slender redhead slipped through. Her hair was wild ringlets around a pale oval face, exactly as Addie had described her. "Hey, Josh," Lucy said, her hand out for him to shake. "I'm glad you're here." Then, to Addie: "I know I'm late, sorry, but I need to wash up. Go ahead and get started without me."

FOR DINNER THEY had braised chicken with rosemary potatoes, which they served with a nice Oregon Pinot. The dining room was long and narrow, and they ate by candlelight. The sideboard was stacked with bottles of wine. A gray painting with one red slash hung over the boarded-up fireplace.

Their conversations flew fast, skipping easily between movies and books and music, stories half told and finished by each other. He felt a little dazzled by them. Estella refilled his wine. "Tell Josh about the Obama niece, Luce."

"Let's not," Lucy said.

Josh thanked her for the wine. Then, to Lucy: "Does President Obama have a niece?"

"Oh God no, this is so embarrassing," Addie said, laughing, and Josh squeezed her hand, saying, "Well, now somebody has to tell it."

Estella tossed her hair. "It was Addie's alter ego in college."

"Ugh, you can't tell a story like that," Lucy said, setting her glass down. Wine slopped on the linen. Then she turned to him and said very seriously, "We'd go to parties and guys would hit on Addie. She could never kick free of this certain type of guy that always gravitated to her."

Estella interrupted. "The saddest, drunkest, most pathetic . . . "

Penelope lifted her eyebrows. "These guys would ask for Addie's number, and she'd crumble, afraid to hurt anyone's feelings."

"Who likes hurting people?" Addie said.

Estella pointed her fork at Lucy. "So Lucy developed her alias. Alter ego, whatever. Remember that first guy hounding Addie for her Instagram handle? So Lucy moves in with something to the effect of, 'I'm sorry, but she's under orders from the Secret Service to observe a strict social media blackout. I'm sure you can understand . . . her uncle, you know.'"

"I was thinking, play her off as some foreign dignitary's kid," Lucy said. "The university is lousy with them. But the guy assumed President Obama, so."

Addie was shaking her head, laughing. "I never said anything about President Obama. I never gave any name. He just said I looked just like my uncle and then everyone started agreeing and it took off from there."

"You look *nothing like* President Obama," Josh said.

"We were treated so nicely after that, remember?" Penelope said. "The guys gave us a security perimeter and kept bringing us free drinks they didn't even spike."

"Wouldn't someone google 'President Obama's niece'?" Josh said. "Does President Obama even have a niece?"

"You're missing the point," Lucy said. "It was funny. Plus, we kept Addie safe."

"From men?" Josh said.

Lucy cut him a look. "From everything," she said.

As the night went on, he noticed Lucy was a good storyteller, good at telling stories that showed her friends in the best light, while keeping herself in the dark. Every story was about other people, nothing about her. She skirted direct questions, which intrigued him. "Addie says you're from an island on the Georgia coast?" he said.

Addie shot him a warning look. But Lucy smiled and turned his way. "In Georgia, we have barrier islands, sure."

Then she eased into a story about her namesake, the matriarch of a robber baron family who, more than a century ago, bought the island and built a great house they called their Winter Palace. Soon after, bad luck fell on the family. A terrible storm came, and the matriarch died, and the great house fell into ruin. After the family abandoned the island, their horses turned feral, although there was some debate about whether the wild horses had an older lineage. Some people believed the horses were descendants of shipwreck survivors that made it to land. Rumor had it the island was cursed.

It was a colorful story that kept everyone rapt. Lucy gauged her audience. She had a good feeling for how far she could push. When she saw him watching her, she stopped the story.

Addie's best friend was a liar. Maybe not as much of one as Josh's father, but Dad had been in a league all his own.

Still, Lucy was good.

CHAPTER EIGHT

ON MONDAY—TWO DAYS SINCE JOSH WAS A NO-SHOW AT WORK— the city was still shut down, government offices and schools closed for the snow emergency. My boss gave me the snow day off.

Addie still hadn't heard from Josh. She was certain he was emotionally in trouble but physically fine. She said she'd feel it in her gut if he wasn't. And hadn't our neighbor seen Josh Saturday night after he'd skipped work and his newsroom had called the police? Mrs. Dalton told Detective Kelley that Josh appeared fine. Now, maybe Detective Kelley had warned us to take the neighbor's account with a grain of salt—Mrs. Dalton's eyesight wasn't as good as she'd led me to believe, for example, and during the interview with Detective Kelley, Mrs. Dalton had referred to Josh as his father. But everyone misspoke from time to time, didn't they?

We stayed inside all that Monday. Penelope built a fire in the hearth. Estella got out her guitar and sang Phoebe Bridgers songs by the fire. I dusted off an old game of Monopoly left behind by a previous tenant. Pieces were missing, but we made it work. Addie kept forgetting her turn, glancing at her phone, until we gave up on the game.

"I feel like we should be doing something," she said. "Should we go out and search?"

"I'd go with you." I nodded.

Penelope frowned. "Where would we go? We don't have a clue where to look."

"You're not talking about searching outside, are you?" Estella pointed out the record cold. Forecasters warning of hypothermia. "There's no way Josh is out in this."

"Here, Ads," Penelope said, "help me with Spelling Bee."

For dinner we threw together food left over in the fridge into a pot—some old beans, half an onion, a green pepper—and called it chili. Estella uncorked a bottle of red.

We ate by the fire and finished the wine. Addie slid closer to me on the sofa and put her head on my shoulder, as we'd done countless times before.

"Isn't this waiting exhausting?" she said.

"It's the worst," I agreed.

She fell asleep on my shoulder for hours, me unwilling to move, not wanting to disturb her. I listened for footsteps in the snow beneath the window, certain any minute Josh would show up at our door unannounced, but more afraid that he wouldn't.

THE NEXT MORNING, my office was operating under a "snow schedule," meaning, if you can get to the office, come in. I was getting dressed to go into the office when a *Washington Post* notification appeared on my phone:

DC POLICE SAY JOSHUA EGAN IS MISSING.

I clicked on the link to a short article on the newspaper's app:

DC POLICE ARE INVESTIGATING THE MYSTERIOUS DISAPPEARANCE OF JOSHUA EGAN, TELEVISION NEWS STAR, LOCAL CELEBRITY, ONLY SURVIVING CHILD OF FORMER PRESIDENTIAL CANDIDATE SENATOR ELLIOTT EGAN.

DC Police are asking for the public's help.
This is a breaking news story. We will have updates throughout the day.

I hurried down the steps toward Addie's room. Penelope came out into the hallway, wearing the rumpled scrubs she slept in. An eye mask was pulled up over her uncombed hair. "What's all the noise?"

"Where's Addie? Where's Estella?"

"Addie took the Jeep about an hour ago," Penelope said. "She's meeting with Detective Kelley. What's *wrong*?"

"Did you see the news? Josh is actually missing. As in, this is not a drill." I shoved my phone into her hand. "Here's the *Washington Post* article."

"Shit, this is bad," Penelope said down at the phone, then looked up at me, stunned. "They couldn't possibly think that Josh is . . . well . . . I don't want to say it."

"Then don't. Why did Addie meet with Detective Kelley?"

Penelope scratched her jaw. "Huh, yeah, I didn't think to ask."

DOWNSTAIRS, ESTELLA WAS at the kitchen table, scrolling through her phone. The TV on the counter blared news about Josh. Estella glanced up wearily. "Good morning, I guess. In the past fifteen minutes, everyone and their mother has been texting about Josh."

I hadn't gotten any texts, thankfully. "What did you say?"

"Nothing," Estella said. "I'm not saying one word I don't clear first with Addie. She's probably getting bombarded, too. Let me know if either of you hear from her."

"The detective's probably telling Addie everything right now," Penelope said, worrying her lip. "We'll know soon enough what's going on, don't you think?"

Estella lifted a shoulder. "Maybe."

"We don't think something bad happened to him, right?" Penelope said. Neither of us answered.

We sat with Estella and watched the news. On the TV monitor was a picture of Josh, the official photograph released by cops: Josh smiling into the sun, a summer glow on his cheeks, and his perfect hair gold in the sunlight.

A female news anchor reported: *Josh Egan, acclaimed journalist and only child of former presidential candidate Senator Elliott Egan, was last seen three days ago on Saturday afternoon in the Foggy Bottom neighborhood of Northwest Washington, DC. The Metropolitan Police have released video of that sighting recorded by an ATM bank camera. Take a look.*

Grainy black-and-white video showed Josh in a dark coat walking along what appeared to be Virginia Avenue, a block from Josh's condo. You could see the Mobil gas station. Also, in the background, a sign for the entrance to the Rock Creek Park trails. Josh was walking fast, body bent into the wind, hair blowing. He appeared to be heading toward the park.

Josh Egan was wearing a dark gray coat. He's six foot four, a hundred ninety pounds, with blond hair and blue eyes. Anyone who has seen Josh Egan or has information on his whereabouts should call the police tip line.

Next, a "related" story about "rising violence" in the city. Then something about Josh's childhood on the campaign trail with his father. In front of Josh's condo, a reporter interviewed a woman who said Josh had saved her escaped parakeet. "My poor bird would've died in the cold," she said. "Josh Egan saved my Caruso." Josh's ATM video played over and over.

An hour later, when Addie still hadn't returned, I texted my supervisor and asked whether I could take a personal day. Sharkey replied: this about Egan? what's going on?

Me: we're trying to find out

Sharkey: how's Addie?

Sharkey had been Addie's boss for the six months before Addie landed her gig at the Smithsonian. Sharkey liked Addie, probably more than he liked me, even though I was his star pupil, his numero uno dirt digger.

Me: think she's okay

Sharkey: lemme know if you need help, okay kiddo?

Sharkey: if you need my skills

I knew what he was saying. He wanted to be in the know, and in return, he would help us however he could.

Outside, footsteps crunched the snow. Then clanged on the iron stoop. The front door slammed. Addie was home.

ADDIE WARMED HERSELF in front of the fireplace. She gave us a wobbly smile that didn't quite reach her eyes. "The police are finally taking Josh's disappearance seriously," she said. "This is good, I think."

Detective Kelley had told Addie they had no evidence that Josh was in a life-threatening situation, or that foul play had led to his disappearance. But three days was too long to be gone, given the circumstances—the bad weather, the reports from his newsroom of his odd behavior. The chief had decided out of "an abundance of caution" to go public with their search for him.

Addie had told Detective Kelley about her attack on the towpath before Josh disappeared that afternoon. I was surprised but also glad. No stone unturned and all that. Kelley called in a police sketch artist to make a composite drawing from the attack, which I did not understand at all. There were photos of Josh everywhere. Why did anyone need another image of Josh?

"Detective Kelley doesn't know if my attack is related," Addie was saying, "but agrees the coincidence is striking."

"What coincidence?" I said, so confused.

"This guy clashes with me on the towpath," Addie pointed out.

"The . . . guy?"

"Yeah, and later that same day, Josh doesn't show up for work. And the likeness, my goodness. You really have to see the sketch."

Addie was pulling the sketch up on her phone.

I found my voice. "*What likeness?*"

Addie glanced up. "The guy who grabbed me."

"The guy who . . . " I sputtered. "*Josh* grabbed you."

"*What?*" Addie said. Three sets of eyes turned my way.

"You told me Josh grabbed you." I said this with force.

"No," Addie said, "I didn't."

For a moment, I was too shocked to speak. Had I gotten it wrong? Alarm needled through me. "You said 'oh my God, it's Josh.'" I was repeating her exact words back at her. "You said 'looked like Josh.' You were talking in code about Josh."

"What code?" Penelope asked.

Estella laughed. "Oh my God, you thought Josh grabbed Addie? Look at your face! You really did!"

"Stop that," Penelope told Estella.

"Josh did *not* grab me," Addie said emphatically. "I told you the attacker looked *like* Josh." Addie's eyebrows knitted together. She got that same confused look she wore the day she was attacked. "So much like Josh, but not," she said, more quietly now. She was looking down at her phone again. "Though I can see how you got confused. I wasn't exactly coherent that morning."

She held out her phone. "Anyway, take a look."

THE DRAWING WAS of a man with dark hair and thick, dark eyebrows. He was attractive and looked younger than Josh. He had Josh's same slant of pale eye, the sharp jut of cheek and long Egan jaw.

He was a young, dark-haired Josh.

CHAPTER NINE

JOSH

One Month Earlier

FIVE MINUTES BEFORE HIS ALARM WENT OFF, JOSH SLID OUT OF bed and shuffled toward the bathroom, drunk with fatigue. His phone said it was 3:10 a.m. He flicked on the bathroom light and saw he was in the bathroom of his DC condo. Not, as he'd thought, in the corporate apartment across from the news studios in New York's Rockefeller Plaza, where he was expected on *The Morning Show* within the hour.

Was he in the wrong city? Had he forgotten to get on the shuttle?

He thumbed open his calendar. Okay, this was the Wednesday he was scheduled to work in DC. Big exhale, he hadn't screwed up. *Friday* he had to be in New York. Then he'd be back for the weekend in DC, before starting next week again in New York. In New York his call time was 4:00 a.m. In DC it was 9:00 a.m. Back and forth. Rinse and repeat. Jesus God, it was exhausting.

This insane schedule had been going on for over a month now, his body clock all screwed up, not sure when to sleep or eat or which city he was shuttling off to.

His bureau chief, Linda, had promised the punishing schedule wouldn't last much longer. Peter, the longtime *Morning Show* anchor he was filling in for, was "getting up there in age," and the network was antsy about losing viewers (which meant losing ad revenue, which meant losing money).

The Morning Show's demo was female. Women liked Josh, and the *Morning Show* executives figured the show would do better with Josh as an anchor. Play your cards right, Linda said, and you'll slip into the anchor seat if (or was it when?) Peter got pushed aside.

So he just had to deal with the sleeplessness a bit longer. He went back to the bedroom and saw Addie sleeping peacefully, and knew if he climbed back into bed, he'd wake her. So he wrapped himself in a blanket and went out onto the balcony to wait for the day to begin.

AT EIGHT, WHEN Josh got out of the shower, Addie was in his dressing room, kneeling beside a document box. She was dressed for work, with her Smithsonian ID hanging over her sweater.

Why did she have to go through that box? But he knew: she was a history buff, a person with a brain that moved so fast he sometimes couldn't keep up with it. She loved nothing more than to dig up clues to the past, and she found his past to be a particularly vexing puzzle. Mostly because he didn't want her digging into it. Damn it all to hell, his home was not an archaeological dig.

A headache was coming on fast. "Um, baby, what are you doing?"

"The box fell over. Look what I found!" She held out her palm. In it were two decades-old political pins: A TIME FOR GREATNESS, one said, and the other, VOTE FOR EGAN. Then she noticed the look on his face. She gave him a nervous smile. "I was just admiring them. You're not upset, are you?"

"No, of course not. That would be stupid. It's just that . . . Listen, Addie—I don't want you going through my father's stuff."

"You make it sound like there's something scary in here." Then she laughed.

"He wasn't a nice man, Addie."

"Oh." She looked at him with surprise. He couldn't believe he'd said those words aloud, either.

"I didn't know," she said.

"No one does."

She took a breath, as if summoning her courage. "Tell me, Josh. In what way was he not nice?"

He felt his jaw set, his expression go flat. He looked down at his hands, which were like his father's hands. What were the words to make people understand? His whole life he'd never found the words.

"I don't remember exactly." It was just a feeling, like this pressure bearing down on him. "I just don't want you looking at his stuff. And I know that makes me sound like an asshole."

"No, I understand," she said, but she clearly didn't. "But it's just stuff, Josh. It can't hurt me, or you."

He felt himself getting jittery, tried to tell himself it was sleeplessness. Why couldn't he have fallen in love with a woman who wanted him for his money or his TV job? Why did Addie push him to talk about his father, his past? "If you want to know about Dad, talk to people who knew him. There are people littered all over the city who'd tell you more in five minutes than you'll find in all these boxes."

"Do you do that, then? Talk to his old friends?"

He lifted one shoulder. "Sure."

"What do they say?" She said this like she wanted something good for him. She wanted a normal and loving family for him.

So maybe he exaggerated a little. He told her about the guy on the tip line, who told him stories that filled in his black-hole memory. The birthday party, for instance. After Dad's friend described it, he saw it all—the silver balloons with blue strings, the Wiffle bat in the wrapping paper, Senator Kennedy's dogs in the hallway. Addie seemed thrilled for him. "Who is this friend?"

"Worked for Dad. I don't know his name."

Her smile turned uneasy. "You don't remember his name from when you talked to him?"

"He calls on a tip line. He doesn't leave a name. The way I have it set up, I can't see his ID or trace it."

"Then how do you know he's a family friend?" she asked with a tilt of her head.

"He sounds like it." It wasn't just the things the guy said, it was something about his voice. It was deep and rich and struck the vaguest hint of a memory. He could almost put his finger on who the guy was, and then the message would be deleted and he'd lose it again. "Anyway, he helps me remember, that's all."

"But why hide his identity? And why would you listen to someone who won't give their name?"

"I've always done that." Anonymous sources were a normal part of his job. It wasn't as if he trusted them without verifying with two sources or official documentation. In terms of news stories, this caller checked out every time. He was even the reason Josh had gone to Andrew Lee Strategies that first day he saw Addie, so he also had that to thank him for. "And when it comes to the stuff about Dad, I don't need to verify anything. I remember what this guy says is true. And these memories, they're good memories, Addie. He helps me remember good stuff about my father."

She came to him and put her hand on his cheek. "I'm glad then. I really am."

"But?"

"I hear what you're saying about your business." She pressed her lips together, considering her words before continuing: "But these calls about your father . . . that's personal. And this person you don't know . . . Should he be dictating what you remember? Or how you remember it? It all feels a little manipulative. What if this caller isn't really your father's friend?"

He felt a smile coming on. It spread slowly across his face.

"Why are you grinning about that?" she said.

"You're protective of me." He said this with a kind of stunned wonder. He couldn't remember ever feeling protected. He took her in his arms and pulled her close. "Don't worry about this guy," he said. "I haven't heard from him in weeks. I doubt he'll call again."

But Josh was wrong about that.

THREE DAYS LATER, he was in his office getting ready for a live shot on the newsroom set. He chugged a Celsius before changing his shirt and tie. He grabbed his laptop from his desk and noticed his desk phone's message light blinking. A glance at the digital wall clock showed he had a few minutes to spare. He hit play.

"Remember Iowa, Josh?"

It was the anonymous caller talking about the last stop on Dad's campaign. After that stop, he and his father had left Iowa to celebrate Josh's birthday in DC with his mother, who'd been left behind with an illness. It was the plane from DC back to the campaign trail that had crashed.

"Remember in Iowa how you ran away?"

Josh stood a little straighter.

"Remember the covered bridge they found you under? The staffers were so freaked out. They'd lost the senator's kid. How the hell did you get so far?"

And just like that, Josh was in his dream—the dream of being chased. He could see the bridge with the red house on it, the long, brown bug on the bridge he was hiding under, the sun setting over the brown creek. People shouting his name.

These people were going to take him back to his father's hotel room. He remembered that now. In the dream, he'd been running from that hotel room.

ON SET IN the news studio, waiting to do his live shot, hit time still twenty minutes away, Josh spun on the studio chair and logged into his laptop just out of camera range. He'd long ago learned the fine art of surfing the net with the cameras on him, pretending it was work.

He refused to think about his dream of the bridge.

New Year's Eve was in two weeks. That was a better thought. He wanted to do something special with Addie. He searched for a good place to celebrate with her. Maybe fly them away to someplace exotic, set it all up as a huge, extravagant surprise.

Addie had told him about Lucy's island, the horses, how Addie always wanted to see it. He could give that to her.

Maybe he'd invite the roommates along. A total suck-up move, but if he had to move to New York permanently, he'd need to convince her to come with him, which would require an entire store of suck-up moves.

He started searching for Lucy's family resort. He didn't know its name, but no matter. Josh could find anything.

"Hey, Josh?" came the producer's voice over his earpiece. "Can you stand by a bit longer? We're having trouble locating the edited story package in the system."

He squinted up from the computer. The set lights were bright in his eyes. "What kind of trouble?"

"If you could just stand by?"

"No problem," he said.

He went back to his computer and searched again. Okay, so he couldn't seem to find the resort. She'd said Georgia, hadn't she? The last name was Ambrose, wasn't it?

"Hey, Josh?" came the show producer's voice over his earpiece again. "So we can't seem to locate your story."

"You lost it."

"No, no. We think there's a problem with the storage in the new editing system. Maybe it was sent to the wrong file."

He hoped she wasn't asking permission to kill his story, the story he'd worked on for weeks. He lowered his head back down to his computer. "Keep looking," he said, feeling his shoulders getting tense. "I'll wait."

Despite the cold studio, a sheen of sweat glistened over Josh's lip.

A makeup artist hurried over and dabbed his forehead and reapplied his powder. He thanked her and turned back to his computer, googled *Joshua Egan runaway Iowa*.

He got no hits because it was an obviously stupid search. Imagine running from his father. Where would he run? He'd been in Iowa, for God's sake.

Joshua Egan lost. No hits.

Joshua Egan rescued. Still nothing.

See? The caller may be Dad's friend and know all about Dad, but he didn't know jack about Josh. And Addie was right, he was not Josh's friend.

He typed into the search bar: *Elliott Egan Iowa campaign final speech*, and got pages of hits. The last speech had been at Winterset City Park in Iowa. "A Time for Greatness" was the speech's title. Senator Egan had been a star.

He searched: *Joshua Egan Winterset City Park Iowa, bridge with red house creek.*

The hit minus Josh's name: *Holliwell covered bridge.*

He clicked on the image link, and there it was, his dream. The red house on the bridge. Except the house was actually the covered section of the bridge that had been painted red. It was made of wood. He could almost hear feet pounding on it above his head.

The voices: *Come out, Joshua. Where are you, Joshua? It's okay, Joshua.*

The bridge was real. The dream was no dream.

But who had been chasing him?

The show producer, in his earpiece, startled him: "Hey, Josh? Your story seems to be lost. We're killing your live shot."

Josh didn't say anything. The tips of his ears got hot. His hand trembled over the laptop as he closed it.

"Did you get that, Josh?" the producer was saying. "Can you hear me?"

A voice echoed in his head: *Where are you, Joshua? You can come out now, Joshua.*

"Okay, thank you," Josh managed. He stood up unsteadily. The studio lights hurt his eyes, and pressure was building in his chest. If he could just get to the quiet of his office . . .

He made it as far as the door before the laptop flew across the hallway and crashed against the wall and broke into pieces. He looked down at his hand, confused.

"Bro, that's wild," said a passing writer.

HE CALLED THE newsroom phone guy and asked whether he could dismantle Josh's anonymous tip line.

He left the bureau and texted Addie. Where are you, i need to see you. She was out for a run. She dropped a pin showing where he could meet her. At the towpath, he followed the pin location and stepped through the brush. The clearing was exactly as she'd always described it: a beautiful white sycamore in the center of black rocks, a glorious view of the river.

She was waiting for him by the tree, smiling at him as he crossed the rocks and kissed her. She smelled of cool woods and clean sweat, and he couldn't get close enough to her.

She put her hand on his chest as her eyes searched his. He avoided her look, kissed her neck instead.

"Slow down," she said. "What's going on?"

"You were right about everything. I admit this." He tugged at her running pants.

She batted his hands away, laughing. "We're outdoors," she said. "There are people up on the towpath."

"No one will see us." He was desperate for her. "I don't care if they do."

Afterward they collapsed against the tree. When he was able to separate the roar in his head from that of the river, he untangled from her.

She stared at him with dazed eyes. "What was that?"

"You're good for me." He slid his hands over her shoulders and up her neck. He cupped her jaw, reverentially, and tilted up her chin so she could see in his expression everything he felt for her. How he needed her. How much he loved her. "You were right about me trusting the wrong people. From now on, I only trust you."

CHAPTER TEN

WEDNESDAY MORNING, FOUR DAYS SINCE THE SNOWSTORM, THE citywide search for Josh was in full swing. Addie and I used the last of Penelope's ink to print out "Missing" flyers. We bundled up and met with volunteers at the Foggy Bottom Metro during the morning rush.

After that, we split up. Penelope and Estella headed north to Dupont Circle. Addie and I migrated toward the White House for the big lunch crowds. We texted Estella and Penelope constantly. Anything new? Anybody hear or see anything?

Midafternoon, Addie and I stopped to warm up and grab a quick bite in the West End. We ate over our phones, thumbing through the latest news. Uniformed officers going door to door, asking about Josh. Police cadets and rescue dogs searched along the tidal basin and East Potomac Park. Horse-mounted police officers worked their way deeper into the rugged, three-square-mile Rock Creek Park. Their efforts were slowed by snow and ice. Forecasters predicted the freezing temperatures weren't going away anytime soon.

Addie pushed her salad away and stood abruptly. "I'm not hungry anymore."

"Same," I said.

"Let's get back to it."

By the early evening rush, we'd handed out all the flyers. Our last volunteer straggled off. Addie took our picture standing in front of the Metro with the "Missing" poster taped on the brown Metro sign. Our post to Instagram: *Come join us tomorrow. #JoshEganSearch, #FarragutNorthMetro, 8am sharp.* Then Addie hopped the Metro to catch up with Josh's friend, Marcus.

I WALKED HOME. A rusted Crown Vic was parked in the tow-away zone in front of the house. Penelope and Estella were in the front parlor with Detective Kelley and some cop I'd never seen before. He wore a buzz cut and a bad suit. His cool eyes narrowed on me.

"Oh, there she is," Detective Kelley said, turning a flat smile my way. "I was hoping to chat with you."

Kelley introduced me to Detective Doylan. He thrust his meaty hand my way. He told me he was partnering with Kelley to try to determine Josh's whereabouts. He had a voice meant to communicate that, now that he was here, everything would be put right.

"We haven't gotten around to chatting in depth with you and your roommates yet," Kelley said. "Now that Doylan's here, we'd like to go over everything again. See if any details got overlooked. Would you mind if we asked you a few questions?"

"Sometimes folks hold a piece of a puzzle they don't know they're holding," Doylan explained. "You see what I'm saying?"

"Sure," I said. "Whatever you need."

Estella and Penelope were interviewed first. Detective Kelley went with Pen into the kitchen. Estella showed Doylan to the dining room, gesturing for him to go inside ahead of her. She winked back at me before she closed the pocket door.

I didn't understand why they'd split the three of us up for these interviews. I went upstairs to wait in Estella's room and tried not to worry about why they were here.

After about a half hour, Estella came into the room.

"What did they want?" I said.

"Oh, you know, the usual," she said airily.

The usual? These were police detectives. In our home. Asking questions about Addie's missing ex.

Estella crossed the room and dropped onto the couch with a loud exhale. "God, it was so stressful, though. I could use some coffee."

I ignored the hint. "What kind of questions did they ask?"

"What you'd expect," she said. "Who is Josh, how well do we know him, had he been acting like a weirdo recently? Did I have thoughts about why he might go out of town or blow off work, blah-blah. Oh, and when was the last time I'd seen or talked to Josh?"

"What did you say?"

"The truth." She lay back and put her feet up on the couch. "That I don't really know him, not really. He doesn't come around. He's never called me to talk or whatever, and the last time I'd seen Josh was New Year's Eve."

"Do they believe something bad happened to Josh?"

She was quiet for a moment, thinking about it. "Couldn't tell, actually."

"So this detective wasn't questioning you like a suspect?"

"Like *I* did something to Josh?" Estella laughed. "Are you out of your mind? Why would anybody think that?"

Penelope appeared in the doorway. "Lucy? They're in the dining room, waiting for you."

"CLOSE THE DOOR, please," Detective Kelley said.

She was sitting at the dining table that'd once belonged to Addie's grandmother, a notepad in front of her. She asked me to take a seat. "We really appreciate you doing this."

Doylan grunted from where he stood by the boarded-up fireplace. He was studying Estella's art above the mantel, his face all scrunched up, like he was looking at bullshit. Or maybe he was one of those people who thought everything was bullshit. I took a seat across the table from Kelley.

She asked whether I was Lucy Ann Ambrose, twenty-three years old, residing at this address; to each of these I answered, "Yes, ma'am." She laughed and said I was showing my southern.

"I'm trying to get a feel for how you all fit together," Kelley said. "Where are you in this whole equation?"

Addie had been my best friend since day one. Josh I barely knew. "We've hung out maybe a handful of times at best?"

"A handful is what exactly?" Kelley wanted to know.

Four? Five? I lifted my fingers. "Five."

"Okay, great," she said. "We're going through timelines here, looking for areas that need filling in."

"Why my timeline?" I said.

From behind me, Detective Doylan said, "Looking for those puzzle pieces, remember?"

He was moving around behind me, where I couldn't see him. It was unnerving, as I supposed it was meant to be, though I wondered why he'd bother.

"Tell me about those times you hung out," Kelley said.

The dinner party at our house last fall, when Addie brought Josh home to meet us, I stated. Twice when Josh had picked up Addie—I couldn't remember the exact dates—but both times he came into the foyer to say hello. I mentioned how polite Josh is. Cool, maybe. Reserved, for sure. Older than we are, more worldly, and maybe that's why he doesn't love hanging out.

"Doesn't love?" Kelley repeated back. "What does that mean?"

"I shouldn't put words in his mouth," I said. "I only meant there was our dinner party last fall, like I said, and then he only ever invited Penelope and Estella and me to his party exactly once."

She nodded. "Got it. And when was that?"

"New Year's Eve."

"I've heard about this party."

"It was a great party. Lovely of him to invite us."

She tapped her pencil. *Tap. Tap. Tap. Tap.* "Four hangouts, by my count. And the fifth?"

"Oh, yeah, next day, on New Year's Day. After we'd checked out of the hotel, Josh gave us a ride home. Saved us from paying for an Uber. He carried Addie's bag into the house. We had a Bloody Mary brunch that Josh stayed for."

Kelley nodded down at her notepad. "So no time between that day, January first, New Year's Day, and now?"

I shook my head. "Nope."

"And if you could confirm for me? On Friday, January twelfth, that's the date Addie and Josh broke up?"

"I think that's the date," I said. "Sorry, you know I wasn't there, right?"

Kelley said, "Time flies, huh? What is it now? Almost two weeks ago?"

"Two weeks on Friday," I said agreeably.

"We're trying to find out about Josh's state of mind," Detective Doylan said as he came around to where I could see him. "From what we've been told, in the week after the breakup and before he disappeared, coworkers noticed Josh's behavior seemed a bit off."

"Yeah, I wouldn't know about that," I said. "I don't work with Josh. You think he's okay though, right?"

Doylan grunted. "He's a guy you notice. Nobody sees him in four days?"

What I would've said, if I had trusted Doylan, was this: If anybody could walk away without a trace, it'd be Josh. He had the money and the smarts and the know-how. He'd been sneaking around as an investigative reporter for years. You watch what the slippery bad guys do, you pick up tricks about how to be slippery yourself, if you are so inclined.

"I'm going to need you to take this seriously," Doylan said out of nowhere.

"This is me being serious, sir." I was at the table with two police detectives. Jesus. How much more serious could this be?

"To hear you girls tell it," Doylan said, "nobody hears anything. Nobody knows nothing. I got three girls at home never stop yapping. All they do is chatter until my ears bleed. Not you girls, though."

"Maybe that's because we're not actually girls, sir," I pointed out.

Kelley cleared her throat. "What Doylan is trying to say, in his own way, is that we're concerned. Josh left his condo in the middle of the day and walked to work. Somewhere along those six city blocks, in broad daylight, he disappeared into thin air. That day in question he placed no phone calls. We can find no electronic activity that afternoon or since. His vehicle's in the garage. We can't find car rentals, plane or train reservations, nothing. Any theories about where he may have gone?"

I was nodding. "Yeah, I really wish I knew."

Detective Kelley glanced down at her notepad again. "Back to the night of the breakup, it happened just after seven o'clock, right?"

"Not sure about the exact time."

"Did Addie say why they fought?"

"She told me Josh had been irrational and behaving in a way that frightened her. She told him she was afraid for her physical safety and thought it best if she left until he cooled out. He told her to get out of there, they were over, never come back, and so she left."

Doylan said, "You wouldn't know why it escalated as it did?"

"No," I lied.

"Did he put his hands on her?" Kelley wanted to know.

"I wasn't there, ma'am."

"She put her hands on him?" This was Kelley again.

"Obviously not," I said.

Kelley tilted her head. "You don't know whether Josh put his hands on her, but you know for certain Addie didn't hurt him?"

"I'm certain because I know Addie." And that should've been enough.

But it wasn't enough. They wanted more, fine. "We've been best friends our whole adult lives. I know Addie better than anyone. I've seen her in every mood. She never loses her cool, let alone her temper. She doesn't like to hurt *feelings*. There's zero chance she'd hurt *a person*. I'd bet my life on it."

Detective Doylan made a sound in his throat. "What about the man on the towpath whose nose she likely broke?"

"He attacked her! You don't think she should have defended herself?"

Kelley tapped her pen hard against the table. "Why don't you just tell us where you were on Saturday the twentieth. No detail too small. Start as early as you can remember."

I told them how I got up, revved about the snow, since I'd never seen a snowstorm. I'd gone down to the kitchen and made coffee and played games on my phone. Spelling Bee and Wordle. I'd scarfed down a bagel and coffee. "Addie came home at ten nineteen," I said. "I remember seeing it on my phone."

"That's specific, good," Detective Kelley said. "And how did Addie seem to you?"

"Like she'd been grabbed," I said evenly. "Like someone tried to drag her into the brush. To beat her or rape her or kill her, who knows." I gave myself a beat to cool off, took a couple of calming breaths. "You have to remember, the towpath is her favorite run. Imagine being attacked in the place you love more than any other. The place you should've been safe."

Detective Kelley wrote down the rest: where I worked, how Bruce, who was in charge of security, had seen me at the office that day, what time Bruce had given me the ride home from the office.

"Great," Detective Kelley said, finishing her notes. "This is all helpful. And why don't you tell me about the last time you saw Josh?"

"Addie told you about New Year's, right?"

Kelley nodded. "I want your take."

JOSH INVITED THE four of us to a small New Year's Eve party he was hosting. It was a hotel party, our favorite kind, at a fancy hotel with city views from across the river in Virginia. Josh booked the presidential suite with an extra bedroom for me and Pen and Estella. He filled the sitting room with more booze than I'd ever seen in my life, and that was saying something, given our college days. We had a lobster dinner right there in the room. Really, Josh spared no expense. It was clear he was desperate to make Addie happy.

Josh saw me struggling with my dinner. I'd never had lobster. But he gave me a tutorial, and when I still mangled it, he picked the meat from its shell like it was nothing at all, while keeping the conversation moving and the glasses full.

After dinner, he handed out tickets to the fireworks viewing party on the roof. We carried champagne bottles up. There was a band and a bar and a big crowd. We danced and enjoyed the view of the monuments. Addie flung her arm out toward the Lincoln Memorial and said it looked like a birthday cake, and Josh acted like he would get it for her. That's how he treated her that night, like all she had to do was say what she wanted, and poof, he'd make it appear.

Eventually, we were all wildly drunk. Josh's friend Marcus kept refilling our champagne glasses. I was wearing a little black dress, no coat, and it was cold on the roof. Josh noticed me shivering and gave me his jacket.

"Sounds like the perfect guy," Kelley said as I finished my recollection of the evening.

"That night he was," I agreed.

"Okay, great. Good." Kelley flipped her notepad closed and slid the pen through the spiral top. Finally, they were ready to leave. I was relieved to be showing them to the door. Doylan went onto the street first. Kelley stepped onto the stoop and turned back. "I almost forgot," she said, snapping her fingers. "The whole reason we wanted to talk to you in particular."

"Me?" My eyebrows shot up.

"The night I crashed your party, looking for Josh, I asked if anyone had information. Why didn't you mention Addie getting attacked that morning?"

"You were looking for Josh," I said. "You didn't ask about Addie getting attacked."

"Our suspect is a guy she'd mistaken for Josh. You didn't think that was relevant?"

"Is it relevant?" I stood a little straighter. Had she just handed me a clue to the investigation? "Is the guy who attacked Addie your suspect?"

From the sidewalk, Doylan said, "We think you girls haven't told us every-thing."

I didn't know how to respond.

"You'd do anything for your friend, wouldn't you?" he said after a moment.

"What's the point of friendship otherwise?" I asked.

UPSTAIRS, I PUT Kelley's card on my desk and let myself remember what I hadn't told them about that night.

On New Year's Eve, on that cold, windy hotel rooftop, Josh slid his jacket over my shoulders. He guided me to the chimney, where the wind was blocked. We were away from the others, though never out of eyesight. No one could hear us over the noise of the band.

Josh said he wanted to be friends. I wanted that, too. He asked whether I was enjoying myself, and I said that this was the best New Year's party ever. It's hard to describe what it was like to be with Josh. On TV he came across as Mr. Cool rational observer, objective reporter dude, very impressive. Up close he was all heat. He had charisma. You wanted to be near him. People watched you talking to him, and you'd feel proud he'd turned his attention your way.

"This hotel wasn't my first choice," he said, looking around at the rooftop party, the magnificent skyline, all the very drunk beautiful people. "I wanted to do something *really* special," he was saying. "Addie was always talking about your island where you grew up. The ocean birds and the horses."

I shifted uneasily. The heels of my shoes felt too high all of a sudden. I made myself laugh. "Addie does love her nature."

"I was going to fly everyone down. Let Addie see the famous horses. And it's warm in Georgia this time of year, right?"

"Compared to here," I agreed calmly, though it felt as if terns were beating against my rib cage.

"Thing is, I couldn't find your family's hotel." He told me how he'd searched ownership records of every resort, hotel, motel, bed-and-breakfast, VRBO, Airbnb, condominium rental up and down the Georgia coast. Nothing. He did a business owner search for anything owned by anyone named Ambrose, any records of any Ambrose hospitality businesses, any businesses at all. He checked on LLCs with murky ownerships. He'd clearly put a lot of work into it.

Why go to all that trouble? What went through a mind like that? And was he going to make a big thing of it tonight, in front of all my friends? Couldn't he see me for what I really was—a person who stupidly told a lie years ago, because (and let's just get right at it) I was ashamed? Of where I came from. Of my father. And, since I'd told it, of the lie itself.

"Do you know why I couldn't find the hotel?" he said.

"Why?"

He was looking down at me, his pale eyes reflecting like an animal's in the dark. "I'm asking you for straight answers."

Just then, Addie shouted from the group. "Hey, you two! What are you doing? It's a minute to midnight." Penelope popped open another bottle and the champagne went everywhere, spraying Marcus and Estella.

"It's in my shoe," Estella screamed drunkenly. "I'll just drink out of my shoe."

"Don't you need more champagne?" Addie said.

I tipped back my glass and gulped it down before starting their way.

When the fireworks started, I stuck close to Pen and Estella, far from Josh. During the finale, when all Josh could see was Addie, despite the sky lighting up all around him, I snuck off the rooftop and took the stairs down to the room Josh had set aside for us. I climbed under the blankets and pretended to sleep.

CHAPTER ELEVEN

JOSH

Twenty Days Earlier

DURING THAT FIRST WEEK OF JANUARY, JOSH FLEW TO NEW YORK while his agent haggled with the network executives over the *Morning Show* anchor offer. *The Morning Show*'s executive producer showed Josh around the studios. Rumors traveled back to the DC bureau, but Josh told everyone he was only trying out for the role. No decisions had been made, Josh lied. Wish him luck, he told people. He truly believed that if he talked about an offer before it was inked, the news gods might snatch it away.

Besides, he obviously had to tell Addie first. But he was nervous. After all, she hadn't signed up to date a dude who lived in New York. He had no idea whether she'd be at all open to moving to New York, as he'd hoped.

Sitting in the seventeenth-floor corner office overlooking Rockefeller Center—the office that would soon be his—he read through the draft contract's highlights. Named anchor of the prestigious and most profitable show on the network. A salary so large he swooned. Clothing allowance. Stylist and personal trainer. A PR person setting up his rollout—interviews with big glossies such as *Vanity Fair, GQ, People, Rolling Stone*. Even *Teen Vogue*.

"Got to hook 'em young," his publicist said. His own publicist!

He got up from the desk. He pressed his warm forehead to the cool window and looked down at the rink below, at the skaters going round and round. He thought of the day his father took him up into the dome of the United States Capitol.

He'd been seven or eight. The spiral steps had been difficult for his small legs. His father held his hand the whole way. On the catwalk far above the rotunda floor, Dad told him not to be scared. Dad wouldn't let him fall, and he hadn't, had he? On that catwalk they were close to the dome's apotheosis, that great fresco of President Washington ascending the heavens, so close Josh could almost touch the paint. Josh was woozy from the height. Below, the tourists on the rotunda floor were like ants. A flock of blackbirds flew past windows at their feet. Josh had marveled. "Up here we're like the birds."

"Oh no," Dad had told him. "What I'm giving you is a view of the gods."

Josh sucked air through his nostrils, blinked down at the rink below. He wondered what his father would've thought of this view, and why Josh was suddenly desperate to share it with him.

THAT FRIDAY NIGHT, he hurried home, contract in hand. He was so excited. He had gotten exactly what he wanted. But there was fear, too. Addie said she loved him, and he believed her, but did she love him enough to change her life for him? Would she move to New York for him?

He poured a whiskey and downed it. He scrolled through his phone nervously before pushing it away. He went to the sliders and looked out the same glass he'd looked out of since he was a child. He had never really moved on from this place, and he was ready to.

The night was clear, the sky beaded with stars. He closed his eyes and made a new wish on them: Please help me make this work. Please let her want this, too.

———

AS SOON AS Addie arrived, Josh told her the good news, everything that happened in New York. She'd known he'd been filling in as anchor but now she was screaming with excitement. She jumped up and down and hugged him and told him she was happy for him, wildly so. She started to read the contract, then stopped and looked up, stunned.

"Uh, Josh? I can't read anything past the salary."

"It's a lot, right?"

"A scary amount."

"Not bad scary though?"

She rolled her shoulders uneasily. "I don't know. How does anyone get that much money?"

"Maybe it's a bit much. But we'll need money. You think it's expensive here? Try New York."

"Uh-huh." She looked down and started reading again. "This says you get a stylist. And wardrobe? And a trainer?" She looked up and grinned. "Estella's going to be jealous of you."

"Can we talk about the important part?" he said, all nerves. "You see the New York clause, right?"

She flipped through the pages, looking for it.

"I have to live in New York," he said impatiently. "Though I can keep the condo here for weekends. So if I sign, we live in New York."

"We do?"

"Well, yeah."

She was silent. Clearly she hadn't seen this coming.

He took the contract from her and set it on the counter. Then he grabbed her hands and started again. "I really want you to come to New York with me. If you give it a chance, we can find a place you'll really like that suits us both. Near network headquarters, but close to a park. There are so many good places to run in New York. Lots of parks."

She started to argue; he cut her off.

"And New York has many opportunities for historians. The best museums in the world are, okay, they're here, but also in New York. I can't imagine it'd take any time at all to reestablish yourself. You're so talented."

"That's fine, but—"

"And we can get a place big enough for your family to visit whenever they want. It'll take some time to find the right place, sure."

"Josh!" she said louder, startling him into silence. "You're asking me to move to New York?"

Good God, he was sweating. An actual lake had formed on the back of his shirt. "I am, yeah. March fourth, I'm supposed to take over the anchor chair."

She let go of his hands and moved away from him silently. A sensation moved through his gut. A premonition of heartbreak. Please, he thought, please don't say no.

Then she turned back to him and said, "We've only known each other seven months. Not even a year."

"I knew the minute I saw you. I knew I loved you, or that I could love you. I knew you were it for me." He was talking fast before she could say no.

"Josh . . . "

"If I lost you, I'd have to just go out and find you again. No matter where you went. I couldn't let a day go by . . . "

"Josh, listen," she said, loud again, and when he stopped, she smiled. "I love you, too. But I move slower than you. And a March fourth move is, gosh, that's only two months away now. That's too soon for me."

"Okay, I hear you."

He watched her shoulders relax.

"I'm asking you to leave everything for me," he said, "when we've only been together seven months. I understand this. What if we started slowly?"

"What is your idea of slow?" she said carefully.

"We start with weekends together. I come down, or you come up, but weekends are ours, with an eye to you eventually moving up full-time." He thought of the dream job, the prestige, the contract with all those zeros. Then he imagined tossing it off the balcony and letting it catch in the wind. It made him feel a little sick.

"I can work with eventually," he said. "But tell me—if you can't move to New York ever, if you know in your heart that's never going to be in the cards, tell me and . . . If that's it then I'll just tell them, thank you for the offer, but I can't take it."

She stared in disbelief. "You'd turn down this contract?"

"If it's the contract or you," he said, "I choose you."

"They're offering you twelve million dollars!"

"I do okay as it is, though. It's not like I'd be unemployed. I'd stay here at the Washington bureau." It wasn't the dream, but he could do it.

She was pacing now. "Are you out of your mind?"

"When I'm without you, I feel like I am." It was the truest thing he'd ever told her.

She turned and looked up at him. "I am so happy for you. This is such an accomplishment. I don't want my uncertainty to ruin this for you."

"Addie, I understand. I'm asking you to change your life, and it's a lot." He decided: "Let's do this. Take as long as you need to think about it. I can probably delay the decision a few more weeks. Lawyers are good at buying time."

She let out a long breath. "Okay," she said, nodding.

He blanched, as if he'd misheard.

"Okay, as in, I tell my lawyer to stall?"

Her smile was shaky, but there. "Okay about New York," she said.

"You'll come to New York with me? You really mean it? You're not just saying it?" He was lightheaded with joy.

Fifteen days later, Josh disappeared.

———

TURNS OUT, THE lawyers did have more finagling to do. Nearly a week after he got back to DC, Josh still hadn't signed the contract, and they hadn't announced his new role. He walked around the Washington bureau with his secret tucked safe inside him, stopping in the newsroom and talking to the writers and producers as though it were the last time he'd see them.

He got a week's worth of mail from his cubby. Behind it, Sharon the receptionist told him she had a stack of messages for him. "One guy's been calling every day," she said, "demanding to be put through to your cell phone. I asked, who's calling? And he goes, none of your business. Then he called me all kinds of stuff I can't bring myself to repeat."

Sharon handed him a stack of messages on yellow while-you-were-out squares of paper. On top, a message that came in an hour ago from a Delia McDowell, returning his call. He didn't remember anyone named Delia McDowell.

"Says she's a former reporter at *Coastal News*, some Georgia paper," Sharon told him. "Says to tell you she sent an accident report for the family you were asking about to your email. Call her if you have questions."

Georgia. *Coastal News.* One of the calls he'd put out trying to find the alleged resort owned by Lucy Ambrose's family. He thanked Sharon for his messages, and then her phone rang again. She looked down at the number. "Great, it's your stalker again. He calls so much I recognize his number now."

"Give me a minute to get back to my office and put the call through," he said. "I'll get rid of his ass."

His desk phone started ringing as he came through the door. He picked up on the third ring and said, "Egan here," and heard labored breathing on the line. Then the caller said, "Why'd you get rid of your tip line?"

It was the same guy who'd used Josh's anonymous tip line to hassle him about the bridge in Iowa.

"Who are you?" Josh asked after a moment.

"Are we really going to do it this way?" The caller sounded more frustrated than crazy, although Josh wouldn't put money on his sanity. "You know exactly who I am."

"Actually, I don't."

"Oh yes, Joshua. Yes you do. What I can't believe is that you haven't come out to see me. Why haven't you? Are you afraid?"

This was exasperating. "You want me to find you?"

"No, I want you to *want* to find me."

"So you called me on an anonymous message line?" Josh said. "Look, I'm at work. I don't have time for games. Just tell me who you are."

The caller snorted. "People say how brilliant you are. The great investigator. I don't know, you seem like a dumb shit to me."

He could hear the caller's heavy breathing, the traffic in the caller's background. The man was on a busy street. Was he on M Street below Josh's office? Outside there right now? He looked out the window at the rush-hour traffic below. Cars four deep at the light. Sidewalks crowded. Everybody seemed to be going about their business as usual.

"You got upset about the bridge, didn't you?" the caller said. "I mention the bridge and you shut down your message line like a little baby. Is that what happened? You didn't like me bringing up what happened at the bridge, Joshua?"

Low in his belly, he felt a fizzle of dread. This guy knew about the bridge in a way that not even Josh could fully remember. There was also the way the guy kept saying his name. *Joshua.* Nobody had called him that since he was a kid.

This caller, maybe he wasn't so crazy.

"Were you ever at the Holliwell Bridge in Iowa during my father's campaign?" Josh said.

"In a manner of speaking."

"See? What the fuck does that mean? I hate bullshit games."

"Still running, aren't you?" the caller said, quietly now. "She said you would. She said this was stupid of me to try to make contact."

She?

He thought suddenly of the woman in his recurring dream. In the dream, he's hiding beneath the wooden bridge with a red house, and in some of the dreams it's so he won't have to go back to the hotel room with the woman on the floor, so pale she was nearly bloodless. Something red around her neck.

"Are you still running because you saw what he did to her?" the caller said. "The great Elliott Egan who liked to choke women?"

Josh found the chair with his hand and lowered himself into it. "What did you say?"

"Choked them. You know this, Josh."

Did he know?

"In his downtime, he liked to do it," the caller said. "When he wasn't running for leader of the free world."

And then Josh remembered the noise behind the hotel door. A sound like an animal hurt. Josh wasn't allowed to open the door. Never, ever, his father said, without being invited first. But the sound scared him. So he pulled the door open.

A woman was on the floor. She was naked, pale. His father wore a suit. He was crouched over her, his red tie dangling. His big, sunburned hands were around her neck.

She didn't move. She looked to be dead.

"Who was the woman?" Josh whispered.

"Claire Ryan."

EXCEPT HE WAS looking at her website now. Claire Ryan was alive. She had an address and a phone number and a business website. There was a picture of Claire all these years later—Josh was looking at it again on his computer screen.

So then, Claire Ryan had survived?

He looked around his office and let that ground him. His awards on the wall. His TVs showing news from around the world. The sofa with the stacks of files of investigations that had seemed unsolvable, until he'd solved them.

He went over again the facts as he knew them. The covered bridge was real. The hotel room he'd been afraid of all his life had to be in Iowa. He knew this because after he'd run away, it was at Holliwell Bridge where they'd found him. He also knew Claire Ryan was the campaign manager, so he believed the caller that she'd been in Iowa.

Was the dream about another woman on the hotel room floor in Iowa? Would Claire know what he was talking about?

Could he get her to tell him?

He typed her Falls Church, Virginia, address into his phone's navigation app on his way out the door. He hurried back to his condo and retrieved his car. The fifteen-mile drive took forever, or at least it felt that way. He lowered the window and let the winter air cool his head.

It was noon by the time Josh arrived. The neighborhood was a typical older suburb with big, newly renovated houses hulking over small, manicured lots. The Ryan house was a two-story Craftsman with a basketball net over the garage. A house for a family.

He wanted to get her alone, away from her family, to talk, although it appeared no one was home. The driveway was empty. He peeked in the garage window and saw the garage was empty, too. He crossed the porch with Adirondack chairs to the front door with its wilting holiday wreath. Nobody answered the door.

She was likely at work. He went back to his car and pushed the driver's seat back and settled in for the long wait. A few hours later, a bus dropped off schoolchildren. Then another bus. Then a third. Neighbors came home from work. The sun lowered behind the trees, and still no Claire. His car grew colder.

"Come on, Claire," he muttered. "Get home before I freeze my ass off."

Just before nine o'clock, a pickup truck rounded the corner and came to a stop with its headlights in Josh's eyes. Josh held up his hand in the universal sign of *get your damn lights out of my eyes.*

A man climbed out and, in the headlight beam, walked toward Josh. The man was tall and had long, thin legs. He wore boots and a puffed jacket. With the light behind the guy, Josh couldn't see his face.

"Well, look who's here, the brilliant investigator," the guy said. "Maybe you're not such a dumb shit after all."

The voice was rough, deep, the voice of his caller. But also the voice of an old man that didn't fit the young guy walking Josh's way now. Then the guy circled to Josh's right, and the light was full on his profile. Josh stared at him, stunned.

He recognized the guy's sharp chin, the slant of eye. The curl of his ear was as familiar as Josh's own. Josh let out a breath, white in the cold air.

"I know who you are," Josh said.

CHAPTER TWELVE

ON THURSDAY, FIVE DAYS AFTER THE SNOWSTORM, THE SUN CAME out. Not the white dinner plate sun glaring through wintry clouds, but a real sun that melted snow off the rooftops, pattering the sidewalk like rain. The cold snap had finally broken. Change was in the air. It felt as if today was the day Josh would come home.

I was getting ready for work when I heard Addie shout, "Lucy, come here." All night I'd heard the TV in her bedroom through my floorboards. She'd gotten this idea she should watch for Josh to show up on a news set any minute. When I got to her room, she pulled the story up on the station's website. The headline read: *Exclusive New Video in the Josh Egan Disappearance, Just Released!*

The video was taken from a surveillance camera in the garage under Josh's condominium. According to the website, the video had been taken Friday night. Less than twenty-four hours before Josh missed work.

The video, shot from a distance, showed a dark SUV—Josh's Subaru— pull into the lot and park in Josh's assigned space. Two men climbed out of the car—Josh clearly visible as the driver. The man from the passenger seat, also tall, was shot from behind; he wore a flannel shirt, jeans, and a dark cap.

In the video, Josh leaned over the car roof and talked to the passenger before the two men crossed the lot. The police were asking anyone who recognized the man to call the police tip line.

"That's the guy who attacked me." Addie was shaken.

I pinched the screen, zooming in, but zooming in degraded the video, made it blurrier.

"How can you tell?"

"Look at them *side by side*. How he holds *his head*. That's what threw me at the towpath when the guy sat on the hill. He holds his head exactly like Josh." She looked up with a mix of hope and terror. "The night before, Josh brought the guy who attacked me into his condo. Why would he do that? I have to tell Detective Kelley."

AFTER ADDIE CALLED Detective Kelley, she printed out another stack of flyers. Connor had been running a special at his shop: anybody willing to take a stack of flyers to pass out got a free coffee. I offered to drop the flyers off on my way to work, but Addie wanted to come along. When we opened our front door, we found a woman climbing our stoop.

She had short curly hair under a winter cap and wore big glasses that magnified her eyes. She squeaked with joy when she saw Addie.

"Oh, oh, oh! You're home! You're Josh's Addie! Addie James!" she said, and then, looking at me, "And you're Lucy the bestie! I follow you guys on Instagram!"

Addie took a step back. "I'm sorry, who are you?"

Her name was Rachel Babbitt—"*with two t's!*" She was a person who spoke in exclamation points. She said she was an internet sleuth who specialized in missing people by digging up visual evidence from the internet. She posted her finds on @RachelBabbittReports. "You should totally follow me! I have nearly a million Instagram followers! I can help find Josh!"

I cut Addie a sideways look. I had no idea what to make of this woman.

Addie gave Rachel a dismissive smile. "I'm sorry, but we're on our way out," she said, stepping around her.

"Already I found something important!" Rachel Babbitt said. "It's a picture. Or many pictures I wanted to ask you about. Just give me two seconds."

Rachel slid her backpack off her shoulder. "The backpack's Fjällräven! One of my product placements!" She pulled a tablet from the backpack and held it out.

We were looking at photos of Josh she swiped through. Josh waiting to cross a light in the West End. Josh walking past chess players in Dupont Circle. Josh in line at a café, maybe Aroma on Pennsylvania Avenue. Another of Josh at a restaurant, shot through the window. "Tell me what you see!" Rachel said.

Addie was bristling. "Josh can't get a coffee without people sneaking his picture?"

Rachel smiled triumphantly. "Two phones!" She pointed down to the picture of a suit-and-tie Josh. "The mammoth phone he carries when he's dressed for success! I bet that's his work phone." She swiped through to another picture. "And here, in Dupont Circle, a phone so small it's barely visible in his hand. I only saw evidence of him using it here. But this small one must be his personal phone, isn't it?"

"He has a second phone," Addie said with surprise.

Call me unimpressed. Most people we knew with important jobs scored work phones yet kept a personal phone. "Come on, Addie. We're late."

"Wait, listen," Rachel said. "In situations with missing people, courts give out geofence warrants like candy. But they can only ask for what they know to look for! Can you confirm for me that police are searching for both phones?"

"Sure they are," Addie said, and I could tell she was lying.

CHAPTER THIRTEEN

JOSH

Five Days Before He Disappeared

THE MONDAY AFTER HE AND ADDIE HAD BROKEN UP, JOSH WENT
to see a psychiatrist. He needed to be fixed fast. "Whatever meds work pronto,
that's what I want," he told the doctor. "Speed over efficacy."

Dr. Mantel put the intake papers down. "Therapy's a marathon, not a
sprint, Josh. There's no magic pill." He talked about coping mechanisms Josh
could learn, but also made sure he understood that there was trial and error
in finding the right medicine. It was best medical practice to start slow until
you found the right doses.

Josh interrupted. "I hear what you're saying. I'll work as hard as I need to. I
can come in every day if you can fit me in, but I have a deadline of yesterday."

"This is your health," Dr. Mantel said, smiling gently. "It didn't take a day
to get to how you're feeling now. Healing takes time."

The one thing he didn't have. "I can't deal with what's going on without
her, and she can't be anywhere near what's going on."

"Why don't we start with that. What can't Addie be near?"

Josh told Dr. Mantel how the whole mess with Leo Ryan started, with an anonymous caller to his tip line. This source, Leo Ryan, claiming to be his father's friend. From the beginning, Josh was suspicious—of his motives, and of his honesty. If that was the case, Dr. Mantel asked, why continue the dialogue? Josh supposed it was because of Addie. She came from a nice, normal family who loved one another. He hadn't realized until he met her that he had always wanted a normal, loving family. He supposed when he first took Leo's calls that Leo would jog a nice memory, something good about his father. But that had never been Leo's intent.

Then, last week, Leo Ryan had called Josh directly and made him remember the bad thing. It involved a woman named Claire Ryan. "She worked for my father, idolized him. I'm guessing she loved him. And he hurt her."

"In what way?" Mantel said.

He felt his mouth go dry. Could he break a cardinal rule to criticize family with strangers? Even though there was no one left to enforce the rule. "Yeah, I don't know that I can get into specifics."

"Everything we say here is confidential," Dr. Mantel said. "I couldn't tell anyone anything you say, even if I wanted to, which I don't."

Josh folded his hand over his knee. His profession was bound by those rules, too. If he said it, would he heal faster? Wasn't that why he was here? The old, terrible pressure was building in his chest again.

"I can't seem to sit still," Josh said. "You mind if I stand?"

The doctor held his hands out. "Please do."

He moved around the room, feeling the doctor's eyes on him. Josh stopped at the shelf of medical books. There was a box of tissues on a small table. Next to it, a green stress ball.

He picked up the ball and squeezed. Then, after a long moment: "The last time I saw Claire Ryan, she was naked, lying on the floor of a hotel room. My father's hands were around her neck." His mind tunneled back. "I thought she was dead."

"You thought your father *killed* her?"

"She didn't move. Maybe she was unconscious. Maybe she was too afraid to move, I don't know. I don't know what I know. It's a head fuck for sure."

Dr. Mantel looked at him, waited.

"For years, I had forgotten . . . or hadn't let myself remember the . . . well, not murder," Josh said. "Claire Ryan is alive. She raised a boy. So, attempted murder maybe?" He looked down at the green ball in his hand, the way his thumbnail was picking chunks out of it. He laughed. "Jesus Christ, look what I'm doing. I'm destroying this ball."

"It's okay. I have a whole closet full of them."

"I'll bet," he said, trying to joke. "I don't want to feel like this. I don't want to hurt anything. Not a blade of fucking grass. I don't want to be like that."

Dr. Mantel waited. Then: "Like what, Josh?"

Like his father. But Josh couldn't bring himself to say that.

"Take a breath, Josh."

From the box on the side table, Josh grabbed a tissue and wiped his face. "What a manly display, am I right?" Josh said with a strange smile. He waved the tissue. "Oh boy, would I have gotten a beating for this."

"For being upset?"

Josh put the ball down and paced. There was the story to finish—the one he'd gotten so wrong as a kid. Josh was an adult now, and as such, it was important to be accurate and fair. Getting the story right for Claire.

"Anyway, I got Claire's info," he said. "Turns out, she's doing quite well for herself. She has her own business, a nice home. So I decide to drive out and see it. Claire Ryan doesn't answer the door, so I stake her out. I was out there for hours, freezing my ass off. Finally this big pickup pulls up, and a guy gets out, approaches me. Big surprise, he's that caller who's been fucking with me. Who do you think that caller is?"

"I couldn't hazard a guess," Dr. Mantel said.

Josh's mind raced back to that first sight of the kid. The jaw, the eyes, the way the guy *walked*. The deep voice that didn't match his age. Once Josh had seen his face, he'd realized that Leo's voice sounded just like Josh's father's. No wonder Josh had never dared hang up on him.

Then Josh laughed without humor. Describing Leo to the doctor was simple once he accepted it. "I guess I should call Leo my brother."

LEO HAD INVITED Josh into his house—Claire Ryan's house. Leo was goofy, lanky, awkward as Josh had been as a teenager. Leo had a mess of dark hair that fell over his eyes. A flannel shirt worn over a blink-182 T-shirt. Ripped jeans that might fall any minute down his ass, and he clomped around in big black combat boots.

He was, Josh was shocked to see, basically a kid.

"You know who I am?" Leo said warily.

Josh tilted his head, studying him. Everything was so obvious now. The voice and face so like his father's that it made Josh's head spin. Even the way the kid held his goddamned shoulders. Still, Josh hesitated. Admitting anything felt like fumbling through a dark room with trip wires and trapdoors.

Carefully, Josh said, "I think you must be related to me?"

Leo smiled his father's smile, and Josh just blinked.

"You're my father's son," Josh said. "Am I getting that right?"

"So you do believe it?"

"Yeah," Josh said, surprised that he'd admitted it. What the hell did this kid want anyway? Was Josh supposed to have some kind of relationship with this kid?

"Ma said be careful, you might not be too happy about it. You might be like Dad."

"Claire? She's your mother?"

His smile went wider. "Yeah."

For the first time, Josh took in his surroundings. The interior of the house was like the set of a family sitcom. Pictures of this kid's face scattered all over the walls. It was the kind of house Josh had dreamed about as a kid. A normal house that probably had a backyard, too.

"Where is she?" Josh asked. "Where's Claire?"

"In Jackson Hole on some political retreat hunting big-money donors," Leo said. "You know, assholes who think they run every damn thing."

Josh laughed.

Leo talked about school, how he was on a gap year, Leo talking in a way that made Josh think he failed out of college or dropped out—not that Josh cared. All Josh could think was, this kid was his brother? And only fifteen miles away all these years?

"I'm working at my mom's, saving money." Leo narrowed his blue eyes on Josh. "That's where I got the stories I leaked to you. Clever, right?"

"It was," Josh agreed.

"Plus, the guys I ratted out were such assholes. They totally had it coming to them."

Josh laughed. "The congressman? When I tried to interview him, he pulled a gun. I nearly punched him in the face."

"Really?"

"Yes, really. I totally lost my shit."

"Man, I hated that guy. He was the biggest asshole of them all. I would've paid to see you punch him in the face." Leo put his finger in the air, the *wait one minute* gesture. "Let me show you something, okay? It's upstairs. You're going to wait, right?"

Why did he? He should have left. But he still hadn't gotten to the bottom of the Claire Ryan mystery. Was she the woman on the floor of the hotel room? Or was that someone else? Was Claire Ryan happy? Why did he need so badly for her to be okay?

Leo came bounding down the stairs, all in one motion. Cradled against his chest was a dollar-store scrapbook with *FAMILY* written across the front.

"You got to see this," Leo said, sitting on the sofa and telling Josh to join him. They opened the scrapbook on the coffee table. The first page contained the DNA report Leo had paid for. Under the "Family Finder" section, it showed Leo shared 28 percent of his DNA with Joshua Egan, the proportion you'd expect for a half sibling.

When Leo was growing up, the story Claire Ryan had told him was that his father died heroically, before Leo was born, in an overseas military adventure much like the plot of ten different blockbuster movies you could binge on Netflix right now. Claire told Leo his father had no family. But as Leo grew older, and the hole he felt for the missing father grew larger, he wondered whether Ma missed someone. Someone could've been out there, say an uncle or cousin his mother didn't know about, somebody who might want to be family with Leo. Or at least tell him something about his father. So he took the DNA test.

Listening to this, Josh remembered a news story he'd filed years ago on DNA tests unearthing family secrets; he'd taken a test himself for the story. During his live shot, he'd waved his own DNA results, saying, "No matches! Phew! No nasty Egan secrets." Thinking of that long-ago story, Josh wondered, did I make all this happen? Did I, by opting out of future messages about possible matches, leave myself open to this kid throwing this bomb in my face?

After Leo got the results back—talk about *mind blown*—he asked his ma whether she had anything to tell him. She told Leo she didn't see his resemblance to her old boss. She denied any relationship. Leo showed her the results, pointing out DNA tests were 99.98 percent accurate. Well, there you go, she'd said, you're the point-zero-two mistake.

Leo told Josh about the terrible fight they'd had, as Josh flipped through the scrapbook. There were notes taken from Claire Ryan's diary that Leo admitted stealing and a sticker from a recent Starbucks coffee with the typed words GRANDE CAFFÈ AMERICANO and JOSH.

"Um, Leo," Josh said, tapping the JOSH sticker. "You been collecting my trash?"

Leo turned the page, saying, "Yeah, so that's kind of embarrassing. I picked that up that time you were on the mall all day, doing these reports in front of the Lincoln Memorial."

Josh couldn't believe this. "So there were other times you were stalking me?"

"Stalking? No. Well, maybe sometimes I watched you. But not in a bad way."

"What would be a good way to stalk me and steal my trash?"

Leo blew out a breath. "You're getting it all wrong. I was only trying to figure out how to approach you. I thought I'd go out and meet you. But I sort of lost my nerve."

"Why?"

"Ma got all freaked out when I said I wanted to meet you. She couldn't stop me, I'm not a kid anymore, but she said I needed to be careful. Learn more about you first and figure out how to approach you."

Josh thought about that for a moment, then said: "That's why you made the dumb calls? To learn about me?" It was astonishing, really.

"Those calls were pretty clever, come on. Ma said the Egans hadn't gotten to where they are by being nice. In other words, you were probably an asshole. That night, I saw you do your reports and afterward you signed autographs and let tourists take pictures of you, and I got this feeling maybe Ma was right. Maybe I didn't know enough about you yet."

A surprising ache moved through Josh's chest. "She was protecting you from me."

"Well, I mean, yeah." His shoulder moved with discomfort. "She showed me a picture of what Dad did to her. You want to see it?"

"SO LEO HANDS me the Polaroid," Josh told Dr. Mantel.

Through the doctor's window he looked out at the river, a cool moody gray. "It's of a woman taking a picture of herself in a bathroom mirror. She's wearing a white hotel robe that gapes open. What grabs your attention are the bruises. They're really bad, a dark purple, almost black, and she's got them on her chest."

Josh looked out the window again, but all he could see was Claire Ryan's image in that Polaroid.

"The marks on her neck are shaped like fingers. I mean, she's alive, that's the good news. She's standing there, in the picture she's recording the evidence of this crime done to her, and her eyes—they're bloodred from the broken capillaries . . . and I remember then how kind she was to me on the campaign trail. And I just sort of lost it. Why didn't I help her?"

"But Josh, you were an eleven-year-old child. What in the world do you imagine you could have done?"

Josh lifted his hands, dropped them again.

"Can you tell me what that's like?" Mantel said quietly.

"When I lose it?"

"Best you can," Mantel said. "Take your time."

He tried to find the words for it. "Imagine falling onto the Metro tracks, on the third rail, and electricity courses through you and needs out and you want it out but something's holding you down, it won't let you off the tracks. So the current can't get out."

Mantel watched him. "And if it doesn't?"

"Then I explode," Josh said with a sigh. "I've gotten worse. I took it out on the kid. Why did I do that? If there's anyone in the world who doesn't deserve a ration of shit, it's Claire Ryan's kid."

"You yelled at Leo?"

"Um, that's one description for it."

"Hit him?"

"No, Jesus. God, no. I've never hit anyone. Scared the hell out of him though."

"I'm curious about this reaction," the doctor said, unfazed. "Was Leo Ryan threatening you personally with the picture?"

"He just showed it to me. Who the fuck knows why. I mean, he's nineteen. Was I that clueless at that age? Probably."

"Did Leo say you should've done something for his mother?"

"I didn't give him a chance. I lost my shit and left."

Mantel nodded, frowning. They sat quietly for a few moments. Josh was glad for the break. The office heater clicked off. Josh listened to the doctor's fingers across the keyboard.

The doctor got up from behind the desk and held out a tablet. "May I show you something?" And before Josh had a chance to agree, the doctor said, "Would you mind telling me what you see here?"

On the screen was a photo of a Little League team. Three rows of boys in uniform, their small faces shadowed by ball caps, all a head shorter than the adult coaches flanking them. Josh had never seen these children in his life.

"These boys are eleven and twelve years old," Mantel told him. "Your age at the time you witnessed your father attack Claire Ryan. Would you please point to which of these boys you'd task with stopping your father?"

"Come on, Doc."

"As an exercise only. Which boy goes against a senator running for president? Just one is fine."

"That's ridiculous." Josh dropped the tablet on the doctor's desk. "They're just . . . "

"Children," Mantel said, smiling. "Sometimes when we blame ourselves for things that happen in our childhood, we forget we were actually children."

Mantel typed again in the tablet before holding it out. Already Josh could see the screen. A boy with sad eyes and skinny shoulders. Josh in 2004, or maybe 2005.

"What about him?" the doctor said. "Could you offer the same compassion to the boy in this picture? Seems to me he deserves it."

CHAPTER FOURTEEN

ON THURSDAY, AFTER WE DITCHED RACHEL BABBITT—TWO *T*'S—
Addie and I hurried to the coffee shop. I was late to work again and stressed
about it. We were going down the hill toward the canal when a helicopter
swooped overhead. *Whomp-whomp-whomp-whomp*. We put our hands over
our ears and looked up. The helicopter was close enough that we could make
out its blue and white markings, those of the US Park Police. Addie's teeth
nervously scraped over her lower lip. "What are they doing?"

"I don't know."

"They can't be looking for Josh in the river, can they?"

The thought made my stomach drop. Back home, helicopters searched
open water for shipwrecked boaters. They were bad-luck birds.

"They're just another set of eyes from a different vantage point," I said.
"They're helping." I really needed this to be true.

At Connor's, the coffee shop had customers lined out the door. Through
the front window, we could see that every table was full. Addie and I nudged
our way inside, and she dropped the flyers at the counter. Connor took off
his apron and came toward me.

"You're on your way into the office?" he said, and when I told him I was,
he said, "Give me a second to grab my coat, and I'll fill in for you."

I wasn't sure what to make of this. "You'll hand out flyers for me? Don't you have a coffee shop to run?"

"I brought in extra help today. The shop can survive a day without me."

Connor hadn't had a day off in six months. He'd always said he couldn't afford to take the day. "How can you—"

He laughed at my confusion. "I can do it because I love you," he said. Watching my reaction, he laughed again. "You're so cute when you get skittish over three simple words."

"I'm not skittish," I said.

"Well, good." He hugged me right there in front of all those people. "Because I love, love, love you."

"Get a room," Estella joked, arriving with the rest of the gang just then. Penelope had gotten someone to cover her shift at the hospital and said she was here to help hand out flyers. Estella brought Henry. He was excited about the helicopter.

"It was hovering by the boathouse. We should go where the action is."

Addie shook her head. "We're meeting volunteers at the Metro station."

"Something's going on in the park," he said. "Helicopters don't hover for nothing."

I saw fear settling into Addie's eyes and wanted to stick a sock in Henry's mouth to shut him up. But he kept going. "My gut says go to the park," he said. "If we want to do something that actually matters."

Addie's phone went off. She turned her back to us. I strained to eavesdrop, heard her say something about being on Potomac Street. "Yeah, just around the corner," she said. Then she slid her phone back into her pocket.

A green Acura coupe pulled up outside, and Josh's friend Marcus got out. Addie went outside to greet him, and through the window I saw her become visibly upset. Then she ran off toward the canal. By the time I got through the door, Addie had disappeared down the steps.

I turned back to Marcus. "What happened? Where'd she—"

But then I saw the look on his face.

"They found someone," he said in the saddest voice I'd ever heard. "They won't confirm officially, but it's him. Out there."

"Where?"

"In the woods above the river."

"*The towpath?*"

I was stunned. I thought of that bad-luck bird, that harbinger of doom. Marcus couldn't be right. "That's got to be a mistake," I said. "The towpath has been impassable for days."

"They found him near the boathouse," Marcus said. "That's what I'm hearing."

CHAPTER FIFTEEN

JOSH

The Day Before

ON FRIDAY MORNING, JANUARY 19, JOSH WAS BACK AT THE DOCTOR'S office. He had come to therapy every day, whenever Dr. Mantel could fit him in. Together they'd parsed his biography until Josh felt beaten-up enough, thank you very much. There was only the breakup left.

Josh's homework for today had been to think about why the breakup happened. What it really was about. Why, when Josh had been so blissfully happy, had he knifed himself by sending Addie away? He was supposed to come into the office, ready to dig down deep.

Josh gazed out the window at the gloom settling over the Potomac. Forecasters were calling for a record snow tomorrow, the kind of storm Josh hadn't seen since he was a boy. The gloom settled in as he thought of Leo, his secret half brother he'd learned about only last Thursday. He still wasn't sure what he felt about him. Leo's mom, Claire, was clearer: he felt sick about what his father had done to her.

So he hadn't been in a particularly good place, emotionally. Not that that was any excuse. The next night, Friday, he got into an argument with Addie. He'd been trying to tell her something about Lucy. He hadn't been able to find her family's hotels. Addie was living with a person who was pretending to be someone she wasn't.

"Addie didn't believe me," he said. And Christ, that hurt.

She'd believed Lucy over him. Addie loved Lucy more than him. Had he been jealous? Why had this enraged him so? "Was I saying the friend was danger-ous?" Josh said. "I didn't *think* Lucy was. She didn't *seem* physically dangerous. Then again, who seems physically dangerous? Nobody thought my father was."

"Love and belief," Dr. Mantel said after a moment. "You've said, more than once, that if she believed me, she loved me. And if she loved me, she'd believe me. As though one is a test for the other."

"To me, it is."

Dr. Mantel tilted his head, skeptical. "You can't have love without belief?"

"Not me," Josh said. "I love Addie because I believe her. She's completely authentic. She says what she means and I can trust her. Love and belief belong together the same way violence and lies that cover up violence go hand in hand."

"Ah," Mantel said mysteriously. "So then."

"And the thing is," Josh said, "all I was saying was that Addie should know. If she decided she didn't care about Lucy's lies, fine. But she should know about them."

"You don't seem fine," Dr. Mantel said.

Josh thought of Claire Ryan again, and Iowa. He got up and paced. He wasn't seeing the doctor anymore, or the office, or the river outside the win-dow. He was unaware of the stress ball in his hand.

He'd learned lies covered up violence in Iowa when his father's men caught him under the bridge and told him he was in for an ass-whooping. And later too, on the plane ride back to DC, when his father wouldn't look at him, told his men to sit Josh at the front of the plane. Through that endless flight, Josh told himself all he had to do was get home. His mother would help once he got home. But when he did, he was made to sit on the bad-boy chair in his mother's dressing room while his parents conferred privately about how Josh had behaved.

When his mother finally opened the dressing room door, she was alone. *What were you thinking? Don't you know people are watching all the time? What if reporters got word of you running away? Bad boys run away.*

But why did Dad do that to Miss Ryan?

Stop lying, Joshua.

Did Miss Ryan die?

There is no Miss Ryan.

He never spoke of Claire Ryan again. Whenever he thought of Miss Ryan, an invisible hand would slide over his mouth. Soon enough he'd forgotten her entirely.

"**WHERE DID YOU** go, Josh?" Dr. Mantel said. "What are you remembering?"

"There was a cover story for me running away and the ruckus I'd caused. In case it got out, though I don't think the press traveling with my father ever had any clue."

Josh explained how the advisors had told the press that Senator Egan was returning to DC for his son's birthday. The boy was homesick, they said, and wanted to see his mother, and what could a great family man like his father do but reunite the family for a birthday? "This became part of the legend," Josh said. "If Dad would take such care of his son, think about what he could've done for the country."

Dr. Mantel looked at him, waited.

"And that night, what happens next?" Josh said. "My father, confident of his media subterfuge, climbs aboard that broken plane to rush back to the campaign trail, pretending everything was fine. And his plane crashes."

Josh looked up at the doctor. "The night Addie and I broke up, when I screamed at her and chased her out of the apartment, it was exactly how I'd seen my father behave countless times. When I yelled at her in the elevator, I caught a glimpse of my face in the mirror, and I knew it'd happened."

"What did?"

"I'd turned into what I was most afraid of," Josh said. "I'd become my father."

EARLY FRIDAY EVENING, Josh drove out to Virginia and knocked on Leo's door. "What do you want?" Leo said, answering it.

Josh read Leo's fear, and it humbled him. He felt his shoulders slump. "Listen," Josh said. "I wish I hadn't lost it about the picture. You didn't deserve it."

Leo leaned against the doorframe. "No, I didn't."

"And I thought maybe I could ask for a do-over. Like, maybe you'd let me make it up to you for freaking out like that? I've been thinking about you a lot."

"You have?" Leo said.

Josh nodded. "Thinking mostly about how confused I'd be if I were you. Maybe I'd even have lots of questions about Dad. Did you know I still live in the same apartment I grew up in? Dad's apartment. A couple of rooms are still floor to rafters with his stuff."

"You're kidding?"

"Mom never wanted to let anything go," Josh said. "She died two years ago and left all his stuff and I have no idea what to do with it. I was looking around earlier, trying to figure out what the hell I'm supposed to do with it before I go to New York. You want to take a look? See if there's anything you want?"

Leo tugged a black knit cap on his head and was out the door before Josh could blink, the kid's big-ass Doc Martens slapping the walkway ahead of him, no suspicion at all. Even though the last time Josh was here, he'd blown up in the kid's face.

"You shouldn't just get into somebody's car," Josh said. "Especially somebody who acted like I did last time I was here."

Leo paused at the door handle and looked back, his forehead crinkled in confusion. "You don't want me to come now?"

"I'm just saying, if you tell anyone about Dad, you're going to have to learn to be more careful around strangers."

"Seems like you're careful enough for us both," Leo said, and climbed in.

On the drive back to the city, Josh could feel Leo's eyes on him. "What is it?" Josh asked.

"You look like shit."

"Gee, thanks."

"Like somebody did you wrong."

"I did it to myself." His hands tightened on the steering wheel. He flexed them and let out a breath. "Do you have a temper, Leo?"

Leo thought about it. "Don't think so."

"Good," Josh said, nodding. He felt himself getting weirdly choked up. So Leo hadn't inherited that from Dad. "I'm really glad for you. A violent temper is so bad. You can lose people you love."

As a cautionary tale, he told Leo about his and Addie's argument in the elevator, seeing himself in the mirrored doors and being shocked by his own behavior, how he scared Addie away. If Leo ever felt like he might blow up, Josh could talk him through it, if that's what Leo needed.

"Know what you ought to do?" Leo said. "Turn it to your advantage. Tell her how fucked-up you are. Ask her to fix you. Chicks dig that shit. If that doesn't work, tell her how it's gonna be. Deal with it, bitch."

Josh cut him a look. "Careful."

"She's the reason you're running off to New York?"

"No . . . I don't know. It's a great job. I have to go. But if she'd wanted me to stay, I would've done that, too."

"You got to take control of your relationship, Josh. Let these women know what's what. Me and my buddies, we don't let the women run all over us."

Josh laughed. "Uh-huh, and how many of your buddies have successful relationships?"

"What do you mean by successful?"

"Existent."

"I can get my girl back anytime," Leo said, settling back into the passenger seat. "Want me to talk to Addie for you? Least I can do."

"You're a real comedian." Josh gestured at his condominium in the windshield. "We're here."

ONCE UPSTAIRS, LEO went straight for the balcony and threw his arms wide, shouting "I'm king of the world" over the river and monuments. Josh dragged him back into the apartment before the neighbors called the cops. Josh showed him the apartment, explaining how he was going to have to move to New York soon, and how the condo was a big chunk of the inheritance.

"What's it worth?" Leo wanted to know.

An odd feeling moved through Josh. What was a home worth? There were bad days here, but good days too, the uneasy peace that came after his father died, he and his mother living like survivors of a war they refused to speak of. When she'd died, Josh had grieved. After everything, he still loved her.

And then he thought of last summer, bringing Addie here, falling in love with her, high above the city.

"What is it worth?" Josh repeated. "I don't know."

On the way back to the dressing room, Leo had marked the things he wanted—the enormous picture of Dad, which Josh hauled down from the wall and stored in the closet for safekeeping. Leo pocketed other things—Dad's World War Two-era knives, a pair of cuff links, Dad's old Senate pin that was property of the US government but was thought to have been lost in the crash. Leo snagged Josh's bottle of Jack Daniel's from the kitchen island as Josh walked him back to the dressing room. He showed him the neatly stacked boxes with their father's papers.

Leo sat next to the boxes and went through them like a kid at Christmas. He held up a memo on details of a security setup. "Why Odysseus?"

"Dad's code name the Secret Service used." Once Dad had clinched the nomination, he was afforded Secret Service protection.

"So cool." Leo handed Josh the bottle. "Odysseus because he was clever? His travels? Or what?"

Josh took a long pull of whiskey, thought about it. "Probably the women."

"So there were others?" Leo asked darkly.

It occurred to Josh then that Leo must've imagined some sort of tragic love affair between Claire and their father.

Leo got up slowly. "I guess the only difference was Ma got pregnant? That's why he hurt her?"

"I don't know, Leo."

"Did the Secret Service know?"

Josh tilted his hand. Maybe yes, maybe no. "They don't miss much," he said honestly.

"Do you think he strangled her because he didn't want me?" Leo said.

Josh had considered this, too. "I'm not going to lie to you, Leo. I don't know what he wanted or didn't want."

"All this stuff you were saying about your anger? I think what you're not saying is that Dad was a bad person."

There was a hunger in Leo's eyes. Josh felt sorry for the kid. He couldn't begin to guess why their father did what he did, but he owed it to Leo to try.

"Our dad was a complicated person," Josh said. "People loved him so much. Did you know the funeral was standing room only?"

Josh laughed without humor. "I mean, he was the key signature on the Violence Against Women Act. *Dad*. And he campaigned for a new Equal Rights Amendment. He always said that an assault on one person's freedom was a road map to stealing freedom from anyone. He had that kind of great mind. Yet in his personal life, he was a tyrant."

"And he did that to my mother," Leo said.

"And he hurt you both, yeah."

PART THREE
PAST IS PRESENT

CHAPTER SIXTEEN

I RAN AFTER ADDIE, KNOWING THERE WAS NO WAY I WAS GOING to catch her. She'd taken the snow-covered towpath toward the woods. I stayed on the cleared sidewalks. Horns blared when I crossed Thirty-Third Street. Soon I entered the park.

Here, above the river, it was windier and smelled of pine trees. I followed boot prints in the snow and what looked to me like dog prints. Searchers must've come back this way.

I wasn't thinking about Josh; my only thought was finding Addie. Yet questions kept cropping up as I ran. Josh had been seen on the ATM video around noon before the snow started, and his next sighting was by Mrs. Dalton during our party late that night. Why would Josh have come back to the towpath in the heavy snow late that night?

The sidewalks had been such a mess when I left work that Saturday that Bruce had given me a lift. By the time we left for Josh's around midnight, we struggled to drive two miles in a *Range Rover*. Five days later, police were finally able to get back into the park.

When, between that night and now, would Josh have gotten back here?

A voice broke through my reverie. It was Addie, calling for me.

I stopped, looked for her. She called again—but where was she?

"Lucy!" she said. "I'm here—look *up*!"

Finally, I saw her, halfway up a spruce pine, balancing herself on a tree branch maybe fifteen feet up. I was woozy looking up that far. From where I stood, the branch looked too slender to hold her weight.

"Jesus Christ, get down," I said, terrified. "You're going to fall."

She pointed to someplace farther up the trail, beyond where I could see. "There's movement just before you get to the boathouse. People wearing colorful jackets. I think they're reporters."

I took a few steps beyond Addie's tree but couldn't see anything. She was leaning farther out on the branch now, trying to get a better look. "I see a TV truck in the parking lot above the boathouse."

She let go of the trunk, and I felt my stomach drop. I hurried back to the tree and stood beneath it. What was I going to do if she lost her balance? Catch her? Throw my body under hers? I really had no idea.

"They're all just too far to tell what's going on," she was saying. "Plus, the trees are blocking my view."

"Please, Addie, you're scaring me."

She glanced down as if noticing me for the first time. "Oh, okay, sorry. Hang on. Be right with you."

She gracefully lowered herself through the tree. The branches barely swayed as she made her way down. She landed in the snow with a thud, planting her feet as though she'd dropped onto a gym mat. I let out a long exhale.

"Holy shit, you were high," I said.

Her brow was furrowed, her eyes trained far down the path. "Not high enough. I didn't see anything that mattered. I need to get closer to find out what's actually going on. Except the reporters will recognize me."

"Listen, I think Marcus heard wrong," I said. "Josh being back here doesn't make sense." I started in with the timeline of Josh sightings I'd already run through in my head.

She cut me off. "I want you to go down there and scout things out."

"Me?" I said, alarmed.

"The reporters won't recognize you. You can find a way past them for me. There's got to be a way for me to get to where the police are."

"Addie . . . *no.*"

It was illegal to trespass on a crime scene. I couldn't believe Addie was even considering it. While Addie was physically brave, she didn't break rules.

She lifted her chin stubbornly. "I need to find out what the police are doing, okay? But I won't make it past the reporters if I'm seen. I need you to find my route past them."

I gazed down the snowy path. "I don't know, Addie."

"You know the woods," she said with her eyes on mine. "Almost as well as I do. You can get through. I know you can."

While I didn't believe whatever was happening back in the woods involved Josh—*how could it*—*someone* was back there. I didn't want to go anywhere near whatever horror was waiting.

"Please," Addie said. In her eyes was a look both wild and desperate. She needed me.

"All right," I said. "I'll do it."

I STARTED DOWN the towpath alone. My boots crunched through the snow. This seemed to me the loudest sound in the world. The trees around me were bare, offering no cover.

Voices carried in the wind. Ahead I could see people moving around the boathouse—Addie had been right. The parking lot behind the boathouse was filled with marked police cruisers, along with a television van with the big dish, plus plenty of other official-looking cars.

Beyond the boathouse, yellow police tape flapped in the breeze. Somewhere beyond that tape was the crime scene.

I studied the reporters ahead. A skinny man in a bright blue jacket had wandered from the others. I was pretty sure he'd been reporting on Josh these past few days, though it was hard to tell for certain. The man looked smaller than he'd seemed on TV.

"Hi, excuse me," I said.

The reporter ignored me, kept writing in his little notebook.

I talked to him anyway. "What's with all the cop cars? I'm trying to get to Gordon's Rock for some bird-watching." Gordon's Rock was far beyond the crime scene tape, another mile or so. "Can I get back there, do you think?"

"No, you can't," the reporter said. "Police found a body in the woods."

"Oh no. Who?"

"Still awaiting confirmation."

The guy went back to his notepad. He didn't seem too disturbed, which I took as a very good sign. If another journalist had been killed, he'd be freaking out, wouldn't he? "It's not Josh Egan, right? Everyone's talking about him being missing." I couldn't help myself.

The reporter glanced up. "You'll just have to watch the news, won't you?"

"Sure, sure, sure. I'm just going to take my bird pictures, so long as there aren't any cops or dead bodies or what have you. You don't know where the body is, do you?"

"You know what crime scene tape is, right?" he said, visibly annoyed now. "Just stay away from it, and you'll be fine." He turned his back to me.

I started off toward the boathouse, sick with dread. Why had I let Addie talk me into this? I studied the sycamore and maples, trees that lost their leaves and offered no cover at all.

But there were evergreens ahead. They'd provide some cover.

At the tape, I glanced over my shoulder back at the reporters. Nobody paid me any mind. I slipped under the yellow tape and headed fast for the evergreens. The snow was icy in places.

Coming up on our hideaway, I decided I'd stop there for a rest. Catch a breath and get my bearings and figure out where to go from there. But I heard voices. I stopped and ducked behind the tree. I heard a man say, "Hypothermia, right?"

Then a woman's voice, softer: "I'd like to hear what the ME has to say about the bruise. That's a good-sized knot."

"He'll say he lived long enough to bruise," the man said.

The voices sounded like they were coming from *inside our hideaway*. But that couldn't be right. Why would the DC police be *there*?

I moved closer. At the edge of our clearing, I crouched in the snow beneath crime scene tape wound through the pine limbs.

"My guess?" the male voice said. "He hit his head climbing."

"Not in those shoes," the woman replied. "More like somebody hit him."

I eased back a branch so I could see what was happening. Snow covered the rocks. Two investigators stood at the lip of rock overlooking the river, that same one we'd jumped off hundreds of times. Then I saw what they were talking about.

First his dress shoes, patched with ice. Then how the man was leaning against a tree in his coat, which was covered in snow. His knees folded to his chest, arms wrapped around his knees. He seemed to be hugging himself. A flash of gold watch at his wrist.

I didn't want to believe what I was seeing. I made myself take in the rest: the hair white with snow, the purple bruise above his ear.

Now there was no choice but to believe. I was looking right at him—at Josh.

CHAPTER SEVENTEEN

BEFORE I COULD STOP MYSELF, I HEARD MY VOICE SHOUTING *no, no, no.* Next I knew someone was yanking me by the back of my collar. A man hauled me out from beneath the trees, my hip banging through the branches, then dumped me at the edge of the clearing.

It was Detective Doylan. He was standing over me, yelling. So too was Detective Kelley, and another female detective next to her, one wearing a big fur hat. There was too much noise, and I couldn't understand anything, except that Josh was dead. And I'd thought so many terrible things about him while all this time, he'd been out here in the snow.

Suddenly the investigators' yelling broke through. They were yelling about how I had no right to be back here. How did I get back here? Detective Doylan looked like he was having a heart attack. His face was scary red.

"Do you understand what you've done?" he was shouting. "These woods are closed off. You had to have crossed police tape as far back as the boathouse. And came all this way through the woods to here, where there's clearly more tape. You could've contaminated a murder scene."

At the word "murder," my mouth clamped shut.

"I've got half a mind to drag your bony ass to the DC jail," Detective Kelley said, and somehow her even tone was scarier to me. She hadn't lost her temper. She meant what she was saying.

"Here, child," said the female investigator in the fur hat. She handed me a handkerchief. "Wipe your face."

She was standing next to Detective Kelley. She was older than Kelley. She studied me from behind wire-rimmed glasses.

"This the friend?" she said to Kelley.

"The quiet one," Kelley said.

So we'd been discussed. What did that mean? My mind kept spinning back to Josh. "I don't understand what happened. How did Josh get here?"

"How did *you* get here?" Kelley asked.

Nervously I ran my hand through my hair. "We heard they'd found a body. There was talk it might be Josh, and Addie was so upset. I came out here to find out what I could. I thought the rumor was wrong. I just stumbled onto this, all of you, him. I didn't mean to, I swear."

"You stumbled with remarkable ease," the female detective said pleasantly. She was smiling at me, and that smile felt like something I needed. It was a motherly, everything's-going-to-be-okay kind of smile.

"I bet you're one of those people with inner radars," the detective went on. "My husband is like that. Doesn't use Google Maps or anything. It's all get in the car and let's go, and somehow he finds his way."

Was she trying to get me to admit something? That this was a place I'd been a thousand times before? Should I admit that?

So I told the truth. "It was Josh's friend Marcus who told us. The journalists at the boathouse pointed this way."

"Anyone else trying to get back here?" Kelley asked.

"Not that I know of."

"You've been back here before?"

I nodded. "Plenty of times, sure. When I was in school, we all used to hang out around here. Everyone did. Detective Kelley, how did this happen to Josh?"

"How about your other girlfriends? Do they come here?"

"Addie runs on the towpath. She told you that already. Detective, please tell me what happened."

The police radio squawked on the other woman's hip. "Lawrence here," the woman said, talking into the radio. She slid the radio back in her coat pocket, telling Kelley they had company coming. "Can you get her out of here?" she said to Kelley, nodding toward me.

Detective Kelley led me out of the clearing and down the towpath. All around us officers cut sharp what-is-*she*-doing-here glances our way. Up in the boathouse parking lot were photographers and reporters with microphones pointed at the police chief. I could hear them shouting questions.

"What were you really doing back here?" Kelley asked.

"I told you."

"Uh-huh. You knew, or had some inkling, he was back here, didn't you?"

I looked her straight in the eye. I did not blink. "Seeing Josh Egan there was the worst surprise of my life," I told her honestly.

"You best not be lying to me," she warned. "I catch you lying, you'll be eating bologna sandwiches with the rats in the DC jail. You hear what I'm saying?"

I nodded solemnly.

She lifted the crime scene tape, gestured for me to go under it, but I hesitated. "I heard what the investigator said," I said. "About someone hitting Josh in the head. Is it true? Is that how he got the bruise?"

She shot me a dark look. "Don't let me catch a whiff of any of this on social media. Whatever you heard or think you heard, you best forget it."

I TOOK MY time going back. I still didn't understand what had happened, or what the police had found, or even what their theories were, but I had a growing sense that everything I'd gotten wrong about Josh—he wasn't like my father, he hadn't attacked Addie—all of it had somehow led to this moment.

The lump in my stomach grew as I thought how to break the news to Addie. I resolved to tell her everything. Every single detail. In that moment, Addie stepped out from behind the tree.

"You look upset," she said.

Her eyes roamed my face. Her mouth opened in a soundless O. The look of disbelief turned quickly into resolve. "What happened?" she said, lifting her chin.

I told her everything. The reporter and the yellow tape. Stumbling onto the crime scene at the clearing, hearing the investigators talk. I told her what the cops said, even though I'd promised Kelley I wouldn't. "I wish with my whole heart I didn't have to say this. But it was Josh. I'm so sorry, Addie."

She didn't say anything at first. She looked off into the distance, nodding her head. "You're sure?" she said without looking at me. "You saw?"

"Yeah, Addie, I'm so sorry, I did."

She was holding herself together. But the strange, shocked look had returned to her eyes, the one I first saw after her towpath attack.

"But why there?" she whispered, staring down the snowy path. "Did they say why Josh was in our hideaway?"

"I don't think they knew it was our hideaway. I didn't tell them. I figured the less I said the better."

She tilted her head and returned her look to me. The lost look was gone from her eyes, replaced by a penetrating one. As if she were trying to see past my face and bones and tissue into the inner workings of my brain.

At last, she gave me a bewildered smile. "But why wouldn't you tell them?"

"Why?" I repeated. "The police said to get out of here or else, which by the way, they are very serious about. We need to go home. They don't know you're here."

"Okay, I do understand," she said, her voice formal, how she sounded when she got upset and was trying hard not to show it. "Go tell Penelope and Estella that I'm okay, but I'll be home later."

"What? No." No way I was leaving without her. "Can't we please go home and talk?"

"I'm staying here alone. You're going home."

"We go together," I argued. "We stay together."

She locked eyes with mine. "I'm not asking you, Lucy. I'm telling you."

———

I **CAME OUT** of the park and onto the Georgetown street. The police heli-copter swooped down again. I had the strangest sense this was all a dream. *All* of it—that I'd never left home, never come to DC, never gone to college. That I'd never met Addie and Penelope and Estella and Connor. That none of those classes had been real, or the parties, or the job at Andrew Lee Strategies, or the beautiful house shared with my best friends—they were all part of the dream. And I thought I really liked that dream; I wish I'd never had to wake up from it.

When I got to our stoop, the front door flew open, and Penelope and Estella came out. Penelope locked her hands in front of her and weaved a little.

"It's not true, is it?" Estella said. "The news?"

I nodded.

"Oh God," Penelope said, and her hand went to her throat.

They wanted to know everything, but I was numb. I blinked down at my hand and couldn't feel that either. I wriggled my fingers slowly, surprised my fingers were working, blue as they were from cold. And I thought of Josh, how he looked with the snow in his hair.

"Where's Addie?" Estella demanded.

I gestured behind me vaguely. The way I'd come. The towpath. Somewhere, I didn't know. "She won't come home," I said, and turned and walked away.

I **HAD NO** idea where I was going. And then, without realizing where I'd been heading all along, I found myself in front of Connor's café. He opened the door and then his arms, and I stepped into them.

He pressed his lips against my hair. "I saw the news. I'm so sorry."

The cold I'd been feeling melted away. Words tumbled out of my mouth—about Josh in the snow, how he'd been in the woods maybe all this time, how the police had threatened me and how Addie sent me away and how I didn't know what was happening, that nothing made sense anymore.

He pulled me closer, so that my bones pressed against his bones. My cheek lay against the pulse in his throat. He was so warm after what seemed like forever in the snowy woods. He whispered, "Shh. You're in shock."

I wanted to crawl away from what I'd seen, hide someplace dark and deep. I shook my head to rid the sight of Josh from behind my eyelids.

"Come on, baby," Connor said, tugging at me. "Let's get you out of the cold."

CHAPTER EIGHTEEN

LATE THAT NIGHT, AS I SLIPPED OUT OF CONNOR'S BED, HE FLUNG his arm across the empty space. I traced the ridge of his forearm.

"Stay," he murmured, the way he always did when I slipped away, his eyes closed, half-asleep.

But I couldn't stop thinking about Addie. I'd texted her all night and never got even a read receipt; the location signal on her phone had been turned off. What if she was still in the park? And what if something happened to her there?

This last thought had me out Connor's door, running back to the woods, to where I'd last seen her. The bright moon led my way. The streets were quiet, the city was tucked away to sleep. I entered the park with the city lights now behind me. Here was a different feel altogether—darker, lonely, scary even. I aimed my phone's flashlight on the path.

"Addie?" I called out, again and again. "Addie? You here?"

From the boathouse, I could hear a generator buzzing. There was a glow in the woods near our hideaway. I wondered whether the detectives had set up spotlights. That would mean the police were still poking around. Detective Kelley wouldn't have to threaten me twice. No way was I going anywhere near our hideaway ever again.

I went to the end of the dock and called Addie's name. When the wind kicked up, I huddled down into my parka. I shivered on the dock for hours, listening to the river and the wind and the skitter of night creatures, all the night's moods, pricking my ears for the soft, sure footsteps that would be Addie's. Any minute I'd feel her hand on my shoulder and she'd say, enough, let's go home.

But she never appeared.

When the lights went out in our hideaway and the generator stopped humming, I gave up and went home.

I GOT HOME at around three o'clock in the morning. Exhausted and cold, I headed upstairs, passing Addie's dark room, and then went up the attic stairs to my room. I tried to sleep. When I couldn't, I got out my laptop and searched the news about Josh.

Thousands of hits to articles that all read the same: *At 8:43 this morning, DC police search teams found TV news star Joshua Egan dead in a wooded area along the Potomac River. Police are awaiting word from the DC medical examiner to determine cause and manner of death. Police aren't ruling out foul play. They have no suspects at this time.*

Article after article, nearly the identical wording, as if someone had copied and pasted it in publication after publication. There was no talk of Josh being struck, or why he was out there to begin with. The "crime scene" was described as a "remote area" in the C&O Canal National Historical Park in Northwest Washington, DC. No mention anywhere of our hideaway.

Nobody knew anything. But I kept reading, searching, hoping for one small detail that might help me understand. Or another article to tell me what tomorrow might look like.

I read until my eyes burned. At some point, I fell asleep.

___

SOMETIME BEFORE DAWN, I felt someone standing over me. I came awake with a jolt. "Oh Jesus, thank God." It was Addie. I pushed my hair out of my eyes and sat up fast. "I didn't mean to fall asleep. Are you okay? Are you cold? You look cold."

"Can I stay with you?"

"Yeah, sure, of course. I'm so glad you're home." What I didn't say: I was afraid every moment she was away, and I never wanted her to leave again. "What time is it?"

"I don't know," she said, pulling off her boots. "I dropped my phone on the rocks. The screen cracked."

She shed her coat next and started shivering. I got up and found some clothes for her to sleep in, an oversized T-shirt, sweatpants too short for her legs. I pulled back the bedcovers. "Get in," I said. "Get warm."

We lay quietly together with my arms around her, a weird reversal from our college days when I had the nightmares and it was Addie who put her arms around me and said, hush, everything will be all right, and made the nightmares go away.

I tightened my arms around her. "Do you want to sleep or talk?"

"Neither."

"That's cool. We can lie here as long as you want." I snuggled down under the cover and closed my eyes. I could feel the tension in her body, almost hear her roller-coaster thoughts speeding along. I had no idea how to comfort Addie. "Just elbow me in the head if you need something."

"I saw you out there tonight looking for me," she said. "I don't know what I'd do without you in my life. I don't think I would have made it through the night."

"Don't say that."

"I'm struggling," she said, her voice so small. She turned back to face me. "I couldn't call out to you. The police were still in the woods. They would've found where I was hiding. I kept trying to get closer, all night. I could see some of what they were doing. Not Josh though. I never saw him. I couldn't get that close."

She closed her eyes, saying, "Kelley called me, you know. Bunch of times, it turns out. You know how iffy it is back there, getting a phone call out. I had all these voicemails from her, telling me to call her back, and I couldn't. One call finally got through. She told me Josh was gone."

She got up on one elbow. Her face was shadowed in the low light, and in that moment, she seemed very strange to me. Then she adjusted herself, and she was Addie again.

"I know what you said about someone hitting him," she was saying. "Tell me again what you overheard at our hideaway. Exactly. Word for word."

So I told her.

Addie was nodding. "I asked Detective Kelley about all that. Said that I'd heard someone hit Josh. And she got short with me. She said, I know where you got that and I wouldn't listen to anything your friend thought she overheard. But that's what you heard, right?"

"One hundred percent, exactly," I said.

Addie flopped onto her back and stared up at the ceiling.

"Want to know a secret?" she whispered to the ceiling after a minute.

"Tell me."

"I knew," she said, her lips barely moving. "I've kept my game face on best I could. But I've known for days." Since last Saturday night on the snowy rooftop, she explained—after we'd danced and Henry told her the police were at our house—she'd felt the premonition. She didn't know whether it was the moonlight, or the cold, or the snow, but she felt the dread bear down on her and go deep, burrow its way inside to a place where there were no words, just knowing. And what she knew was: Josh was gone.

She tried to convince herself that it wasn't real. It was just a feeling, and it would pass. There would surely be an explanation for where Josh had been. But the dread only got stronger.

By the next morning, what she was feeling was not only that Josh was in trouble, but also that he was beyond her help. Beyond anyone's help. We all kept reassuring her, putting up posters, staying hopeful—but she knew. After he'd broken up with her, ripped them apart and left her bleeding at the edges, she'd felt the steady drip of sorrow, like blood.

"Only a few weeks ago, he'd begged me to move to New York with him," she said. "He was so excited about it. We were going to be so happy, he said."

"I remember."

"Then a week later, we have this insane argument. It happened so fast I still don't understand it. And even though I told myself I'm not supposed to feel anything for him anymore, I can't help but feel everything."

I nodded without saying anything.

"Saturday night, though, after Detective Kelley left our party, something had changed," she said. "My body knew before my mind could put it together. And now I feel like I'm falling apart."

"It's okay if you do. We'd help put you back together."

She turned then and looked at me. Her eyes were so big and dark and fathomless. There was so much pain there, and the pain seemed to go on forever.

"I'm so afraid of falling apart," she whispered. She turned back to the ceiling. "How do I get through today even?"

"We'll get you through it." At that moment, if Addie had asked me to walk naked through Georgetown at rush hour, I would've done it. I'd have done anything for her. "We might not always know how to. You might have to tell us what to do."

She reached over, squeezed my wrist. "I don't know if Detective Kelley will let you hold my hand through her interview later."

"Wait, Addie—what? Detective Kelley wants to interview you?" I said, dizzy with the abrupt mood change. "They don't suspect you, do they?"

"Why would they suspect me?"

She was right, of course. Innocent people talked to cops all the time.

"They should suspect the guy who grabbed me." Addie's hands slid over her stomach, as though protecting it. "That's what I'm telling Detective Kelley. That man who looks like Josh, he did this. I feel it in my gut."

CHAPTER NINETEEN

ADDIE WAS STILL ASLEEP IN MY ROOM WHEN I GOT UP TO GET READY for work. I tiptoed out of the attic with my work clothes bunched in my arms and carried them down to the hallway bathroom.

As I got changed I noticed a bruise on my hip from when Detective Doylan had hauled me like a rag doll through the tree branches. My fingertips gently probed the edges before I pulled my trousers up.

My phone buzzed on the counter. The headline of a *Washington Post* news alert: *DC Medical Examiner Says Joshua Egan Was Murdered.*

I had overheard the detectives say it, and it shouldn't have surprised me, but still, a low thrum of terror moved through my veins. I looked up in the mirror and shrank at my reflection. I looked awful—pale, frightened, the face of a person who was losing faith in her ability to understand what was happening around her, my instincts off-kilter since the snowstorm.

But Addie wasn't confused. She believed the guy who had attacked her had killed Josh.

Her attacker had been videotaped with Josh the night before. The next morning he'd been on the towpath grabbing at Addie—the same place where later Josh was found. The location couldn't be coincidence.

Also, we knew he was violent—seen what he'd done to Addie.

———

THAT MORNING, I left the house, started my walk to work, turning everything over in my mind. An idea was slowly forming. A fix to the most pressing problem now—who was this guy who attacked Addie? Had he killed Josh? Would Addie be next on his list?

Would he come to our house?

I knew how to find this attacker, I was pretty sure. I had a copy of his sketch on my phone. Addie had shared it with us the day Kelley gave it to her. I also had access to Andrew Lee Strategies' powerful, expensive reverse image search engine. All I had to do was run the sketch, and I'd find this guy.

What would I do then? I had no idea. I walked faster.

Halfway to work, I got a text from Connor: you okay?

heading to office now, I replied.

Connor: can you drop by for a sec? Kevin Thompkins here wants to talk to you. it's stupid, but you ought to deal with it, or tell me if you want me to

Kevin Thompkins, the guy who had taken a picture of Addie talking to Detective Kelley during our party and posted it to social media. As far as I knew, Kevin had taken the picture down. I didn't know what else he would want to talk about.

I replied: tell him I can give him two minutes tops. I'm around the corner.

Breakfast was rush hour at Connor's café. Customers three deep, employees bustling behind the counter. I took off my parka and saw Connor waving from the far end of the counter. Kevin Thompkins towered over him, gawky and uncomfortable.

Connor kissed my cheek and offered us his break room for privacy. Kevin followed me back. There was an old sofa and a café table and a TV that'd been muted showing news of Josh.

"Talk fast," I said.

"Somebody wants to buy the picture. You know, the one of Addie getting grilled?"

Again with the goddamned picture he'd shot of Addie. I didn't have time for this nonsense. "She wasn't getting grilled," I said. "Who wants to buy it? Why?"

He didn't want to give me a name. He would only characterize her as a newsperson working on the story of Josh's murder. He gestured toward the silent TV still flashing old pictures of Josh. A garish red banner at the bottom of the TV said *Continuing Coverage: The Josh Egan Murder.*

"It's a big story," Kevin said excitedly. "This newsperson says it's all anybody cares about today. Her paper has a whole reporter team on it, they're piecing it all together. And she wants the picture I took."

"Again, why?" I said, interrupting him in a harsh voice.

"I mean, duh. Addie's got to be a suspect, don't you think?"

I counted one . . . two . . . three. I let out a long, slow breath. I forced a smile. "You know Addie didn't do it. She's not a suspect. The police don't suspect her."

"Then it doesn't matter if I sell it?"

"You can't possibly be that naive. How would you like to have your picture out in the middle of a murder story? You're a bright guy, Kev. Think about it."

"I probably wouldn't like it."

"Good, then don't. Now, I have to get to work." I had started for the door when he said, "It's a lot of money though."

That stopped me. "Kevin, come on."

"I'm just saying it is. It's a lot, and I've got bills. And look, I really like Addie, and I'm willing to let her put in a bid. She can match the top price."

"You're supposed to be Addie's friend."

He ran his hand through his messy hair. "What can I say? I'm getting a lot of interest. Nikki's offering big bucks."

"Nikki Banks?"

———

I LEFT THE café with Kevin's promise he wouldn't sell anything yet. As soon as I got around the corner, I called Estella and told her what her friend Nikki was up to.

"You understand how bad this is?" Images lasted longer than words. They were suggestive, subject to interpretation. People saw different meanings in images, and it wasn't always the truth. Innocent people got hurt.

"Yeah, yeah, yeah. Lucy, I got this," she said impatiently. "I'll take care of Nikki."

I was nodding into the phone, so relieved. "You will?"

"And Kevin's not going to sell that picture."

"He won't?"

"Not when I'm done talking to him," she said, and hung up.

CHAPTER TWENTY

THE ANDREW LEE STRATEGIES LOBBY WAS CROWDED; IT ALWAYS was this time of morning. I swiped my badge and went in the second set of doors. Every eye turned my way. A hush came over the lobby as Tom and Mandy, my two favorite coworkers, cut a path to me, asking how I was doing and what I could tell them.

"Everything's fine," I said, and winced. "Well, okay, it's awful actually." What did people say to this sort of thing? "We're managing best we can." I gave what I thought was a brave smile.

The crowd moved closer, straining to listen. Tom turned around and said, "Hey, guys, give Lucy some space." Mandy walked with me to the stairwell, where I escaped.

In my office, an email was waiting for me from my boss, Sharkey, with the subject line "NEED ASAP RESEARCH." The work was for a pol wanting us to find dirt on the guy he was running against. But I'd already searched and couldn't find anything actionable. This infuriated the client. He told my boss I was incompetent and accused us of being in the bag for the guy he was running against. These accusations didn't bother me. Nobody ever sees themselves as the bad guy. In your story, you're good; in your opponent's, you're not. Where that leaves the truth is anybody's guess.

My priority was the police sketch of Addie's attacker. I dropped it into the image search bar and let the computer do its work. While I waited for results, I tried to get started on the research that Sharkey wanted. But my nerves were too jittery. I couldn't seem to focus. I kept glancing back at the image search.

All it retrieved were hits on Josh Egan. The search program thought the sketch was of Josh.

I needed a more powerful search engine, and we had them—they blasted past paywalls and poked through keyholes of private social media pages. But those engines were expensive and required a client code to charge searches to. I couldn't charge a client for a personal search of my own private obsession— that was stealing. Not to mention, I'd get caught.

No, I needed permission from a higher-up. So I called Sharkey, known as the best opposition researcher in the city. His feats were legend. Word was, he'd toppled another country's prime minister with a well-placed whisper campaign. A rumor Sharkey steadfastly denied, always with a mischievous smile.

Sharkey picked up on the second ring; we skipped past the how-are-you-doing-with-everything niceties. I asked whether there was a training code for the more advanced image search programs. He laughed and said I was a dirt-digging savant, what did I need with training?

"I need to do a little research off the books," I said. "Is there a code for that?"

He hesitated. "This search is of a personal nature?"

"That might be accurate."

I could hear him smiling over the phone. "Would this search be related to the mystery turning the city upside down today?"

"Depends."

"On?"

"On if a yes gets me a code."

He laughed. "Come around to my office, kiddo. Let the phenom give you a hand."

SHARKEY ANSWERED HIS door wearing his usual all-black Chuck Taylor All Stars. A worn Jets cap covered his mop of dark hair. He had the prime corner office on our floor. Windows on two walls, one overlooking the river, the other the canal. Man cave–cool decor. A retro fridge full of classic Cokes in glass bottles. A basketball net on the wall, and a trash can full of balls of every size. A table with computers and video monitors.

"Can you keep this a secret?" I said, closing the door behind me.

He held up his hand like for the Boy Scouts' honor. "Secrets are the only things I keep."

I handed him my phone. On its screen was the copy of the police sketch. He stared down at it a long time, giving nothing away. But I could feel his quicksilver thoughts sliding fast through possibilities. Finally, he looked up. "You think this guy offed Egan?"

"This sketch was made from Addie's description of a man who jumped out at her in the same location where Josh was killed. This man grabbed her wrist. We think he was trying to drag her back in the brush. This happened around ten on Saturday morning, before the snowstorm. Days later police find Josh murdered in the vicinity."

"And police think it's this guy?"

"It's their sketch."

He rocked back on his heels. "If police thought it, you'd expect this picture to be distributed far and wide. On the news, police say they got nothing. This looks like something. Why isn't this all over?"

"I don't know," I said honestly. "Maybe they're still building their case and don't want to spook this guy." I held his eyes, let him see my desperation. "He's already attacked Addie. Who's to say he doesn't come after her again?"

"I hear you," Sharkey said, looking down at the phone again, studying it. "Am I allowed to say the obvious?"

"Please."

"Look at that face," he said. "This bozo's got to be related to Egan, am I right?"

"I've searched the Egan family tree several times. Josh did a news report on family searches a few years back. He took a DNA test for the story. In the story, he reported that the findings proved he was the last Egan. There's no tree left, Sharkey. I can't even find a leaf."

"There's always another leaf, Lucy. Let's go find it."

WE SAT AT a table with two laptops and a PC with three monitors and pulled up the search engine Sharkey liked best for social media websites. I dropped the JPEG of the sketch into the search bar. Sharkey typed in a code I'd never seen before. Results came in fast—again all Josh.

Sharkey started typing again. This time, he excluded the blond hair. He went for a younger age range. We got a match on TikTok under a profile for Leo the Lyon. We maximized the profile pic showing a guy in his early twenties, bare-chested, standing in front of a lit barbecue grill with a can of gasoline. He had dark wavy hair, sharp cheeks, the trademark Egan pale-eyed squint.

The account was set to private, though. We couldn't access his real name or hometown or schools or friends. I zoomed in on the background in the profile pic. The barbecue was set up in a front yard. Behind it was a porch with a door, and the door had a house number on it: 1310.

"Bet you a beer he's local," I said to Sharkey. I screenshotted the picture of the house and ran that image through a geo-browser reverse image search accessing satellite map imagery with street views. My search parameters included the screenshot with a 1310 house number in DC or suburban Maryland or northern Virginia.

We got a hit: *1310 Windswept Way, Falls Church, Virginia.*

He gave me a wolfish smile. "The student becomes the master."

Google Earth showed a Craftsman-style single-family home with a porch resembling the porch in the TikTok picture. Next came the property tax records search. The property was owned by a Claire Ryan. Sharkey typed the name and address into Virginia's motor vehicle database. Her driver's license pic filled the screen.

"Holy shit," Sharkey said. "Claire Ryan. I know her. I've talked to her—here in the building." She'd had her own boutique messaging firm, Sharkey remembered, and had partnered up with Andrew Lee when she had to kneecap a client's powerful enemy.

"Is that not an incredibly weird coincidence?" I asked.

Sharkey shrugged. "DC's the smallest big city in the world," he said.

On her short wiki page, Claire Ryan was described as a party activist and messaging consultant. She started her firm in 2012. Between 2005 and 2012 she had no employment history. It was as though she'd dropped off the face of the earth. But before that . . .

"Uh, Sharkey," I said with excitement. "Back in 2004, she was the campaign manager for the Elliott Egan presidential campaign."

A look of astonishment washed over him. "I don't know that she ever mentioned that. I would've remembered. Wouldn't you find some way to drop it into every professional introduction you ever had?"

"I would've dropped it." I pushed my sleeves up to my elbows. "Let me do a family search for Claire Ryan."

Five minutes later, we had it all laid out in front of us. In February 2005, Claire Elizabeth Ryan had given birth to a boy, Leo Ryan, at Inova Fairfax Hospital in Fairfax, Virginia. Father unknown. He'd been born seven months *after* the death of Senator Elliott Egan, killed in that famous plane accident in July 2004.

"Had there been any rumor of an affair in the months leading up to his death?"

"None that I remember." Sharkey told me to pull up Leo Ryan's Virginia driver's license. We stared at Leo Ryan's picture on his license.

"Look at this kid's fucking face," Sharkey said. "Except for the dark hair, that kid's the spitting image of the Sainted President That Never Was."

I felt the hair rise on the back of my neck. "Which means . . . "

"Looks to me like you just dug up Josh Egan's long-lost brother."

LATER, BACK IN my office, I used Sharkey's super-secret password to run a full background check on Leo Ryan. Far as I could tell, he'd had a normal and largely uneventful upbringing. He'd played lacrosse at Falls Church High School, graduating in 2022 with honors. He then studied at William & Mary—but dropped out after his freshman year. On his Facebook page, he marked himself as being in a relationship with a woman named Hailey Waters, a sophomore at William & Mary, studying poli-sci. The only sign of trouble was a 911 call for trespassing and possible stalking at her home address. Leo Ryan was questioned at the scene and released with a warning.

Here we go.

I dialed her phone number of record and left a message, said I was conducting a background check on Leo Ryan and asked whether she would talk to me. I made it sound official, like this was the government calling. Two hours later, I got a return call.

"Who are you with?" Hailey Waters wanted to know.

"I can't really talk about the application," I said, like I was an NSA official or something, confident and no-nonsense. "Tell me about the stalking."

"I wouldn't call it stalking. Is Leo in trouble? Who did you say you were again?"

"Does your boyfriend get into trouble?"

"Leo's not my boyfriend. Is he still telling people that?"

She told me they'd been high school sweethearts. They'd both applied to her dream college, where he struggled. He took sophomore year off to go home and work for his mother. Hailey broke up with him eight or nine months ago. Leo didn't take it well. He kept coming around, begging for another chance, talking about how he was coming into this big fortune. Like she believed that.

"My parents caught him throwing rocks at my window at three a.m.," she said. "They called the cops."

"This was May twenty-seventh last year?"

"I guess."

"Your parents feared Leo would hurt you? Was he acting violent?"

"My parents fear *everyone's* violent," she said. "They watch *Dateline* and Fox News."

"Did Leo ever mention Josh Egan?"

"Josh Egan?"

"So that's a no?" I said, and then: "This big fortune Leo told you about, did he say where it would be coming from?"

"His imagination?"

"Then he didn't, to your knowledge, actually come into that windfall?"

"No offense," she said. "But if Leo came into a fortune, would he need this background check for some job?" She hung up without a goodbye.

NOTHING IN LEO Ryan's background indicated a predilection for violence. Yet he'd attacked Addie. And this big fortune Leo Ryan had told Hailey Waters he was coming into—what was that about? I didn't know exactly how wealthy Josh had been, but he'd been heir to the Egan fortune, and surely he'd been earning a king's ransom from his prestigious job.

If Leo Ryan was related to Josh, did he think he was getting his hands on Josh's money? Or was that windfall talk a desperate effort to get his ex-girlfriend back?

I kept searching for anything that pointed to any signs of Leo's violence and coming up short. At five o'clock, coworkers lumbered noisily past my office to the elevator. They were done for the day. I thumbed through the latest news headlines on my phone.

DC Medical Examiner Confirms Josh Egan Was Murdered

With No Suspects, DC Police Turn to FBI for Help

DC Police Chief Tells Frightened Residents Parks Are Safe

This One Hurts: A City Mourns One of Its Own

Just past five thirty, when I was running out of ideas for how to prove Leo Ryan was the guy who was ruining our lives, Estella texted: Meet me at Cafe Milano for happy hour?

First off, there was no "happy hour" at Cafe Milano, a Georgetown hotspot. One martini would set me back a week of Dollar Menu meals. Besides, were any of us up for hanging out at a bar? Talk about not reading the room.

And there was my ASAP research I promised Sharkey.

I replied: can't do it, still working. How's Addie?

Estella: hasn't come home

Estella: you asked me to deal with Addie's picture, this is how i deal with picture, but i need your help

Damn it, I'd forgotten about Kevin's picture of Addie. be there in ten minutes, I texted.

CHAPTER TWENTY-ONE

THE RESTAURANT WAS PACKED. AS SOON AS I CAME THROUGH THE door, I saw Estella at the bar in her red print Prada coat, her hair in an elaborate updo that shone under the lights. Strangers surrounded her. This was Public Estella in her element, charming and glittering with a social grace I envied.

At the bar we did air-kisses and moved to the end for privacy. She introduced me to the bartender. At all our hangouts, Estella made friends with every bartender, best I could tell. Tonight, she ordered focaccia and bought me a whiskey. When the bartender was out of earshot, I leaned toward her and said under my breath, "What are we doing here?"

She gave me a big smile. "Letting the game come to us."

She explained that after work on Thursdays, Nikki Banks always came here, usually with people from her office, which Estella knew from Nikki's weekly Instagram post *#ThursdayNights* at *#CafeMilano*.

"You know how she got her job, right?" Estella said.

She'd told the story a thousand times. Nikki had seen Lena Leamas, the columnist who'd become her boss, walking to Cafe Milano and followed her inside. After she'd cornered her at the big table, the one by the window, Nikki gave her the whole song and dance about how she was Lena's biggest fan, had read every column she'd ever written. Next thing you knew, Nikki was hired as the famous columnist's assistant.

"Nikki's been reaching out to me for days," Estella said, "pretending like she's all broken up about Josh. I should have known she was trying to get a scoop from me. I can only say I'm so glad I blew her off. But I figure, why not let her stumble on us here? Get her to tell us what she and Lena Leamas are up to, why exactly they want Kevin's picture. But we don't tell her anything, okay?"

I nodded. "Right. Of course not."

"Maybe I bring up Addie's lawyer. Let's play that by ear."

This lawyer was news to me. "Wait, when did Addie get a lawyer?"

"Today," Estella said. "Addie's dad hired him for her interview with the cops. The point that Nikki might need reminding about? Lena Leamas can report whatever she likes about Josh. He was a public figure on account of his father and his celebrity TV job, and this might sound cruel, but anyway, he's no longer around to sue. Addie, though, is a whole other ball of yarn. She's a private individual. Any lies they'd tell about her would be libel, and she's got a good lawyer now."

"So the lawyer threat is how we get Nikki not to publish Kevin's picture?"

"If Kevin knows what's good for him, he won't sell her that picture," she said. "Anyway, he's already trying to shake me down. He figures he can get more money from me. No, tonight we find out *why* Lena Leamas has Addie in her sights."

Estella's red coat was the bait—and a few minutes later, just as she'd predicted, Nikki came into the restaurant with her boss. The two stopped at a table of men who looked vaguely familiar. Were they on TV? Had I seen them in the elevator at Andrew Lee Strategies? They all laughed together. Nikki glanced up and, seeing Estella, gave her a big smile.

"Gotcha," Estella murmured, ducking her head to hide her smile.

My phone buzzed with a text from a strange number. This is Addie. Come home.

"Sorry," I told Estella, "but I've got to go."

———

THE HOUSE WAS too quiet. The downstairs rooms were dark, except for the light over the staircase. I went up, calling Addie's name, but got no reply.

I found her in my room, standing by my bed, wearing a hoodie that dwarfed her. A picture of my mother and me was in her hand. In the picture, our faces were sunburned, and we were laughing on the beach—I was maybe ten. This was my favorite picture of us, the one I kept by my bed.

She set it down carefully and turned. "I talked to Detective Lawrence"—the detective in the fur hat—"and Detective Kelley at the Homicide Branch."

"How did it go? Are you okay?" She didn't look okay. She lifted her hand in a gesture indicating she had no idea how she was. Or maybe she didn't want to talk about the police.

"After the interview," she said, "Dad dropped me off at Josh's."

"Oh? Why?"

She was shaking her head. "I don't know. I guess I just felt like being surrounded by his stuff. A shirt that still holds his shape. A pillow that smells like him. I get it, he's gone, but I still love him. You think I'm crazy."

"I absolutely do not."

"Anyway, the concierge wouldn't let me in. He said the apartment was closed off by police. I got so upset right there in the lobby, and then the concierge got upset, and it was becoming this big, awful scene, so I excused myself and went to the restroom."

A hard expression settled on her face. "The restroom is next to the indoor pool and the lockers," she said, and I had the oddest feeling she was mad at me. We had never argued, not even once, the entire time we'd been friends—I'd made sure of it.

"Did something about that locker upset you?"

She nodded slowly. "Josh has his own locker he shared with me. I went in it and found this." She pulled a small phone from the pocket of her hoodie. I had never seen that phone in my life.

"Whose is that?"

She turned it in her hand. "The ID in the settings shows it's registered to Josh's mom."

Now I was even more confused. "Didn't she die years ago?"

"Two," Addie said.

"Why is Josh's dead mom's phone in his locker?" And then I knew, too late, this was the phone that internet sleuth, Rachel Babbitt, had shown us a picture of. This must've been the second phone Josh carried in that picture of him in the café last summer. I wondered why he'd used his mother's old phone. Then it occurred to me he'd probably used it for calls you couldn't track to him. "Did you bust into Josh's mom's phone?"

"Yeah."

"How?"

She said the phone was too old for facial recognition. It had a simple passcode, the same one Josh used to enter the condo building, the code he probably had used for everything. Then in a cold voice, she told me what she found on the phone: that Josh had been in therapy, which she hadn't known about. The phone contained notes he referred to as therapy homework. There he recorded his feelings and anxieties and fears.

"Do you want to see them?" she said.

"Josh's therapy notes? Oh no. God no." That was private. I did not wish to know the inner workings of Josh's mind. I held up my hands to ward her off. "His therapy isn't my business."

"But you should read the last entry," she said, holding out the phone. "It's about you."

IT WAS A journal entry titled "WHAT TO SAY" and addressed to Addie, like the way I wrote to my mother. An odd mix of understanding and numb fear moved through me.

first the apology: there's no excuse for how I blew up last week. you were right to run, I'm ashamed of having frightened you. I know I got (get!) too angry. I'm working with a therapist. I'm going to fix it, I promise

at time of fight I was having hard time dealing with stuff surfacing about my dad. He wasn't the person everyone says (though I guess I always knew that)

He hurt people

I should've told you, but when I tried to speak up as a kid, nobody believed me, and what does talking matter if nobody listens?

"Aloud," Addie demanded.

I cleared my throat and read:

"point is, I'm not going to be like dad. I want to fix me and have healthy relationship, i.e. never scare you again

but Addie, what I didn't say (and maybe this only matters to me), when you didn't believe me about your friend it was a major trigger (sorry for psych jargon). And the truth is your friend did lie, okay? She lied

this is me expressing my hurt calmly, as I should've that day (see proof of therapy!)"

That was it. Josh's last entry written the Saturday he died. I looked up to find Addie waiting for my response with a kind of angry impatience. Somehow I managed, "He was talking to you about my parents, I guess?"

"Yes."

So she knew.

"Makes sense," I said with a shaky smile. "It's the only thing I ever lied about." I was in a panic, sweating now, the back of my neck moist. "I don't know how to talk about this. I've never known how to tell you. It was always too big, too scary, and I always thought tomorrow would be a better time to set the record straight with you."

I waited for her stance to soften. I expected her to do her usual thing. Tell me everything was okay, all that mattered now was us, the past was just that—past.

But she stood there, silent, tilting her head. She was studying me, as though I were a stranger. That look scared me more than anything.

"Maybe I can just show you? Is that okay?" And without waiting for her to respond, I said, "Let me get the report."

CHAPTER TWENTY-TWO

At 4:18 p.m. on March 1, the 18-foot center console pleasure boat (*Endless Summer*) upon returning to port struck a ten-foot all-steel day marker on a rock pile, known as Day Marker 4, located 0.5 nautical mile east of Cumberland Island, Georgia.

It is believed the impact of the crash caused one passenger, 36-year-old Katherine Ambrose, to fall into the water. The driver of the boat, 40-year-old Samuel Ambrose, struck the windshield, and died on impact. His body was transported to the Glynn County Coroner & Medical Examiner's Office for autopsy, where Ambrose was found to have a blood alcohol concentration (BAC) of 0.18 percent, a BAC level requiring charges of aggravated DUI under Georgia law.

The US Coast Guard conducted a search and rescue (SAR) mission for Katherine Ambrose, who remains missing. A minor was rescued from the wreckage, treated and released at the scene.

Glynn County Sheriff's Department investigated the incident, with help from the state's Maritime Accident Reconstruction team. This report concludes that Samuel Ambrose operated the *Endless Summer* at a high rate of speed through a no-wake zone while intoxicated. The boat rammed into the structure known as Day Marker 4.

Despite low visibility due to weather conditions and the day marker's lack of illumination, maritime law is clear: the captain of a moving ship is presumed at fault when crashing into a stationary object, absent strong proof otherwise.

Sheriff Ed had given me this copy of the report, along with a bus ticket and a hundred bucks to get myself to DC for college. On that seventeen-hour bus ride from Gwynn County, Georgia, to DC's Union Station, I read the report again and again and again.

Boat speed (twenty knots through a no-wake zone). Weather conditions (advection fog, wind at nine knots, five-foot seas). Witness list (the fishing charter skipper and his drunk sports fisherman passengers). The search over open water lasted for days.

I'd lingered over the part of the report that still confuses me:

Katherine Ambrose remains missing.

The captain is presumed at fault.

ADDIE TOOK THE report I offered without looking at it, saying she'd already read a copy of it on Josh's mom's old phone. I no longer had any power over anything that was happening around me. It felt like being out in the wreckage again, the ocean threatening to pull me under.

"The report makes it sound like my father killed himself and made my mother disappear," I said.

"Yes, I read that."

Everything inside me clenched. I felt as I had as a kid waiting for the crunch of Dad's car tires on the gravel, on alert for advance warning of what kind of mood he was in. Could I defuse it or should I run?

I tried something new. I told the truth.

"That's not what happened," I said.

———

THIS IS WHAT I told Addie:

Let me tell you about my dad, a person both so good and so bad. Charming as you please, but he could turn on you quick as a copperhead. He coached my T-ball team and collected coins in a big Lucky Leaf glass jug, and when he was in a good mood he'd let me help sort the coins, "paying" me with wheat pennies or a buffalo nickel, whichever I thought prettiest.

During his good days, he made me feel rich, though we struggled financially, and safe—until I wasn't anymore. One day he loved me to the moon, and when he laughed, I felt it deep in my rib cage. But if his dinner was not to his pleasing, the wall would wear it, and an emptied bank account was the only warning he was fixing to roll out.

Was he mentally ill? I really don't know. What do you do with a person like that? I have yet to figure it out. Nor why it is my mother never made one complaint against him.

Years ago, after Sheriff Ed found my father in the closet with a knife (Sheriff Ed saying, *Don't drop the knife, give me a reason to shoot you*) and made Dad leave, the sheriff sat on our porch swing all night, begging my mother to press charges. "At least petition for a restraining order."

"And what?" she said, a deadness in her voice. "Make him madder?"

"He's going to kill you one day," Sheriff Ed told her in a low, somber voice, unaware I was listening through the screen door. "Then what happens to Lucy?" he said.

None of this is an excuse. I'm just laying out my reasons.

THE *ENDLESS SUMMER* was a gorgeous girl of a boat, a center-console Maxum, not particularly big but fast—eighteen feet of raw power. She had a sleek jut of bow, a blue and gold racing stripe along her hull. Dad bought her the day after I got my college acceptance.

I have never liked the ocean. Let me play in bay water ankle-deep. Give me a kayak on the river so long as I can see a coastline. To me, the ocean is terrifying in its vastness. Then again, I had never had my mother's feel for its currents or the way the winds control it.

But that first day of March, my father wanted to take us out on the *Endless Summer*'s maiden cruise. He told us it was to be a celebration.

We put in on St. Mary's River. My father drove, one hand on the wheel, a can of Budweiser in the other. As we cruised through the inlet, my mother pointed out the osprey on the channel marker. An osprey is a good-luck bird that bodes well for a safe voyage. My mother turned her face into the wind and smiled, her red hair flying all around her. She was never happier than when she was on the water.

Around three thirty, according to the report, we passed a sports fishing vessel coming in from a day of hunting marlin on the shelf. My mother radioed its skipper, asking about sea conditions. The skipper radioed back: windy, five-foot seas.

With the right captain—say, someone like my mother—the *Endless Summer* could've handled seas twice that size. That boat drove beautifully.

Two or maybe three miles out, Mom noticed the weather turning and suggested we head back to land. Dad cut the engine and popped his third Bud—or maybe it was his fourth. He was frowning in a way that told me his buzz had turned bad.

"Congratulate me," he kept saying. He'd gotten this boat for a steal. "Get it?"

We didn't.

He told us the *Endless Summer* cost the year's tuition my mother had saved in what she'd thought was a secret account.

The wind kicked up. The boat swayed in the chop. My father's eyes flickered dangerously. "A secret account," he said again. "The account you thought you could keep secret from me."

"You emptied out the college fund?" she said in disbelief.

This fund was news to me. My mother had squirreled away that much money? How? I was stunned into silence.

What my mother said next were fighting words: "I will never forgive you. Not so long as I have breath."

"No, no, no, it's okay," I said, holding out my hands, like *everyone please be calm*. This was my job: separate if possible, de-escalate if not. I had never expected money, I explained. My financial aid paperwork was already filed. I'd go to school on borrowed money, like everyone else I knew at that time. "I love you so much for trying," I told her.

And he exploded. I was making him the bad guy, he said. My mother and I teamed up against him always. "Your mother's why we never have money."

"Can we just get back?" I begged.

The chop was making the boat rock woozily. Fog had disappeared the shoreline. "Mom, the front's coming in."

"The weather's fine," she said. I don't even think she saw it. She said, "Your father is *not*."

Stupidly, I left them in the transom and went to the helm, turned over the engine. I did not know this boat, or how to drive in rough seas, and started off at an easy ten miles per hour, then fifteen, pointing the bow through the fog due west. Any minute Dad would take over the helm, I was sure of it. If Mom thought I couldn't handle these conditions, she'd be up here in a hot minute.

They thought I could handle this, didn't they?

The wind at my back carried snatches of their argument, and when it got loud I glanced back, as Dad pushed her down in the transom seat. She shook out her wrist as though it'd hurt.

"Don't push her," I yelled before I turned back to watch where I was driving—faster now, standing so I could see better over the windshield.

Sea spray soaked my hair, stung my eyes. Why wasn't land visible yet? We'd only gone out a few miles, hadn't we?

Had I gotten us lost?

I glanced back again. "Mom," I shouted over my shoulder. "Could you come up and help?"

But he was standing over where he'd pushed her, shouting accusations—half of which were lost in the engine roar—and by the look of her, she was giving it right back.

She had decided, for whatever awful reason, that after all these years of taking his abuse, she was finally going to take a stand. Here, on the boat, with nowhere to run. If we were going to make it back to land, it was up to me.

THIS IS WHERE memory shatters. Like pieces of a broken mirror I try to reassemble but what it reflects back isn't quite right.

As we headed in, the wave pattern became tighter, choppier, whitecaps everywhere. My jacket flapped madly, like a warning. I was more worried about what was going on behind me with my parents than what was in front of me with the waves and fog—that was the big mistake. I wasn't minding the odometer. Was I really speeding as the report said? The following seas may have pushed the boat faster than I'd realized. In seas that rough, anything felt too fast.

Over the engine, I heard my mother say, "What kind of a man steals from his child? No kind worth having."

"I'm warning you," he yelled back.

"The fog's getting worse," I cried.

My mother started forward, gripping a seat handle for balance. Seeing her, I nearly cried with relief. Then my father pushed her out of the way. It was his boat, he said. He staggered toward me, bent into the wind.

"Turn it at an angle," he shouted, and I looked at what he was pointing at—the biggest swell yet. I turned the wheel, bracing myself. I stupidly hit the wave head-on. For a brief, terrifying moment, the boat was airborne before it slammed back down with an ear-shattering *crack*.

Dad was cursing, bleeding; he'd fallen and cut his mouth. Just as he shoved me aside and grabbed the wheel, the fog parted like a curtain, and my mother screamed. I saw the buoy the instant before we hit.

———

WHEN I CAME to, I was wedged beneath the steering console, where my father had pushed me. My head felt woozy, strange. The bump was tender where I touched it. Getting up, I slipped in blood.

My father—he was dead.

The seat my mother had been holding on to was still intact, but where was she? I looked around frantically. I screamed her name into the fog.

The boat listed, its starboard side sheared away. I scampered around what was left of the boat and leaned out over the side, peering down into the dark water.

Broken boat parts bobbed against each other. Flotation devices skimmed across the waves. Into the fog, I screamed her name and waited, listening, before I called out again.

All I heard back was the lap of waves.

Had she gotten trapped beneath the boat? I looked down at the dark chop, terrified by what lay beneath. Then I took a deep breath and dove in.

The water was bracing, colder than expected, and dark. I had to feel my way along the bottom of the hull. I recoiled from the sharp edges of broken pieces and searched until my lungs felt on fire, coming up for air. I coughed out salt water.

How many times had I gone under? How long had it been since the crash?

In the ocean, you lose your sense of time and place. I gave in to the waves that carried me up and up, and from each crest, I scanned the surface frantically for a glance of wet red hair, only to have the wave drop me back down again. Eventually, I made my way to the buoy and climbed for a better look. From there I screamed her name until I was hoarse.

That's where the helicopter found me. A man in a red suit fell from its belly, and despite my kicking and screaming, he pried me loose from the buoy and shoved me in a basket. I screamed, *Leave me alone! Find her!*

The basket lifted higher.

Give me my mother back.

CHAPTER TWENTY-THREE

WHEN I FINISHED THE STORY, I SAT DOWN NEXT TO ADDIE ON THE edge of my bed. I felt exhausted, emptied out, scared. The walls of my room had fallen away, and I could almost smell the ocean. Addie sat there quietly.

"What are you thinking?" I said.

She blinked down at the report in her hand. Then she looked up with stunned eyes. "Oh, Lucy," she whispered. "Is that story true?"

"Yes."

"But I don't understand. Why couldn't you tell us that?"

I thought of her first group text to me all those years ago: I think we're all roommates? That summer before freshman year, only months after the accident, those texts ushered in a kind of magical thinking, a pretend life with those pretend friends who were gorgeous, almost fantastical. They seemed to me flickers of light in the darkness I'd found myself in. Missing my mother so bad. Out on the beaches searching for her every day. Wondering whether it would've been better if I'd died out there in the wreckage, but too mentally exhausted to do anything about it.

And of course the ever-persistent shame. I had not been strong; I'd been weak. I had not kept her safe. The moment my mother needed me most, I'd failed to get her back to land.

I explained that first bus ride from Georgia to here. "The entire way, I was thinking I'd have to fix the lie I told you about my parents," I said. "But once I got here, every time I tiptoed toward it, I had this terrible fear. Would you think I was damaged? If you knew I was different from you, would you call university housing and ask for a roommate switch? Would I lose you? I was so afraid to be alone. And I wanted the three of you to love me like I already loved you."

For a long moment, she considered what I said, then nodded once, decisive. "Look, I understand not wanting to tell strangers. That's what we were when we first met, I get that. I would've been the same way. But why hide the accident now? After all these years? Did I do something to make you mistrust me?"

That was a terrible thought, one I couldn't allow her to believe even for a second. "You never do anything wrong," I said. "You've been the best friend I've ever had."

"Then why?"

"You don't know how you affect people, I don't think. When you talk a certain kind of way, you make people feel loved. You give hope. You said we could start fresh. When you talked, I could imagine a new way to live. People can't live without that kind of hope."

Addie got up and was moving around the room restlessly now, looking at everything in my room anew. The horseshoe crab on my shelf, the clamshell that held my earrings. The rustic floors and low ceiling, small, dark corners at the attic's edge. A mishmash of furniture, sagging bed, dented lampshades, the decor of the college student I sometimes forgot I wasn't anymore. Or maybe just the room of a person trapped in the past.

At the table beside my bed, she gazed down at the picture of me and my mother on the beach.

"You're still grieving," she said, in a way that almost made my heart stop. "What happened to you," she said, and stopped, struggled. "I don't even know the words. I don't know how I'd react either, if my mother died."

"But . . . she's not dead, Addie."

She blinked at me.

I said it again: "My mother's not dead."

"The accident report says—"

"That she's lost," I said, cutting her off. "Lost means she can be found. The buoy we hit was half a mile from shore. My mother is an amazing swimmer. The strongest swimmer I've ever known. That distance is nothing for my mother."

Wind ripped across the copper rooftop. The old windows in the turret groaned. Addie's gaze on mine was steady, intense. There was so much love in that look, and a kind of fear, too.

Finally, she said, "You think your mother swam to shore?"

How did you explain to someone who'd never been lucky enough to meet my mother? "She knows those waterways like the veins of her own wrist. We used to joke she was part mermaid. There were flotation devices all over that wreckage. It would've been, for her, a piece of cake."

And not an unusual story, either. The annals of maritime disaster are filled with survival tales. Three teenaged boys lost in the middle of the South Pacific for fifty days—rescued by a passing boat. A sailor adrift on an inflatable raft for seventy-six days in the West Indies before he made it back to land. A Chinese sailor aboard a wooden crate for 133 days, surviving on blood from the liver of a shark who lost its battle with the sailor.

"And it's been how long?" Addie said quietly. "Six years?"

"On March first, it will be, yes."

She raised an eyebrow at me. "Can I ask . . . where do you think she is?"

"I don't know. The fog was thick. I never spotted her." Then, helplessly: "I don't know that she's not upset with me. Obviously I shouldn't have wrecked the boat."

"But it was an accident."

"Doesn't matter."

"Oh, yes it does. It wasn't your fault, Lucy."

"Okay."

She grabbed my wrist, as though I might fly away. "Your mother couldn't possibly think it was. Lucy, look at me. If your mother survived, why hasn't she come for you? Why didn't she, in any of these six long years, reach out to say what happened was not your fault?"

PART FOUR
THE MATCH

CHAPTER TWENTY-FOUR

AFTER OUR TALK ABOUT THE BOAT ACCIDENT, ADDIE PACKED HER overnight suitcase. She promised she'd be back in a few days. She said her leaving had nothing to do with what I'd told her, only that she needed to get away from the noise of the neighborhood. Her parents' house, a lovely Colonial in leafy upper Northwest DC, was on a street so quiet you might mistake it for the suburbs. There she could get her head straight.

I waited with her by the door for her father to come. When he pulled up in front of the house in his big Mercedes, she turned to me, fear on her face. "What you told me, that's everything?"

"Yes," I said, nodding.

She hugged me before she left.

ON SATURDAY, I hung out in my bedroom all day, keeping myself busy reading the news about Josh. There was a lot. I read everything I could find, as though it were a research project at work, looking for anything that stood out, any leads, and found nothing new. I lurked on the page of the internet sleuth who visited us. I read every rumor on social media.

According to all the reports, Josh Egan's murder appeared random. Police reportedly had no suspects, no witnesses, no murder weapon—or at least not that police were willing to talk about. It appeared to be a buttoned-up, disciplined investigation. No leaks, no *sources say.*

That night, I dreamt of the ocean. In the dream, I was drowning in water like mercury, its shiny, burning surface reflected my face. A rescue helicopter came, but it wasn't the Coast Guard; it was the US Park Police still looking for Josh. A woman's voice—my mother's—shouted through the bullhorn: *Plant your feet.* When I did, I was standing hip-deep in the stagnant water of the C&O Canal.

Get out, came my mother's voice through the bullhorn. *Help Josh.*

I woke in a sweat. My room was dark, freezing cold. I got out of bed and slid my arms through my robe, and, belting it tightly, walked across the cold floorboards to my desk against the turret window.

Still lost in the dream, I rubbed sleep from my eyes and turned on my laptop. Through the turret window, I noticed a man across the street, standing just beyond the yellow dome of light from the gas streetlamp.

He looked big and was wearing dark clothing, but otherwise I couldn't make him out.

Our street was a cut-through from the university to the bars. Lots of people passed by after the bars closed down. The man was probably waiting for an Uber. He could've even been trying to sober up in the cold. All this made sense. But still, I felt like we were being watched.

I ran down the three flights of stairs and flung open the front door. On the stoop my toes curled from the cold. But the man was gone.

If there'd been a man.

IN ITS SUNDAY morning edition, the *Washington Post* reported the medical examiner's preliminary findings: Josh's time of death was the Saturday of the snowstorm, afternoon or early evening. The bruise on Josh's temple had reportedly led to a fatal brain bleed. He also had other bruising to his torso, though no defensive wounds. To the medical examiner, this suggested Josh may have known or been surprised by his attacker.

I went downstairs to Penelope's room and asked whether I could borrow a book. Penelope spun around on her desk chair, rested her feet on the radiator. "I haven't read anything good lately," she said. "But sure."

"I'm looking for an anatomy textbook. Biology maybe."

"Why?"

My hand went to the spot above my ear where I'd seen Josh's bruise. "What's this called?"

"Your temple?"

"The medical term."

Penelope's smile went flat against her teeth. "You need to go outside and get some fresh air. Take a walk. Go see Connor. He came by twice yesterday. He's worried about you."

"I can't see him yet. I'm busy with my research." Though the truth was, I didn't want him to see me like this. I hadn't showered in days. God only knew what my hair looked like—I'd been avoiding mirrors lately. I went to Penelope's bookshelf and pulled out *Human Anatomy*. The book was heavy. "Have you heard from Addie?"

"No, sweetie." She said "sweetie" in a way that meant she was tired of the question. For whatever reason, Addie wasn't returning our texts.

"You think she's okay, though?"

"As okay as she can be, sure." Then she said what she'd been saying all weekend: "Give her the space she wants, Lucy."

I went back to my room and wrote a letter to my mother. I told her how much I loved her and missed her. Then I thought about what Addie said, about how she should've reached out to me. I wrote that I needed her to come forgive me.

And that was how I passed my first weekend without Addie.

MONDAY MORNING, THE three of us were getting ready for work. Estella was all glammed up in a white button-down and black merino wool trousers, dressed to the nines for her new job.

She'd landed it last Thursday night at Cafe Milano, when the columnist Lena Leamas had been so charmed by Estella, she'd asked her to come in for an interview the following day. At the end of the interview, Lena Leamas offered Estella a research position on her staff.

This didn't surprise me at all. Estella was a world-class schmoozer and had a gift for talking her way into anything. This would be her third job offer since graduation. I congratulated her for what I hoped could be the start of a serious, wonderful career.

"Yes, well, my primary purpose is spying," Estella said, correcting me. "I already put the kibosh on their Addie suspicions. Kevin Thompkins won't be able to sell that picture if he tried."

"Good," I said.

She grinned. "I'll let you know what else I hear around their newsroom today."

"And Addie's cool with this spying?" I said, starting down the stairs with her.

"Sure."

"When did she say that?"

"She didn't have to. I'm finding out what I can for Addie." Estella stopped on the stairs. Her eyes narrowed on the front door. "Asshole!" she shouted.

Estella raced down the stairs to the foyer, stepping over the pile of business cards beneath the front door's mail slot. Its metal flap was currently being held open by someone's finger. Then I saw an eye. Someone was peeping through.

Estella picked up a boot from the tray and smashed the finger. A man shouted, "Yowch," and the flap clanged closed. Estella got down on her haunches and lifted the flap. Through it, she shouted, "Next time I gouge out your eye!"

Penelope hurried down the stairs. "What happened? What's wrong now?"

"The outside keeps trying to come in!" Estella whirled around with wild eyes. "We have to do something to keep this mail slot closed. Can we board it up? Would gaffer tape work?"

"You can't close the mail slot," Penelope said. "What would happen to our mail? I'm still waiting for med school invites."

Estella flung her arm toward the front door. "People are peeking in! Whoever killed Josh is out there somewhere. For all we know, that was him!"

I looked through the French window at the man retreating. It was some middle-aged dude scurrying off. Not Leo Ryan. "Josh's killer was not peeping through the door. Things are *fine*."

Even though things felt so far from fine.

"Really? You think this is *fine*?" Estella said. "Josh is dead, and his killer is probably running around the city. Strangers keep showing up and banging on our door all hours. Do you notice any of it, Lucy? You're upstairs, hiding away in your attic room, oblivious to all this. I for one am sick to death of it. This is not how I wanted to become famous."

"This will all blow over," I said, and it sounded weak even to me. "We just have to be patient until we get our lives back."

"Patient?" Estella scoffed. She turned to Penelope. "I love this house, I do. But it's in the middle of everything. We have no privacy here." She waved her hands. "Addie was smart to get out."

"Oh, come on," I said.

Penelope held up a hand. "Let her say her piece, Lucy."

"Should we plan for a move?" Estella said. "At least start our search for a new place, if we have to get out quick?"

I glanced around the foyer. I loved this house, every beautiful room of it, every broken part, too. The old chandelier that didn't work. The walnut railing that wobbled under your hand. The big front room, our favorite hangout spot. All the memories we'd made here. If I had my way, the four of us would never leave.

"Maybe Estella's right," Penelope said, eyeing me nervously. "If we don't feel safe here, why would we stay?"

"Things will settle down," I assured them. "Everything will go back to normal as soon as the police arrest someone."

Estella cut me a look of disbelief. "An arrest, huh? And when's that going to be?"

WHEN I GOT to my desk at the office, I was still distracted. An uneasy feeling kept coming back, a churn in my gut that if Leo Ryan had actually killed Josh, something about him should've been reported by now, even if it was only police declaring Leo "a person of interest." Three days ago, I'd found Leo Ryan's identity using the police composite sketch. Detective Kelley had that same sketch. If I had found him, of course she would have, too.

What if the investigators were talking to Leo right now?

Or Leo was already being detained? If we knew Leo was in the slammer, wouldn't we all feel safer?

If we were safe, we could all stay together in our house. Addie would come home. I logged into the speedy, expensive database. I searched DC Courts records for active arrest warrants with the keywords "Leo Ryan." But got nothing.

Then I tried "murder of Josh Egan" and "Josh Egan homicide," and it was the same—no hits.

From public reports—mainly the newspapers—I made a list of key players in the police task force. An FBI agent, a quoted assistant US attorney. The Metropolitan Police detectives whose names were already known to me. In the search for all warrants and court orders with their names listed, I constrained the search to court filings within the last seven days.

Bingo, I got a hit.

Last Thursday's search warrant for Josh's apartment was issued by a DC Superior Court judge. It authorized:

Metropolitan Police Detective Edna Lawrence to search the premises of 2700 Virginia Avenue NW #1408 and personal vehicle described as 2019 Subaru Outback located in parking space 1408 in underground garage of same address. This warrant directs police to seize computer, phone, and other digital media including written media for evidence of threats and motive.

And to seize "footwear, shoe, including boot" for physical and other impressions, to perform chemical, scientific, and other tests or experiments. Police have reasonable cause to believe such "footwear, shoe, including boot" described in attachment matches footprint impression found at homicide scene located on federal parkland within the C&O Canal National Historical Park near Fletcher's Cove, NW, DC, and constitutes evidence of and demonstrates commission of that homicide.

This warrant shall be executed during daylight hours within ten days of issuance. An inventory of property seized must be returned to the court on the next court day after its execution.

I read it again: The judge had given the investigators the okay to go into Josh's apartment looking for computers, electronic devices, and specifically a shoe that had left some kind of evidence at the crime scene. But why search for this suspect's shoe in Josh's car and condo? I couldn't seem to connect these two things. How could a shoe that'd been at a crime scene make its way back to Josh's condo or car?

I remembered the garage surveillance video of Leo Ryan getting out of Josh's car. Josh and Leo walking across the parking lot on that video. You had to assume Leo Ryan was going into Josh's apartment.

Is that why the police were looking for the shoe in the apartment? I started a new search for warrants issued for Leo's home address, and Claire Ryan's business in Arlington, Virginia, and for Leo himself in the Virginia jurisdictions.

Again, no hits.

I was frustrated. The warrant showed that the investigators had a critical piece of evidence. Why not name whom it belonged to? It felt as if I was looking right at the answer but couldn't see.

Okay, Lucy, *think*.

Maybe the investigators suspected Leo Ryan but were holding off on court filings for some reason.

Or maybe Leo Ryan met with the investigators voluntarily, as Addie had, and voluntarily gave up his shoes.

As Addie had, a small disloyal voice inside me said.

I brushed that thought away. Focused instead on police looking for shoes that they believed could be found in Josh's apartment.

. . . which Addie had access to, that same small voice whispered.

I didn't like that thought at all. I stared at the computer screen blankly. Addie wasn't a suspect, was she? She had an alibi. The three of us were her alibi.

Why did her dad get her a lawyer? the voice asked. *Why not run her name in the system?*

I told myself that would be a waste of database time and money, even as my hands hovered over the keyboard. A knock on my door made me jump.

"Hello, hello, can I come in?" Sharkey said.

I closed the search window before reaching over and opening the door.

Sharkey's Jets cap was flipped backward. The sleeves of his black blazer were pushed up to his elbows. He wanted to know where my ASAP research project was. Since last week, he'd been asking for the dirt I was supposed to find on a pol's opponent. Instead of doing the client's research, I'd been spending my office time trying to figure out what was going on in Josh's murder investigation.

"Not quite finished," I said weakly. "Might need a little more time."

"The research was due days ago, Lucy. The client complained to Andrew. Then Andrew called and complained to me. Where exactly are you on the project?"

"I'll get to it right now, promise."

He was studying me. "What's going on with you, anyway? This is not like you. You're not sick, are you?"

"No, I'm not sick."

"You look sick," he said, backing away. Sharkey had a fear of viruses. His hands were permanently cracked from hospital-grade sanitizer. "I'll reassign your project to someone else. Go home, feel better."

That was the last time I saw him.

CHAPTER TWENTY-FIVE

I LEFT THE OFFICE AND WENT OUT ONTO THE STREET. I PULLED OFF my coat right away. The temperature had shot up. Warm air curled over melting snowpack, creating a fog. I could smell the river but couldn't see it. I didn't want to go to Connor's café, which was surely crowded, or home, which would be empty. But I had nowhere else to go.

At the turn onto our street, our house was shrouded in fog. On the corner, a man leaned against a white van with a TV dish on its roof. A big television camera was by his feet. I was pretty sure he was staking out our house, and if that was true, I wasn't sure I could get inside without his seeing me.

I texted Penelope: you home?

After a few minutes, she responded: at work, want to get drinks after? was hoping to talk to you

What about?

Bubbles appeared on the screen. They seemed to bubble on forever.

Finally, it came: Addie called.

I can meet now, I typed.

Can't, too busy. How about this afternoon

Lunch?

A long pause. Then the bubbles started up again. If you can meet me at work, she replied.

———

THE HOSPITAL RECEPTIONIST asked for my government ID. She handed my driver's license back with a sticker with my name and face printed on it. I stuck it to my shirt and took the elevator to the floor where Penelope worked. You could tell it was the pediatric ward. The walls were bright yellow and covered with watercolors and sketches clearly made by children, some surprisingly good.

There was a metal bench in the corner of the waiting room shaped like a giant butterfly. I sat there and texted Pen that I was here, no rush.

Finally, Pen came out from behind a big electric door that said NO ENTRY. She wore her hair up in a messy twist showing her hank of purple hair, and shoved in it a bright pink pen.

"Ready for lunch?" she said, and didn't wait around for me to say yes or no.

I hurried along beside her. "What's going on with Addie?"

"Let's get food first." She was moving so fast. "I only have thirty minutes."

In the cafeteria, we waited in the lunch line. Penelope ordered a cheeseburger and fries at the grill. I grabbed the first thing I saw, a sad little salad from the refrigerated section. While we waited for Penelope's burger, she asked why I wasn't at the office.

I told her about my boss sending me home while I was doing research about Josh's murder but avoided mentioning Leo's name. I still had this feeling Addie ought to be told first. Also, if I was being honest, I wanted credit for finding Leo Ryan. It was important Addie see how hard I was working to fix this problem. I guess I was hoping for a kind of redemption after Addie found out I'd lied about my parents.

After I told Pen that Sharkey had sent me home, her eyes went soft with concern. "But I do wonder why you're getting all wrapped up in the investigation aspect of this. Why not let the police do what they're going to do? They have an entire team of professionals working on this. They'll figure it out."

"I don't think they're playing straight with Addie."

"That's funny. Because Addie seems to," Penelope pointed out.

The cafeteria chef slid Penelope's burger under the heat window. We carried our trays to the main dining room, where I stopped in the middle of the room, tray in hand, and stared at the windows. My hands gripped the food tray. "Can I ask you something? It's foggy outside, right?"

She looked over at the bank of windows. "I mean, yeah," she said, puzzled. "What's wrong, Lucy?"

"Nothing. Just wanted to make sure you were seeing it, too."

"I've got an idea," she said in a cool, professional voice. "Why don't we take our food someplace private? Where you'll be more comfortable."

WE LEFT THE crowded cafeteria, and Penelope took me to what she called the sin bin. Basically, a giant storage closet. Shelves of linens and pillows and towels, the faint hint of bleach. "You don't want to know what goes on in here," she said with a twisted smile. "Hang on, let me get something to put our lunch trays on."

She disappeared around a shelf and came back with a big cardboard box. She put her tray on the box and sat on the floor, crossing her legs. I sat across from her and said, "Do people hook up back here?"

"Not me." She laughed about that. "Others, maybe. That's the word on the curb."

We ate in silence. She watched me from under her eyelashes. She was considering her words, I could tell. After a couple of minutes, I couldn't help it. I told her: "Just say it."

She nodded. "All right, I was thinking about how you found Josh. And how you took it so hard. Which makes sense. I mean it is traumatic, isn't it? Seeing someone you liked, out like that in our clearing."

I shivered. "Horrible, yes."

"And you must've been so worried for Addie. Estella and I love Addie of course, but you and Addie, it's different, isn't it? She always treated you more like a little sister than a friend." Penelope was gnawing at her lip. "Addie and I spoke over the phone this morning. She told me about your parents."

I stiffened in anticipation of Penelope's judgment. I had lied to her, too. But she just kept picking at her French fries, talking as though we didn't have a care in the world.

"Addie's mad at me," I said.

Penelope shook her head. "Not mad. Confused. Worried. She wanted to know if I could help you get help. Mental health help, I'm talking about."

I looked at her blankly. "Why?"

"Anybody who'd been through what you'd been would struggle with grief . . . guilt." The words hung in the air between us. I didn't like either word. Then she said, "None of this, by the way, am I qualified to offer my opinion about."

She sat very straight when she explained all this. She respected the rules of the profession, and while she might trust her own emotional IQ and ability to read people, my "situation" required someone properly licensed. "We have some really good doctors here," she said. "If you give me the green light, I can work to set you up with someone who specializes in unresolved trauma."

She explained how our subconscious mind is always trying to repair our traumatic wounds. Especially traumas from an early age. She described destructive impulses, unconscious needs to relive that old trauma through a mirrored event. To gain power over a situation similar to one in which you'd been powerless. A way to right a perceived wrong. The ever-present hope for a do-over to ease unresolved guilt.

Then she pointed out, as an example, how people who suffered abuse often got into relationships with abusive people. Not because they liked being abused. But because of a compulsion to come to terms with the earlier abuse by reenacting it.

I stared at Penelope, surprised I hadn't put this together before. It made such sense. My mother must've had something bad happen in her childhood, which could have been why she'd taken so much shit from my father. "That's why my mom stayed with my dad, isn't it?"

"Um, maybe?" Penelope shook her head. "What I was talking about is you."

"Me?"

The boat wreck, she explained, was—psychologically speaking—my unresolved trauma. "It could explain why you've been so heartbroken about Josh. You could be working out your unresolved feelings for your mother through his death. Addie says your mom was missing?"

I pressed my lips together. "*Is* missing."

"See? You could talk about that with a good doctor. Somebody who's way smarter about all this stuff than me."

Penelope swirled a French fry in ketchup. It was kind of her to try to help me. And she was right—I had been so upset. At the same time, talking to a professional seemed like something other people did. The whole thing seemed a bit of an overreaction.

Then she dropped the other shoe: Addie was going to stay with her parents a bit longer. This was not because Addie was mad at me, she said; it was only that Addie needed to work out her stuff alone, without having all my feelings intrude on hers.

"But she'll come back?" I said.

"Think so, yes. Listen, I want to introduce you to a doctor friend. He's not really taking new patients, but I sort of explained how I had a friend struggling in his area of expertise, blah-blah-blah, and as a personal favor, he thought he could fit you in at the end of his shift tonight."

"What area of expertise?"

"Grief."

"I don't know, Pen. I appreciate it. I do. But, I mean, he's probably expensive, right?"

She told me not to worry about all that. She'd help me figure out the insurance and out-of-pocket crap and all the rest. "You just get better, okay?" she said, smiling. "I want us all back together, happy and healthy and feeling like ourselves again, right?"

That was what I wanted more than anything.

"Okay," I said. "I'll do it."

CHAPTER TWENTY-SIX

ESTELLA TEXTED AS I WAS COMING OUT OF THE HOSPITAL, WANTING
to know where I was and whether I was busy. I told her I'd just finished lunch
with Pen but why wasn't she at work? She said she'd explain everything when
she picked me up in five minutes.

An ambulance came screaming up Reservoir Road. Trailing behind it
was Penelope's Jeep. Estella hopped the curb, part of the Jeep blocking traffic.
Horns went off. The Jeep's window slid down and Estella said, "Hurry up,
get in."

"Where are we going?"

"Addie's. We have to warn her."

We cut across Georgetown and took the parkway north. Estella told me
about her first day in the office, the morning meeting with Lena Leamas and
Nikki. Apparently, Nikki had been working the concierge at Josh's condo,
and he'd told her confidentially about a fight Addie and Josh had had in the
elevator. Estella glanced away from the road over at me. "Lena sent me out
to ask Addie if she'd agree to an interview."

So this was why Lena had hired her. Lena had been planning on using
Estella for access to Addie, same way Estella had hoped to use Lena. "Don't
worry," Estella said. "I'm not going to talk Addie into anything. But we do
have to warn her. Do you know about an elevator fight?"

"That was where the breakup happened."

"Oh, okay, that makes sense," Estella said, thinking it through. "That's what it looked like to me, though there wasn't a date stamp. So I wasn't sure when the video was recorded."

My heart dropped. "What video?"

"Videos," Estella corrected. "There are two. Lena has them both."

Estella described surveillance video shot from two different cameras in Josh's condo. From the corner hallway camera, you could see Addie hurrying down the hall with Josh hot on her heels; she punches the elevator button repeatedly, like she can't get away fast enough.

"While she's waiting for the elevator, Josh stands over her, yelling at her, and he's so much bigger, and all you can think is, what a jerk," Estella said. "Then the elevator doors open, and Addie gestures for Josh to go away, but he follows her in. From the elevator camera, you see Josh pacing, Addie shrinking. Josh waving his hands. Addie trying to ignore him. You see it in the mirrored walls, like a goddamned Stephen King fun house."

Estella shuddered. She described Josh's face—all red and contorted. The way he paced the elevator—like a maniac. She kept thinking that he was going to hit Addie. "The whole time he's raging, looking totally batshit, she just stands there, trapped. Then something really weird happens. He just stops."

"Stops what?" I breathed.

"Everything. Moving. Talking. Maybe even breathing. It was like someone flipped a switch on him. So *weird*. Like he'd caught a glimpse of his crazy in the mirror."

"What happened then?" I whispered, afraid to know.

"The elevator door opens, and Addie bolts."

We were in Addie's parents' neighborhood now. Estella parked the Jeep in front of Addie's house, a gray stone Colonial with bright blue shutters, a US flag over the three-car garage. A tire swing hung from the oak tree in the snowy front yard. Framing the house were the trees of Rock Creek Park.

Before we got out, Estella turned to me. "I'm worried about how Addie would handle the questions the video raises. If she and Josh had a volatile relationship? Did Josh harm her? Lena wants to ask if Josh abused her, because it fits Lena's view of what happened to him."

"And what the hell is that?"

"That Addie was defending herself. Lena actually said, 'I've been in this business forever. I've seen everything there is to see.'" Estella was mimicking a deep female voice. "'It's always the person you love who kills you.'"

ADDIE'S MOTHER ANSWERED the front door. Dr. James was an older, curvier version of Addie—perfect hair and red lipstick, a glitter of jewels at ears, throat, wrists. She said hello as Addie's three dogs came tumbling out. They were the worst-behaved dogs you'd ever seen, shelter dogs Addie had saved but had never been able to train. They were jumping all over us.

"Inside," Dr. James said in a stern voice, and the dogs lowered their tails and slunk back in. Then she turned on us a polite, dismissive smile. "Addie's not here, girls."

"Oh, but we have to talk to her," Estella said. "Do you know where we can find her?"

"Afraid not."

"We haven't been able to reach her. Her phone's broken."

"Yes," Dr. James said. "I'm aware."

Estella, who'd never met a brick wall she didn't try to climb over, pressed on: "It's kind of urgent we talk to her ASAP. Are you sure she's not in her room?"

"I feel quite certain I know what goes on in my own house," Dr. James said coolly. "Now, if you'll excuse me," she said, and went back inside and shut the door.

———

ESTELLA WAS QUIET on the drive back home. Turning onto the parkway, she glanced over at me. "Can I ask you something?"

I didn't like her guilty expression, or the way her eyes crinkled around the corners in a wince.

"What if Addie—" she said in a low, somber tone.

"Don't."

"Then who?"

"The guy who grabbed her," I said. "Come on. We know this."

She let out a shaky laugh. "You're right, yeah, we do," she said. "Sorry. That video's got me all turned around. And Lena suggesting Addie would've been right to defend herself from that kind of thing, you know, if it happened in the woods. Because she would have had the right to defend herself."

"Except that didn't happen."

"No, of course not," Estella agreed.

"We know that because we know Addie. End of story."

"Right, right," she said, nodding again. "Thing is though. Why not tell us what the police asked? Why run off and hide at her parents'?" She said this all really fast, as though she hated herself for asking. "And where is Addie now? She's been acting so weird, hasn't she?"

All this annoyed me. Mostly because I had wondered briefly, too. But hearing it coming out of Estella's mouth, it sounded so disloyal. "Dr. James will give her our message," I said. "Then Addie will call, I'm sure."

It was quiet in the Jeep after that. The trees along Rock Creek Park flew fast past our windows.

"Did Addie ever say why she got a lawyer?" Estella asked.

"Anybody in her position would get a lawyer." I had just gotten this calm. Penelope had worked so hard, talking me back to feeling calm. Now Estella was messing up my head again.

"No, you're right. You really are. I've been thinking that maybe I should get a lawyer, too. You know, I did lie to that investigator."

"Doylan?"

"He asked three times where was I during the snowstorm, where was Addie, and I said Addie and I were together, and he was like, all day? So I told him we never took our eyes off each other. He was annoying, so pushy. Why couldn't he leave me alone? I just wanted him to leave."

"You were with Addie."

She bit her lip. "Actually, I wasn't."

"Yes," I said, "you were."

"Nope, I was hungover from the night before. I took a nap and didn't see Addie until Penelope came home."

Oh no. "That can't possibly be true."

Estella had the grace to wince. "I think I came out of my room around five."

"*O'clock?* You left Addie alone *for four or five hours*? On the day she was attacked?"

"You didn't tell me she'd been attacked," Estella said. "Why am I always the last to know anything? If Pen hadn't said anything, I probably still wouldn't know. And now Lena's got me all messed up in the head, acting like, I don't know, *police could start looking at us.*"

I passed a hand over my eyes. "Police are not looking at us."

"Henry says lying to a cop is against the law."

My eyes snapped open. "*You told Henry?*" The guy she'd been dating for, like, a minute, who seemed harmless but also, quite frankly, like an idiot.

"Henry's in law school," she said. "I didn't tell him it was me I was asking about. Problem is, if I do lie, I'll get in more trouble. But if I come clean, they'll know I lied in the first place."

"Quiet," I said. "Let me think."

I put my head down and rubbed my temples. I was trying to focus. The video of Josh and Addie's explosive fight would soon be out in the world. Addie would be humiliated—she was a deeply private person, after all—but would it also put her in legal jeopardy by suggesting she had a motive? And now Estella was two seconds from calling the police and admitting she'd lied, and that meant Addie had no alibi—that was very bad.

All this, I decided, was Leo Ryan's fault.

Leo Ryan was violent. He'd attacked Addie on the towpath where Josh was found dead. The night before, Leo had been in Josh's apartment, and now police had a warrant for his shoe. Leo had obviously killed Josh. Why hadn't the police arrested him?

Would an arrest come soon enough to help us?

We turned onto O Street and parked in front of our house. "Go in without me," I told Estella. "I need the Jeep for an errand."

AFTER ESTELLA WENT in, I thumbed open Instagram on my phone. I put in a friend request for Leo Ryan. Within minutes, he accepted. Immediately, I sent him a DM. *I want to talk. Do you know who I am?*

Him: *oh hello Lucy*

Him: *come over, bring Addie. you know my address?*

Me: *I know everything about you*

CHAPTER TWENTY-SEVEN

IT WAS LATE AFTERNOON WHEN I GOT TO LEO RYAN'S HOUSE. I checked my face in the rearview mirror. It looked exactly how you'd expect someone confronting a killer might look. Face pale and drawn, eyes wide and mouth trembling. Nobody to back me up. What the hell had I been thinking, coming out here alone? Was I desperate—or just stupid?

Leo answered the door. I had a brief stomach-churning moment in which I thought I was looking up at Josh.

He was tall like Josh but young—even younger than I was—with a kind of awkwardness about him, like a puppy that hadn't yet grown into its paws. He wore a rumpled flannel shirt over a faded Nirvana T-shirt. A flop of dark hair fell over bright eyes. He had Josh's squint.

"Lucy, right?" he said in a deep, scratchy voice, an old man's voice. "Where's Addie?"

"She sends her regrets."

He stepped out past me on the porch, looking around the yard as though Addie were out there, lying in wait. "You said she'd come," he complained.

"Turns out she was otherwise engaged."

His shoulders drooped, like those of a kid whose plans had been ruined. "So you lied to get here," he said, surprised.

"Yeah, Leo, I lied to get you to talk. So let's talk."

After a moment, Leo turned and went through the door.

In the foyer, he turned back and waved impatiently. "Well, are you coming in or what?"

INSIDE, THE KITCHEN was big and modern, the kind you see in fancy magazines. Shiny appliances and stone counters and a windowsill of spiky plants over a sink. Knives like art on a magnetic block. Leo Ryan was a grown man who lived with his mother, a woman who'd worked for Senator Egan.

The house was quiet. "Your mom home, Leo?"

He stopped at the kitchen island and turned back with a thin smile. "Nope. This is just you and me."

I'd wanted him alone so I could talk with plausible deniability. Now that we were alone, I was scared. At the hideaway, Detective Lawrence had said Josh had been struck on the head. Leo Ryan looked strong enough to knock Josh out. Mean enough to leave him in the snow. I kept the kitchen island between us. "Do you expect your mom back soon?"

"She's out of town," he said. "Business. About the only thing that'd keep her away from all this Josh stuff."

"Josh . . . *stuff*? So you know Josh?"

He frowned with disappointment. "Don't act like you don't know who I am."

"Why don't you tell me?"

"So you do want to play games," he said, rolling his eyes. "Whatever."

He opened the massive refrigerator and asked whether I wanted a beer, and I said I did. He opened a can of Rolling Rock and slid it across the island counter. I took a sip but set the beer away. My stomach was in knots.

He slouched with his own beer in hand. "What's up with your friend anyway? Telling cops I attacked her. I was the one walking away with the bloody nose."

His nose didn't look so bad to me. He deserved worse. "If you don't want a bloody nose, don't go grabbing women on the towpath."

He pouted. "All I wanted was to talk to her."

"Talk. Right," I scoffed.

"She was making Josh go through it."

I couldn't believe this. It wasn't believable. "You wanted to talk to her? About Josh?"

"Let me ask you something," he said. "Why did he put up with her? I'd seriously like to know."

"Why did *he* put up with *her*?" Now he was trying to gaslight me. I told myself not to get distracted. Focus on his shoes that matched the footprint in the search warrant. Find out about the shoes and get out.

"Josh was rich," he was saying. "He was on TV. He could've been dating models. Instead, he gets all obsessed with this random chick and lets her shit all over him."

"So you stalked Addie to the towpath? Like you stalked Josh?"

"What?"

"You hurt them."

"She hurt me," he said, thumbing his chest. "I called out to her from the hill, but she kept running."

"So you chased her?" I was boiling. "You're a stalker, aren't you, Leo? You were obsessed with Josh and his relationship with Addie, which is none of your business."

"You're one to talk! How is this any of *your* business? I only invited you if she came. I want to talk to Addie."

"I'm as close as you're getting. Addie and I are best friends, practically family—"

"*Family?*" he said, interrupting me. His jaw worked furiously. "You and Addie?"

"Like a family, yes."

"Well, get this. I *am* family." He slapped his palm on the island counter and leaned forward. "*Josh was my brother.*"

The way he said it gave me chills. Sharkey and I had guessed who Leo must be, but hearing Leo say it outright, through angry tears, made me nervous. I shrank back.

"All I ever wanted was a guy in my life," he was saying. "I mean, Ma's great, all right, but I need a dad, a brother, a guy to do guy stuff with. Then I found Josh. Maybe it took him a minute to warm up, but he invited me to our dad's place. He gave me Dad's things. He told me stuff I deserved to know. I thought we could be like real brothers. But then he talked about moving to New York because your asshole friend broke his heart. All she had to do was take him back, and Josh would've stayed, and I could've been happy. That's all I was trying to say. Just have a little pity. And what did she do? She hit me."

Surprisingly, I believed this. Part of me understood Leo not wanting Josh to move. I hadn't wanted Addie to move to New York either. But I wasn't such a maniac that I'd kill somebody over it.

"So you got mad at Josh for leaving you," I said.

"I was mad at Addie."

"Did you tell the cops how angry you are?"

"Sure, I told Detective Kelley."

My eyebrows shot up. He talked to Kelley? Why wasn't he already locked up then? "Detective Kelley questioned you?" I said in disbelief.

"I'm Josh's only relative. She called me a next of kin."

"And she suspects you?"

A tiny smile played across his lips. I didn't like that smile at all. "Meh, I wouldn't say that."

"What would you say?"

For a long moment he just stared at me, calculating. I watched a decision play across his face.

"First she asked some pretty tough questions," he said finally. "Scared the shit out of me, not going to lie. When she came back the second time, she got a good look at this."

He swung his foot up on the counter. He was wearing a black combat boot, the biggest shoe I'd ever seen in my life. A sense of alarm rushed through me. My body understood the disaster first.

"Size fifteen, baby." He turned his boot this way and that, admiring it. "This here is how Detective Kelley said I was in the clear."

Blood drained from my face. "I don't believe you."

"Her exact words? I was excluded as a suspect. They found a footprint where Josh got killed, and the footprint didn't match my shoe." There was that smile again. Flirty, almost mean. "Apparently snow and ice are great for preserving crime scenes. Kelley told me that evidence gets frozen underneath. The snow's like a big, protective blanket just waiting for the right person with the right tools to sift it away and find out what happened. She said Josh had been kicked—"

"No," I said, shaking my head. "He'd been struck on the head. Detective Lawrence said it at the crime scene. I saw the bruise."

"Yeah? Well, Kelley told me kicked. And they're looking for a shoe smaller than mine. I bet a lady's shoe."

"You're wrong." He had to be.

"My money's on her looking for Addie's shoe," he said.

I buzzed with adrenaline. I needed to get out, *now*. I had to warn Addie.

"Addie has an alibi," I said, eyeing the door. "She came home at ten nineteen a.m., and I was with her. We all were. The rest of that day Addie was never alone."

His eyes burned like Josh's. It was like looking at Josh again. "I think you're up to your ears in this," he said. "You're covering for her, aren't you? I wouldn't be surprised if you and your buddies helped her kill him."

I slid to the side and started for the door. He was beside me, quick as a snake. "Tell me what you did," he said, grabbing my arm.

"Let go. You're hurting me."

He squeezed harder. "Know what else I told Detective Kelley? Josh was obsessed with that woman." He said this so bitterly. "He'd have done any-thing for her, gone anywhere she wanted. The detective asked if I had any idea why someone would do this to Josh, and I said I don't know why. But I know how. There's only one person who could lure Josh into the woods on a day like that."

CHAPTER TWENTY-EIGHT

BY THE TIME I LEFT LEO'S, IT WAS DARK OUT. ON THE DRIVE BACK to the city, I called Addie. When she didn't answer, I hung up and tried again. And again.

Should I leave a message? What if the police took Leo's ridiculous suspicion of Addie to heart? Would police have gotten a warrant for our electronic devices? I didn't know whether I was being paranoid or smart.

I played it safe: *Call me back, please. No matter how late. It's important. A hideaway swimming hole sort of importance.*

In my head, I heard Estella's voice saying *What if?*

Why not tell us what the police asked? Why run off and hide at her parents'? She's been acting so weird, hasn't she?

"The police do not suspect Addie," I said aloud.

Okay, but what if they do?

I grabbed my phone and texted: CALL ME and NEED TO TALK. Then I remembered Addie's phone was broken. She probably wouldn't have responded anyway. Deep inside I already knew she'd left home because of me.

I'd handled everything all wrong. If I drove out to her house now and begged her to talk, she'd probably turn away from me again.

In my gut I knew all this.

I should've told her the truth about everything from the beginning. I should've told her about the boat accident and that it killed my father and made my mother go missing. What had I been so afraid of, anyway? That she'd find my part in it unforgivable? Addie is a kinder person than I am.

I DROVE TO Addie's. The front of the Colonial was dark. The Jameses, it seemed, were either out or tucked in early for the night. The dashboard clock said it was only nine o'clock.

When I got out of the Jeep, there was a stillness in the air, as though the neighborhood were holding its breath. My boots hit the porch—*boom-boom-boom*—and got Addie's dogs barking. Through the window, I watched the dogs leaping over each other, trying to scratch their way out. Nobody came to the door.

I went onto the dark lawn and looked up and saw Addie at her window with a faint light now behind her.

She seemed so far away. I missed her so much. Her face would always be my favorite face in the world, though at that distance, I couldn't read her expression.

She stared down for a long moment before she turned away and closed the curtains. Her window went dark again.

I stood on her lawn, waiting for her to come down. Five minutes turned to fifteen, thirty. All around me, the lights of her neighbors' houses went out, one by one. I waited until the entire street went dark.

I got back in the car and drove to the next block before I pulled over and sat in the cold car on the dark street. I didn't actually know how to get through this without my best friend. I had always thought Addie would be there. I bit the skin along the edge of my fingernail and was relieved when it bled and hurt. My teeth started to chatter. I rested my forehead against the steering wheel and let myself have a good cry.

———

I DROVE BACK to O Street, intending to return Penelope's car. But I passed our row house and kept driving toward the river. There were no other drivers on Canal Road. The fog from earlier had lifted, and my mind seemed to be functioning properly again.

Probably I'd overreacted to what Leo Ryan said. Yes, he'd known about the footprint, but maybe he knew because it was his footprint. Because he killed Josh. I had to believe he killed Josh.

I left the Jeep in the boathouse parking lot and used my phone's flashlight to find my way down the hill. A few times, I lost my footing on the slushy ground beneath me. Then I was on the towpath.

There was a strange energy in the woods that night. A squirrel crashed through the brush. An owl screech made my insides jump. I zipped my jacket to my chin and followed the path to crime scene tape fluttering in the breeze.

I took a breath to calm the trapped-bird beating of my heart and pushed through the brush as I'd done hundreds of times before. Then I found myself in our clearing.

Unbelievably the snow was gone completely. The white tree flashed like a ghost in the beam of my phone's light. Then, at the base of the tree, the light picked out something odd. A white pebble in the dirt.

I got down on my haunches, balancing myself with a hand on the tree. I bit off my glove and touched the pebble with one finger. It felt like plaster, like the kind that came off our row house walls and that I was always sweeping up and tossing away. It crumbled between my fingers.

Then I angled the light down on the dirt and saw what the plaster had been resting in. Knowledge moved through me like an electric shock. Slowly I lowered myself next to it.

It was the boot print.

The police must've taken a plaster cast of this print. I ran my finger over its indentation, which was deeper at the heel. The toes pointed away from the tree. It had a distinctive tread—tiny *x*'s in the sole, perfect for gripping snow, which made it recognizable as a Moncler boot. A high-end, expensive boot. The kind you didn't see around DC very often. Why shell out that kind of cash for shoes that were only useful a few weeks a year?

But Moncler boots lasted forever, and though I could've never afforded a pair, Addie had given me her hand-me-downs years ago.

With shaking hands, I slid my black boot off my right foot and set it onto the footprint. Spots danced in my vision. I pawed at my eyes and waited for my vision to clear.

My boot was the perfect match.

PART FIVE

O STREET LOST

CHAPTER TWENTY-NINE

JOSH

The Day He Died

LATE SATURDAY MORNING, JOSH WOKE TO A PHONE RINGING. HE'D been dreaming of Addie.

He put a pillow over his head to block out the sound. He had a wicked hangover from the night before, when Leo had emptied the last of his bottle of Jack Daniel's before moving on to the rest of his whiskey shelf. Good God, the kid could drink. Why Josh thought he could—scratch that, why he *should*—try to go drink for drink with a nineteen-year-old was anybody's guess.

Leo had gone through the apartment, pocketing every piece of Dad's old junk that Josh offered. In the dressing room, Leo had pulled out storage boxes and Dad's old notes and diaries and campaign material, searching for anything Dad might have written about Claire Ryan. Something loving or even kind, Josh supposed.

Josh warned Leo that he wouldn't find anything like that there. But he let the kid flip boxes and crumble up historical documents, challenge the artifacts of a career their father had loved more than his own family. It was all "boring" and "stupid," Leo announced, everything he read.

Josh decided to let him have at it. Trash the place if he wanted. Better to get it all out than pretend everything was cool—Josh was tired of all that. *You missed a box*, Josh had pointed out as he'd poured himself another drink.

The phone stopped ringing, and after a moment started up again. Josh pulled his pillow from his face and opened his eyes with a groan. A Post-it note was stuck to his chest:

Good times, called an Uber, catch you later.
   Leo

Josh laughed. That kid, he was something, all right.

The phone rang a third time. It was his personal phone, the one that'd once been his mother's. He reached for it.

"This Josh Egan?" a man said.

The call was from the fishing charter captain Josh had, weeks ago, left messages for everywhere, an eyewitness to Lucy's family boat accident. As the captain launched into his story Josh had already figured out, Josh felt himself back in the elevator with Addie again.

She was calling him a liar. His father's voice got loud in his head: *Make her shut the fuck up.* Josh's hand had tingled with the overwhelming urge to punch the mirrored elevator walls and let it all shatter around him. At the last moment, he saw Addie in the mirror. Her beautiful, terrified face. His own cartoonish, pathetic version of his father's.

And it had broken him.

So Josh thanked the captain for his return call. He said he wasn't working on that story anymore. The captain kept talking anyway, described Lucy—the little redhead, he called her—on the boat. This was no surprise. Josh had assumed Lucy was the "unidentified minor" passenger in the accident report. But how did that information get Addie back? He had already decided he could be right, or he could be loved.

Once he and Addie got back together, though, they were going to figure out how to talk to each other. They had to discuss things rationally—kindly, but rationally. She couldn't just jut her chin and stick her fingers in her ears whenever she didn't like something he said. She could not call him a liar when he was right.

And this captain was reminding him: He wasn't a liar. He was right.

He felt himself getting all revved up again.

"Man, I couldn't wait to get out of that backwater hellhole," the captain was saying. "You got no idea how corrupt it is down there. If you're friends with cops, you're in. If not, get ready for a hassle. For a long time I been saying, somebody's got to look into this. Those cops ruined my business. All on account of me seeing that girl kill her parents."

Josh sat up so fast, his head spun. Josh had known there was something off about Lucy. But he never could have imagined this. "Kill them?"

"That's what I told that sheriff," the captain said. "You got a whole ocean out there. How do you hit a buoy? You got to *want* to do it, that's what I was saying. I saw her going full throttle, straight for that buoy. Killed her parents dead."

CHAPTER THIRTY

I DON'T KNOW HOW LONG I SAT NEXT TO THE FOOTPRINT IN THE clearing, too tired to move or think. My knees were to my chest. I was curled up against the base of the witchy tree. I put my hand in my boot print to make sure I hadn't imagined it.

It was real, and it was damning.

Beyond the print, I couldn't keep a single fact straight in my head. The river below roared angrily. The woods, which had always been our respite, seemed to close in, press down on my shoulders. I imagined out there in the darkness something of Josh left behind, Josh at the edges of my periphery, glaring out from behind a tree with his bright, eerie eyes:

You did this.

Look what you did to me.

It made no sense. The day I stumbled on the crime scene, I'd over-heard investigators say Josh had been struck on the head. I couldn't have imagined that, could I? But Detective Kelley told Leo that Josh had been kicked and fell. How could his fall have been so grave?

That was not how I remembered it.

———

THE DAY OF the snowstorm, my phone had rung when I was putting Addie's bloodstained track jacket in the washing machine. A number I'd never seen before crossed the screen. Like with every call I didn't recognize, I let it ring through to voicemail.

Later, I checked the message. It was from Josh. *I need to talk to you today. Call me at this number as soon as you get this.*

But I didn't call him back, not after what I thought he'd done to Addie on the towpath.

Instead of returning his call, I went to Estella's room and stewed about Addie's bruises and the blood on her jacket and wondered what the jerk who'd caused them would want to talk to me about. Then I went to work.

On the way, Josh called me again, and again I let the call go to voicemail. But he was really pissing me off now. From the office mail room, I returned his call.

He demanded we talk in person, right now, and it couldn't wait a day.

"Yeah, I can't," I said. "I'm working."

"You take lunch, don't you?"

"That's when I take my walks. What's this about?"

"The towpath, right?" he said. "I'll meet you at Addie's hangout by the boathouse."

This was Josh saying hop, and I better damn well hop. I heard the threat beneath it—come or else. I thought of Addie's terror when she came home that morning. It was that *or else* threat that got me agreeing. I hung up and went out the mail room door.

I went to the woods to stop a person I believed was a violent man. I was doing it to keep my friend safe. This was what friends did, I believed. I also believed I could reason with him. Whatever else was going on inside me, deep underground, darkly subconscious, I really can't say. I got to the clearing ahead of Josh. I waited in our tree.

As each minute ticked by, I thought how impulsively stupid it was to meet a man like Josh in the woods. Hadn't he just attacked Addie here, in almost this very spot? Was anyone near if I needed help?

And it occurred to me how furious Addie would be with me if she learned I'd come out here to meet Josh. With that sick feeling in my stomach, I hopped out of the tree to get the hell out of there. Just then, Josh came crashing through the brush.

Talk about a city boy through and through. He wore a suit and fine coat and fancy shoes—not boots, as the woods demanded, or a hat and gloves in that terrible cold. His black mood was written all over his handsome face.

"You took too long," I said. "I have to get back to work."

"I'd rather talk."

He stepped in my way, blocking my path. My chest buzzed with adrenaline, like my body was preparing for a fight. I told myself not to engage, don't say anything. Just get out. But there was something about that man. He made me so mad.

"You really scared her, you know that?" I said with contempt. "She came home in bad shape because of you."

I was referencing Addie's attack on the towpath. To this day I still don't know why he didn't correct me.

I told him what I'd never been able to tell my father. That he would not be allowed to hurt Addie ever again. I felt this was a reasonable thing to say. Then I explained how I'd ensure Addie would be kept safe. Like it or not, guys in his esteemed position were vulnerable to credible allegations of violence against women. Think #MeToo. Think famous celebrities blacklisted for grabbing women. Think about that creepy movie mogul in jail.

There was an electric snap in the air. His cold eyes narrowed. "You're talking about consequences?" he said softly.

"Yes."

"You'll tell people I have anger issues. You'll get me fired."

"I don't want to."

"But you'll do it?"

"Can't you just leave Addie alone?" I mean, what the actual hell. "How hard is it not to hurt someone?"

He tugged at his collar. "Like you hurt your parents?"

He had cornered me on the New Year's Eve rooftop party about this very thing. I should've been prepared. Still, I stumbled. "I can't . . . that was . . . that's not the point."

"You did it? You really did?"

I didn't say anything.

"You're admitting it?" he said, shocked.

"Yes, but the accident—"

"That's what you're calling it? An *accident*? If it was, why would you need to hide it?"

My face got hot. "My parents are none of your business."

"Get this straight," he said, pointing his finger in my face. "Addie is my business. And you're a danger to her."

Everything sped up, both of us talking over each other, neither listening. It was clear this was a terrible mistake. "You grabbed her," I shouted, unable to help myself. "You terrified her. You're the danger."

"*You killed your parents.*"

"What? No—"

"You crashed your boat purposefully into a buoy."

"Excuse me? *Crashed purposefully?*"

His temper crackled, electric in the air. Any minute he might blow. "I have an eyewitness who saw you drive straight into that buoy," he said.

"Jesus Christ. What eyewitness?"

"Captain of a fishing charter. Says you murdered your parents."

"*Murdered?*" I put my hands in the air. There was no reasoning with him. "Are you insane, Josh? That's a serious question I'm asking."

His ears went red. "And you're living under the same roof as a person I love."

"Get out of my way," I said angrily. "I'm going home."

"Good idea. Let's clear this up with Addie." He grabbed my arm.

"Let go of me." I twisted out of his grip. He was still blocking the way out. "Don't touch me."

"Oh, come on," he said, reaching out again. I backed away from him into the tree. I scrambled up its branches. We were both breathing hard. It was as though we'd come too far too fast and had no idea how to back down. My chest was tingling with adrenaline. "Touch me again, asshole, and I'm calling the police."

"You're being ridiculous," he said. "Get down before you hurt yourself."

I climbed a branch higher. Just to spite him.

"Let me ask you something," I said, not even bothering to hide my scorn. "Did this captain of yours tell you the weather that day?"

He looked up at me through a hard mask. "Why would that be relevant?"

"Weather conditions during a boat accident?" Jesus, this guy. "That day on the water, the fog was like pea soup. You couldn't see three feet in front of the bow. I didn't see that buoy until we were on it." I was suddenly so, so tired. I just wanted this to be over. Make him go away, so I could go home. "If this captain of yours had such extraordinary powers of sight, and saw what happened to us on the water that day, why didn't he stop? Your friend could've helped me find my mother. Why didn't he do that? What kind of person leaves us alone, dying in the ocean?"

He shifted on his feet. "I don't know."

"Did you even ask him? Or did you just believe what you wanted to hear?"

I stared down, watching the emotions play across his face. It was clear I had hurt him, but I didn't care. He had hurt me, too.

"Listen," he said finally. "I should've asked. I'm sorry."

"Fine, now go away."

"Maybe I jumped to the wrong conclusion."

You think? "Whatever. Just please go."

"Not until you get out of that tree. Can you come down? And we'll talk about everything calmly?"

"I'll get down as soon as you leave," I said.

But he came closer. He gave me the smile he used on TV. It was actually a warm smile, the kind you might think was real. He was trying to talk to me like a friend. Come down. Everything's okay now. He was sorry.

My father had always been able to turn on a dime, too. That was when he was most dangerous.

Josh stopped at the base of the tree, where I was now trapped. He held out his hand.

"Don't," I said, panicked. I kicked at his outstretched hand and missed. My boot hit him square in the chest, and he fell down.

WHAT DID I know of head injuries? On my father's boat, I'd hit my head when we struck the buoy, and aside from a huge forehead knot, I was fine. A few months back, during an all-nighter, Penelope fainted and hit her head on an iron radiator, and then she came to, hopped up and mopped away the blood, took two Tylenol, and got back to work. People who play contact sports routinely hit their heads.

That day, I jumped out of the tree and left my print, I approached Josh cautiously. I suspected he was playing possum on the rocks. I bent over and poked at his shoulder, saying, "Josh? Get up now," the way we woke up drunks passed out at our parties.

Josh groaned and pushed himself up on one hand. He maneuvered into a seated position.

"You okay?"

It took a moment for his eyes to find me. Another minute still to focus. Then he said, "Yeah."

"Sorry for kicking you like that. I didn't mean to."

He was looking around, like he wasn't sure where he was. I said, "You need a doctor?"

"What? No."

That was the answer I wanted to hear. "You sure?" I didn't wait for a response. "Okay, great."

I watched him get to his feet. Now he was moving toward me, lumbering really. He looked *fine*, handsome even, though he was getting too close again. I pointed behind me, toward the towpath home. "So I'm just going to go now."

"Okay," he said, and then he lifted his hand, saying, "Wait."

But I was afraid of him. What if he snapped again? So I ran.

CHAPTER THIRTY-ONE

JOSH

The Day He Died

WAIT, HE SAID.

White stuff danced in front of his eyes. What was that? Oh, right. Snow.

Wait, he said again into the snow, but the redhead was gone. She'd run like she was being chased.

He touched his hair above his ear and it came away wet with blood.

Maybe he ought to sit down.

WHERE WAS HE? Why was he here? Was it . . . The redhead. Oh, right, he wanted to tell her something.

He couldn't—

NEXT HE KNEW, the snow blanketed him where he sat. Around the river's bend were city lights. They were so beautiful to him. They marked the way home, and home meant Addie. Somewhere among those lights, she waited.

When he tried to get up, his head swam. He leaned back to catch his breath. A short rest was all he needed. Then he'd get up and go home to her. As soon as the dizziness passed.

CHAPTER THIRTY-TWO

ON THE DRIVE BACK TO GEORGETOWN, MY HEAD WAS FILLED WITH noise. I did this? *I killed Josh?* I wasn't a bad person. I looked out for my elderly neighbor, ran errands for her, made sure she got her medicine. I was a loyal friend.

How was my life any different from everyone else's? I was ordinary, I made a point of being so. All I'd wanted was an ordinary life. And I'd gotten that, hadn't I? My life had been my friends and boyfriend and work and paying the bills. I never stood out. I never made waves. Aside from the boat accident—I flinched away from thoughts of the accident—I followed every rule.

Even my decision to meet Josh—which, okay, I should have told Addie about, and oh God, how I wish now I'd never gone—my *intentions* were good, weren't they? I had only been trying to keep her safe.

And you certainly failed at that, that awful voice inside me whispered.

The light at M Street was red. I stared up at the spires of the university buildings and beyond that, the starless sky. What made me like this? I didn't want to be like this. A danger to everyone I loved. Then it hit me, a punch to the chest: *the boots.* I'd been walking all over the city looking for a bad guy *while I was wearing the boots the police were looking for.*

Boots that had once been Addie's.

And where were the police looking for them?

Josh's condo. Where they must've thought Addie left them. I could explain they were mine now, but would anyone believe it?

I didn't know anything anymore. Only that I had to get rid of these boots.

But how? I couldn't leave the boots in the woods, *obviously*. Someone would find them and turn them in to the police. Police might do some jujitsu computer thing and retrieve a purchase receipt for them in Addie's name.

Dumping them in the river was out. What if they got caught in the rapids? What if they didn't sink?

I could toss them in a dumpster behind one of the restaurants on Wisconsin Avenue, but what about surveillance cameras? What if someone saw me and called the police? Not even the trash seemed safe.

You could jump in the river with them, that old voice in my head went.

The traffic light turned green. I just stared up at it. *Everyone's going to hate you anyway. Addie most of all.*

That voice had been getting louder ever since I left Leo's house. It was too loud for me to think. Nearly as loud as that summer I'd searched for my mother along the beaches, but still—

Jump and the boots don't matter.

A car behind me honked, and I hit the gas. Then I was on O Street. I was home.

PENELOPE AND ESTELLA had left the front room curtains open again. From the street, I watched them through the big French windows. Their smiles were wide. They laughed and gestured wildly with their phones. Estella lifted a bottle of champagne and filled Penelope's glass. Penelope tossed it back with abandon and held out her glass for more. Something good had happened tonight.

I dropped back into the darkness and went around to the alley, came in through the back gate. The rose trellis to the roof was icy, but I had no other choice. On each rung as I climbed, I made certain of my footing until I scrambled onto the kitchen roof.

Addie's bedroom window was dark. I stood outside and listened but there was no sound. I shoved all my weight against the window until I heard it crack and the wood gave. Then I pushed the window up, climbed in.

I left the boots by the window, and by memory made my way around the furniture in Addie's dark room. At the door to the hallway, I listened for Penelope and Estella. Their laughter drifted up the staircase like music.

Quickly, I went up the attic stairs, careful to avoid the weak spots that creaked. In my room, I changed quickly into athletic wear and slid on my running shoes. I shoved Mom's letters in my backpack and carried the backpack down to Addie's room.

Someone was coming up the stairs. I stopped and listened. Then someone else joined her on the floor below, and now they were outside Estella's room, laughing. I hurried into Addie's and eased the door closed. I went to Addie's window and retrieved the boots, held one out. Definitely not heavy enough to sink. I got on my hands and knees and felt through the darkness to the corner near the hallway door. This was where Addie kept her workout equipment.

I moved aside a mountain of running shoes. I reached under a yoga mat. Bingo—the fifteen-pound dumbbell.

I shoved the weight on top of the letters at the bottom of the backpack and followed with the boots. The backpack's zipper wouldn't close. Oh no, oh no. I pulled at the zipper with all my strength, struggling to close in the boots.

"That's okay, I'll get it," Penelope said, shouting her way up the staircase.

Then she was in the hallway just outside Addie's door, and I thought, please keep going to your bedroom, please. She stopped and knocked twice. "Addie, you in there?"

I backed into the corner, crouched down in the dark. This was so, so bad.

Penelope called back to Estella, "Did you shut Addie's door?" To which Estella hollered up the stairs, "No, why?"

"It was open, wasn't it?" Penelope said. Then she opened the door. "Addie?" she said, turning on the overhead light.

PENELOPE'S HAND FLEW to her throat. "Holy shit," she said as we stared across the room at each other. "You scared the hell out of me."

"Sorry."

"Wow, whew. That was like a defibrillator to the chest." She gave me a drunken smile. She was weaving on her feet. "What are you doing?"

I came up slowly out of my crouch with my hands out. The backpack was still open at my feet.

"Pen, listen," I said.

"Oh, you heard, didn't you?" She flew across the room and hugged me hard, saying, "But did you hear I got both? *Two* invites, Lucy! Georgetown and GW med schools *both* want to interview me! Both invites on the same day!"

"You got into med school?" I said dumbly.

Her champagne smile went crooked. "Well, I could botch the interviews. But likely not both! Maybe I won't have to leave DC for school! We'll be together forever!"

"I'm so happy for you."

"For us!"

She pulled back from me and held me at arm's length, wrinkling her nose. "Where have you been? You smell like outdoors. And your jacket is cold."

From the hallway, Estella was moving fast, saying, "Is that Addie? How'd Addie get in?" and then she slid in her socks stopping at the doorjamb.

"Lucy's here!" Penelope pointed out.

"I see that," Estella said, smiling.

"She came home to celebrate with us," Penelope told her. She pulled a face. "And I know, I know, maybe we shouldn't be celebrating without Addie. But we have to take a win when we can, don't we?"

"Of course you should," I said. "You've worked for this your whole damn life."

Estella was leaning against the doorjamb, silent. She always drank champagne like water, but in that moment, she seemed completely sober. "You don't look right," she said. "What is it now?"

I lifted my hands. "Happy for Pen. Worried for Addie. Same as always."

"You sound . . . weird," Estella said.

"Just tired."

"What's with the backpack?" Estella was eyeing it curiously.

"You're not leaving us for Connor, are you?" Penelope said. "Come down and have one glass of champagne at least."

Estella narrowed her eyes, studying my face. Then down again to the backpack. "Why are your boots in your backpack?"

My chest fluttered. I didn't say anything.

"What's wrong?" Penelope said to Estella. She looked from Estella to me and back to Estella again. You could hear the heater click back on. Penelope's smile wobbled. "What's with the vibe change? It's a buzzkill. Let's just go finish our champagne, okay?"

"In a minute," Estella said, sauntering into Addie's room, close enough I could smell her Chanel. She was trying to get a better look into the backpack at my feet. She scrunched up her face. "Is that Addie's dumbbell in there?"

To answer that question, I'd have to explain everything. And I loved them, I did, but if I were to tell anyone what happened, it would be Addie. I would always tell everything to Addie first.

"Why do you have a weight in a backpack full of boots?" Estella said.

Then she turned to Penelope. "Know what I was telling you earlier?" Estella said conversationally. "About that weird rumor going around that Nikki told me? Unconfirmed, so Lena won't report it yet." Estella turned back to me. "Want to hear the rumor?"

"No."

Estella leveled her eyes at me. "It is rumored that police found a boot print at the homicide scene. Distinct from Josh's footprints, totally different tread. Apparently, Josh had worn dress shoes. This boot print, so it goes, is evidence of the second person at the scene. If they could find this alleged boot that matched the alleged print, then maybe they'd have their murderer."

"Huh, yeah, interesting," I said weakly.

Penelope tilted her head and sniffed something in the air, like danger. "Somebody please tell me what's going on."

"What else is in that backpack?" Estella demanded. "You're hiding something."

"No." I was shaking my head. I couldn't look at her. "I'm not."

Estella made a move for the backpack. I snatched it off the floor and took a step back. Estella grabbed at its handle and tugged. "Let me have it," she said, trying to yank it out of my arms.

"Let go," I said, yanking back.

"Stop it, Stelly, you're being too rough." Penelope was trying to pull us apart. But Estella was stronger than she looked.

"I'll show you rough." Estella was tugging so hard. "Give me—"

The backpack zipped open. The weight and the boots fell out. Dozens of envelopes scattered across the floor.

"Oh," Penelope said. "Oh no."

I fell to my knees and scooped up as many envelopes as I could manage. Penelope helped me gather them. She held a handful out. Estella snatched one.

"What the hell?" she said.

Then she read the address. "'Katherine Ambrose'? 'Care of Sheriff Ed Brown'?" Estella glared down at me. "What is all this?"

"None of your business," I muttered. "Leave it all alone." Then to Penelope I said, "They're private. Between me and my mom."

Penelope helped me with the rest. Estella leaned with her back to the wall, watching us both.

"You told me she was sick," Estella said to Penelope. "You didn't tell me she was delusional. Jesus Christ."

"Do *not* stigmatize," Penelope warned her.

Estella threw her hands in the air. "Oh, I guess I'm the bad guy! Look at that boot!" Then she swung around and gestured to Penelope. "What do you think that boot means, Penelope? Come on, use that big brain of yours. What about Addie's dumbbell?"

Her voice chilled me to the bone. I hung my head lower.

"Tell her, Lucy," Estella said. "Tell her you were using the weight to dump the boot in the goddamned river, weren't you?"

Penelope was looking at me, panic-stricken. "Why would you do that? Lucy, tell her it's not true."

"She's not denying it," Estella said. I saw the knowledge in her eyes, though there was disbelief, too.

"Look at her face, Penelope," she said quietly. "The guilt's written all over it. Goddamn you, Lucy. Those are the boots the police are looking for, aren't they? You killed Josh, didn't you?"

CHAPTER THIRTY-THREE

MY ATTIC ROOM WAS BLUE WITH MOONLIGHT. I KEPT THE LAMP lights off as I packed. I didn't want to see everything I was leaving behind—all the reminders of our school days together, the pictures of the four of us sweeties, the clothes we shared and the books we talked about and the bottles we'd emptied when we sat around and laughed and talked as though there were nowhere else in the world for us to be but in this house, the luckiest place in the world.

I tried not to think of Addie at her bedroom window earlier in the evening. But my mind kept circling back. By refusing to come to the door, she'd been trying to tell me something, hadn't she? I looked down at my mother's suitcase open on the bed. At the sweaters and the wool socks, as many clothes as I could fit.

Was I really running away? How could I leave without knowing my best friend was okay? Without telling her what happened? What if, while I was gone, someone blamed Addie for what I'd done?

I got out my phone and called and texted her again, knowing she might not have replaced her broken phone. I checked her location services, but she still wasn't sharing it with me. Was she seeing the calls come in but ignoring them? If so, what did that mean? I had no way to know for sure.

Penelope came up the stairs. "What are you doing in the dark, silly?" she said, bustling in as if she'd already forgotten the big fight the three of us had had only moments ago. Penelope turned on the light by my bed and then did the same with my desk lamp. "Can we talk?"

I braced myself. "Sure."

"Is Estella right? You know, about what she says," she said delicately. Pen, always leading with empathy and kindness, the soft touch.

"I need to talk to Addie about this first," I explained. "Do you know how to reach her? I've been texting."

"I don't think she replaced her phone," Penelope said. "Can we slow down for a minute? Talk about how you're doing at least? I guess you met Josh out at the hideaway, do I have that right? But you didn't mean to . . . " She paused. She couldn't bring herself to say what I'd done. Instead, she said, "It must've been a terrible accident, right?"

"What does that matter?" I lifted my hands helplessly. "Anyway I'm getting out of here, don't worry."

"Why?"

I gaped at her. *Why?* Was she kidding me? "Estella hates me."

"Well, that's not true." Penelope waved her hand in dismissal. "She's shocked. This is all very shocking. You know how Estella gets. Hotheaded, overly reactive, for starters. Anyway, I calmed her down some."

My eyebrows were up at my hairline. "Is she overreacting, though?"

"Are you going to Connor's?" Penelope asked, avoiding my question.

"Sure," I lied.

There was no way I could face Connor right now. Or maybe ever again. I was unsure where to run. Maybe back to the river, I didn't know.

Penelope moved to the bed, gesturing toward it. "Mind if I sit down?" She settled with her legs crossed on the bed. She was sitting next to the backpack, though she didn't look at the letters. "Why did you write all these?"

I didn't answer right away. She just waited me out. So I let out a sigh and explained my deal with Sheriff Ed. At the time, I couldn't see how I could stop searching for my mother and leave home to go to college. He'd said my mother wanted me to go to college. She was so proud. That was all she'd talked about for months before the accident.

He and I came to a deal: I'd leave for school, since that's what she really wanted, but only if Ed promised to keep looking for her. Meantime, when I was away at school, he said I could write her letters and send them to him, and when he found her, he'd give them to her. So she'd know I hadn't stopped loving her or missing her. I had never given up.

Then the day before Parents' Weekend, freshman year, I got the note from Ed telling me to stop writing. It was the number of letters that bothered him. Plus, my mom had been missing for six months. He had lost faith. He had given up.

With that, I lost Ed, too. All the people I'd once loved were gone from me. My first home, my community, gone. "But that day Addie took us to the swimming hole for the first time," I said. "And you know, jumping in the river did feel like a kind of baptism, and we did start this new life, and you all didn't mind my letters. You hardly noticed. So I kept writing, knowing that when my mother came for me, she'd see how sorry I was. How she was always in my thoughts. The letters were my proof."

Penelope nodded. "Thank you for explaining," she said quietly. "I don't think any of that was clear to me before. But I understand now. I really think I do."

Then, without asking, Penelope opened the backpack and flipped through the dozens of different stuffed envelopes addressed to *Katherine Ambrose c/o Sheriff Ed Brown, Glynn County Sheriff's Department, Georgia.* Some of the envelopes had preprinted return addresses. They were like a map of all the places I'd been. The Tombs and Andrew Lee Strategies and the Georgetown Inn and the Ritz-Carlton. A few Smithsonian Museum envelopes swiped from Addie's office. Earlier letters stamped with the university crest. I always wrote about the places I'd been, so my mother could be there with me, too.

Penelope stacked the envelopes carefully and returned them to their place in the backpack.

"I don't think you should leave tonight," she said, looking down at the quilt we were sitting on. She plucked nervously at the frayed edges. "For one thing, it's so late, and it's cold. Also I don't think it's safe for you to go out tonight."

"I'm okay, Pen."

But all she said was, "This is your home, where you're most safe. If you feel you can't be here, I could drive you to an inpatient treatment center. For tonight, I mean. That would be the second best option before whatever comes next."

The road. A life of hiding. Or the police.

"You agree with Estella?" I said. "You think I'm delusional, too?"

She shook her head. "Estella shouldn't have said it that way. First of all, she talks too much. She never has any idea what the hell she's talking about."

"But you don't think I'm well."

She looked up at me with clear eyes. "No," she said. "I don't think you are."

CHAPTER THIRTY-FOUR

PEN CONVINCED ME TO STAY THAT NIGHT, AND I WAS GLAD SHE did. Because I finally figured out how to reach Addie.

The idea came at dawn. I'd been sitting at the turret window, thumbing through the call history on my phone, wondering whether somehow I'd missed a call or text from Addie. Maybe from one of the numbers I didn't recognize. I searched the call history all the way back to that horrible day of the snowstorm, where the incoming calls from Josh's second phone were recorded.

Unless she'd turned it over to the police, Addie still had his phone. A chill went through me. The phone had the evidence of my return call to Josh from the mail room.

Then came the next realization, the most obvious of all, the one that hit me in the soft spot behind my knees and made me woozy:

Addie would've checked the call history. She must've seen my call from the mail room. She was too smart not to piece together what happened with Josh before I did.

She *knew*.

That was why she hadn't come home or answered the door to me when I showed up at her parents' house. What she was signaling me from her bedroom window last night. Addie had probably known *for days*. Perhaps as early as the day she found Josh's phone.

I glanced out the turret window at the city coming awake. Traffic noises drifted up from the street below. I tapped Josh's number and sent Addie the text: can you talk?

My hands shook. there's something i didn't tell you and i need to, in person.

A read receipt popped up. I let out the breath I'd been holding. She responded immediately: where?

Suddenly I worried, what if this wasn't even Addie texting me? If she turned Josh's phone in to the police, I could be walking right into their trap. I thought of the DC jail images on Google. Green cells and tiny block windows near the ceiling. The two cots and the toilet in the middle of the cell.

Detective Kelley had warned about hauling my ass to the DC jail if I kept fucking up. She promised me bologna sandwiches with the rats.

But those worries only lasted a moment. Memories of Addie took over. Addie that first time I saw her in the dorm room, standing tall and strong in the golden slant of afternoon light. Addie in the swimming hole, her shoulder under my arm as she swam me up out of the river I would've drowned in. Addie whispering through my dark nightmare, saying *shh, it's okay, I'm here.* Fun Addie and Bossy Addie and Addie who'd found this house and organized our routines and shepherded us through this postgrad life I loved. Addie laughing with her hand over her mouth. Rolling her eyes at my ridiculous stories. Addie taking off on her run on the paths under the trees, where she felt freest, happiest.

Dazzled Addie in love for the first time, dumbstruck by it.

Through my tears I typed: meet me at judiciary square

I LEFT BEFORE rush hour was in full swing. The sky was gray, somber with clouds. I waited at the corner of Wisconsin Avenue and M Street, a usually busy corner now hazy and half-asleep. The Circulator bus stopped. I got on.

I said good morning to the driver and chose a seat farthest from the door, settled back to watch M Street speed past my window. Georgetown disappeared behind me like a dream.

A westbound Circulator drove past from the other direction. This was the Union Station to Georgetown route, the first bus I'd taken in DC, the one that carried me to campus on move-in day freshman year.

In the bus window was a girl, maybe eighteen at most. I wondered whether she was going to college, whether she was sick with fear. Did she have her mother's old suitcase pressed between her knees? Did she have, waiting at the end of her route, roommates she'd luck into and love the rest of her life? I pressed my palm against the window, fingers spread like a starfish, a wish for her. Then she was gone, too.

At the Farragut stop, a big woman with a tattered Target bag got on. She shambled down the aisle and took a seat directly across from me.

I unzipped my backpack and pushed aside the boot for something to read. There, at the bottom, beneath the boots, were my mother's letters. I ripped the first open: *School's unbelievably hard. It's very different here. I don't like being so far from you.*

Then another letter: *Went to a party last night and drank too much. In the morning, Addie made us run. That's how you get the poison out, she says, do good to get rid of the bad. Addie reminds me of you.*

And another: *I think of you all the time. I'm sorrier than you'll ever know.*

Too many letters. Ed Brown had been right about that. Delusional letters. Estella had been right, too.

The big woman cleared her throat. I looked up from the letter and saw a Kleenex box in my face. She said, "You okay, hon?"

"My mother died." Years ago, or maybe just now.

"Oh no," the woman said. "Honey, I'm so sorry." She squeezed my hand tenderly. "What a sad thing for a girl to lose her mama."

CHAPTER THIRTY-FIVE

JUDICIARY SQUARE WAS A CLUSTER OF BUILDINGS THAT INCLUDED the courts and the US Attorney's Office, as well as the DC Police Headquarters. I crossed Indiana Avenue to the wind-tunnel courtyard separating it from Superior Court.

I found a bench in the corner that was partially sheltered. When I sat down, cold seeped from its concrete through my jeans. I dropped my location pin and texted it to Josh's phone, then settled in for the anxious wait.

Court opened, and employees filed in through the side door. Police cruisers parked two and three deep. Officers jogged up headquarters steps, and though nobody paid me any mind, I pulled my hoodie over my head and shivered.

Finally Addie was coming up off the Metro escalator. She was wearing her track team captain's running jacket, the one we'd washed the blood from, and I noticed even from that distance how thin she'd become.

She stopped in front of me and looked down coolly. Loss had changed the angles of her face. Her cheeks gaunt, her eyes hollowed out, a tightness around her mouth I'd never seen before.

And I thought, I've done this to her.

I gave her a weak smile. "Thanks for coming." I gestured to the bench space beside me. "You want to sit?"

"No thanks, I'd rather stand. You have something to say to me?"

"I do, yeah."

Except I hadn't practiced what I was going to say, and now that she was standing over me, staring down with cool eyes, I couldn't think of how to say it. I had no idea where to start.

"I don't totally understand it all myself," I started, faltering. She took a deep, impatient breath and I pressed on: "Imagine seeing people through an old lens. Confusing the motives of innocent people with those who'd once hurt you."

At the word "innocent," her eyes snapped to mine. "You need to do better than that." She gave me a hard look. "You brought me here to tell me something. I want to know exactly what happened. Any philosophical bullshit, and I'm gone."

"Okay."

"And this is it," she said. "Your last and only chance."

"Understood," I said, nodding.

And so I muddled through the story, slowly, every word a struggle, with a feeling I had broken out of myself and was floating high above, looking down below at these two sad, lost women in a windy courtyard.

From that distance I could tell it. The compulsion to go out to meet Josh at our hideaway, even though I was scared, and despite the fact I knew Addie wouldn't want me to. I described the argument and how he lost his temper and I lost my nerve, and when he came near, he held out his hand. I thought he was trying to grab me, so I was trying to kick his hand away.

Every word seemed to beat her down. At the end of the story, she said quietly, "You didn't mean to kill him?" Her voice was remarkably steady. "That's what you're saying."

"I didn't even know he was really hurt. I thought he just, you know, bumped his head."

"Okay."

But I could see it wasn't. Of course it wasn't.

"Listen, Addie."

"Stop," she said. "I need a minute to process this."

She slumped onto the bench next to me. She rested her elbows on her knees and held her head in the basket of her hands. We were in a courtyard between some of the busiest buildings in the city, and Addie couldn't have seemed more alone, more unaware of her surroundings.

When she looked up at me, her eyes were still wary. "Why not tell me you saw him that day? At any time during any of those days I searched for him?"

"I really thought he was fine," I said.

"Are you telling the truth now?"

I nodded. "I was afraid to tell you. I thought you'd get mad."

She gave me a look of amazement. "*That's* what worried you? Me being *mad*?"

Like a little kid, I thought. Clocking her mama's every expression, worried her mother would get upset. When was I going to grow up? Well, I was getting there fast now, wasn't I?

"I was so worried I made a mistake by meeting him, getting in your business, that I missed the thing I should've been most afraid of. That Josh was hurt."

She put her head down, nodding. She was thinking about it. "I can be unforgiving."

"No, Addie. You did nothing wrong."

"I have my regrets," she said mysteriously. "And frailties. We all do." She glanced off, and a distant look came into her eyes again. "And I believe what Penelope says about things running beneath our surfaces, terrible things that compel us to do what we otherwise wouldn't. Like you arguing with Josh. Thinking that would keep me safe. It was bad, though."

"Yes," I said. "It was."

"Still, I do understand what Pen says about pain and grief and guilt making us process things the wrong way. I saw that in Josh, too. He struggled in the exact same way as you. In some ways, he was like you." After a moment she added, "I was prepared to hate you for the rest of our lives."

"I'd understand if you did."

But what I heard: *was prepared*. As in, those bad feelings were in the past. Now was something different: a glimmer of hope.

She got up and paced, as though something inside her was propelling her. Little by little she told me about these past few days at her parents' house, alone in her room, going through Josh's phone for call history, messages, emails, feeling like she was going crazy. She'd seen Josh's calls to me on the morning of the day he died. As well as the return call from my office mail room. She remembered I'd been at my office that afternoon.

"Josh was my heart," she said simply. "But then I loved you too and so I believe you when you say why you did what you did. And if I love the good in you, I have to try to understand the other parts of you, don't I? And I think maybe I could. I could try to, anyway."

"Addie," I said with a broken voice. "I don't deserve that."

"But what's so complicated, what I keep arguing with myself about, is the other half of this. I really do think I could work hard to get past what you hid from me, but how do I get past what you did to Josh? You barely knew him. Like, did you know he loved to wake with the sunrise through the blinds?"

The smallest, sweetest smile crossed her face as she remembered him. "Or that he was so impatient for spring? He knew the name of every bird. He used to point them out from his balcony." She laughed quietly. "And his dream job. He was so excited for it. But now . . . now . . . " Her forehead crinkled as her smile died away. "But now he won't have any of that. He won't know if he could get healthy again. Or see if he and I could get back to what we were. Or find out if we could become what he wanted so badly for us to be."

Tears streamed down her cheeks. "All that got taken from him," she said through them. "And I can't pretend it's okay. It's not my place to do it. It'd be a betrayal to what I feel for him to even try."

I nodded. "I understand, I do."

She wiped her eyes with her sleeve. She let out a long breath, gave herself a moment to get herself under control.

"And then there's the police," she said finally. "They want to know about those boots I gave you. They think they're still my boots. The lawyer bought me time, but I've also got Josh's phone, which I'm afraid those detectives will figure out, too. What do I do with the phone? Do I cover for you, which part of me wants to do. But if I cover for you, that's disloyal to Josh, isn't it? Ever since I found this damn phone, I haven't been able to sleep or run. My mind keeps racing around and around. But there's no way out, Lucy. I can't find my way out. Everything's just so jumbled up."

"It's not, though," I said, looking up, and for the first time since Josh had been found, it was true. I glanced over at the courthouse, where people were milling in and out. The wind had died down. The sun was struggling to make its way out. And I knew how I'd fix things with Addie, to make things right. To make everything okay again. I could do this.

"Give me the phone," I said.

She made a pained noise. "What? No." I could see her apprehension. Maybe she thought I was going to run off with it.

"It occurs to me," I said, surprised by how straight I sat, how easy it was to lift my chin, "that this isn't jumbled at all. You're doing exactly what's right for Josh but in your own way, on your own time."

We used to joke about it. We called it Addie's Time. She took things slowly, made her decisions thoughtfully. She hated mistakes.

"You're getting this right for Josh," I said, "and you know that I'm going to help you. That's what we've always done. Together we'll do it this one last time."

I smiled at her calmly. I wanted her to remember me like this, in control of myself. "You see where we are," I said, gesturing to the court building. "I just needed to talk to you about it all first."

She glanced around, her eyes wide, as if just now understanding. The busy courthouse, the US Attorney's Office hulking over D Street, waiting for me. I hauled my backpack on my lap, and from its top pouch I pulled out the business card Detective Kelley gave me. "Do you want to place the call to Detective Kelley, or should I?"

HOW DID YOU explain to someone who didn't know the ocean its vagaries, its dark depths and many moods? What it was to be pulled out to sea and want only to make it back to land? I'd been out too long. I was so tired of treading water.

"I want to do this," I said, and it came out serenely. "If I tell the detectives what I did, come clean, maybe I'll even *feel* clean." And Addie would be able to run again. "Please give me the phone."

She handed it over with a suspicion I understood, though it devastated me. When Kelley answered, I told her how I was calling from Josh's phone, and if she could come to retrieve it, I'd explain everything I knew about what happened to Josh. Then I hung up and looked over at Addie.

Addie stared down at me, slack-jawed. Then she glanced back up quickly, surveying the courtyard with terror. "Detective Kelley is coming *here*?"

"Any minute," I said. "You have to go. It's no good for her to see you with me."

But she just stood there, shifting her weight from foot to foot, uncertain.

This, of course, was the flaw in my plan. How to get Addie out of here fast. But then I thought of Connor, and my chest ached.

"Could you hurry over to Connor's?" I said. "Tell him what happened? I feel terrible I didn't do it myself. If you could just explain that everything I ever said about what I felt for him, that was true."

When she didn't go, I said, "Don't let Connor hear about it from the news. I need you to do it now, Addie."

"I will."

To my horror she dropped on the bench beside me again. She bit off her glove and wiggled her fingers beneath my sleeve, pressing her warm fingers against my wrist. "Are you scared?"

"No," I lied, though my pulse must've been throbbing like crazy. I was terrified. What if Detective Kelley caught us together and took this as evidence that Addie was somehow conspiring with me?

I yanked my wrist from her grasp. This seemed to freeze her up, so I pushed her away. "For God's sake, *go.*"

She grabbed me quickly and whispered something I didn't quite catch. I like to think it was *I love you.* Probably it was goodbye.

Then she ran off the opposite way she'd come—out of the courtyard and away from police headquarters, across C Street, then through John Marshall Park. She hooked a sharp turn around the corner, and I couldn't see her anymore. But my mind followed her to the gravel path of the National Mall down to the Potomac, where she looped past Josh's condo on her way to the Georgetown waterfront. She was getting close now, I could feel it.

The sun slid from behind the clouds, and the whole world brightened. I closed my eyes and tilted my face up and let the wintry light bathe my face. I imagined Addie reaching home, going through the front door to Penelope and Estella, and they'd look out for her. I could trust Penelope and Estella to do that for me.

Soon enough, heavy footsteps came from behind me. I knew exactly whom they belonged to. I kept my back to her, smiling that crazy, closed-eyed smile up at the sun. I felt so thankful that Addie had gotten out. Addie was safe.

When her shadow fell over me, my eyes snapped open.

"What's this about a phone?" Detective Kelley said. "Where is it?"

I pulled Josh's phone from my jacket pocket and, handing it over, said, "This is how Josh reached out to me the day he died." My voice was strong. It surprised even me. Then I told her, "I'm the one you're looking for."

CHAPTER THIRTY-SIX

THROUGH THE DIFFICULT DAYS AND MONTHS THAT FOLLOWED, I
carried with me the memory of Addie's last run from Judiciary Square. Even
now, I close my eyes and there she is, taking off like a shooting star, zinging
across John Marshall Park so fast you'd expect contrails in her wake. Sometimes I can see Josh right alongside her, as though he couldn't get close enough.

Josh, though, is harder to hold in my mind. More often than not he catches
me watching and turns his gas-burner-blue eyes my way, as if to say, *See what
you've done.* Before I can say how sorry I am, that I never meant for any of
this to happen or wanted anyone hurt—poof, he's gone again.

The most difficult times come at night. After it's lights-out and the walls
feel like they're closing in, this place in which they've put me comes alive
with its strange sounds like I've been swallowed whole. In the darkness, I
hear people breathing all around me, and sometimes a skitter, a clank of bars.
Occasionally a woman cries out.

But I never cry. Whenever I get sad or scared, I simply close my eyes
and dream my way back to that wonderful old house on O Street, slipping
through its big front door and climbing up the curve of stairs, where I cross
Addie's bedroom to the window that still sticks. I push my weight against it
and shoulder open the window to a fresh burst of cold air.

And there they are—out on the snowy rooftop, Addie and Penelope and

Estella, so beautiful my heart hurts. Always my dream travels back to this last perfect moment. Before Henry called through the window for Addie, or we go downstairs together to meet the detective. Long before we had any inkling that Josh was already gone.

Addie turns to me in the moonlight. "What took you so long?"

"Get out here already," Estella says.

When I do, Estella opens the bottle of Fireball and pours us each a shot in little Dixie cups. We raise our drinks, and Addie makes a toast that sounds like an incantation. We are the sweeties, she says. Nothing will ever come between us. We will love one another till the end. After we toss back the shots, Penelope says, "Pull up our playlist, would you, Stelly?"

The music comes on—Addie's favorite pregame song—and we dance together in the snow, screaming the lyrics about London werewolves and Chinese menus into a starlit DC sky, Addie's voice loudest among us. Then comes the famous refrain, and we link hands and lift our faces to the moon, and from our unbroken circle, we howl.

ACKNOWLEDGMENTS

IN THE SUMMER OF '22, I TURNED IN A DRAFT OF THIS NOVEL, called it *Watch Us Fall*, and months later, my much-loved brother-in-law, Paul Loebach, fell. Throughout the edits, I agonized. What if somehow I'd thought this terrible thing into happening? What if, by the act of making this book about falling, Paul fell? Crazy, grief-stricken, writer-brain stuff. It took a long time to realize what Paul himself would've said: *Stop being stupid. Finish your edits, make my brother some money, take my wife and kids out for dinner and drinks*, but also, being Paul: *set it to music* (I'm not that kind of writer, Paul), *so I can play the lead role* (he was a performer, total main character vibe).

So first I'd like to acknowledge Joe Loebach, the love of my life, for picking me up and carrying us all through; and Lauren and Jack Loebach, who are my joy; and all the rest of that big, wonderful Loebach clan I so luckily married into—especially Pam and Katie and Michael, and Amy and Matt. My parents, Sharon Taylor and Tom Burns, gave me a room to write when I needed it most, and my forever-bestie, Kimberly Sneed, taught me everything good about friendship.

Special thanks to my very talented editor, Carina Guiterman, and—as always, for everything—Dan Conaway, my agent who every day goes above and beyond.

Heartfelt gratitude for early reads go to Angie Kim, my brilliant friend

ACKNOWLEDGMENTS

whose books inspire me, and to Dana Cann and Kathleen Barber, both wonderful authors who patiently read again and again, and to Kathleen Wheaton, Jim Mathews, Jim Beane, Carmelinda Blagg, Jeff Blount, Fernando Manibog, Carolyn Sherman, Beth Thompson Stafford, Dennis Desmond, and John Benner, who also kindly provided important early thoughts.

ABOUT THE AUTHOR

CHRISTINA KOVAC writes psychological thrillers set in Washington, DC, where she worked as a television journalist before turning to fiction writing. She lives outside of Washington, DC, with her family.